ABOUT THE AUTHOR

Born with an obsession for the written word, Rowena Spark navigated her youth armed with pen, paper and an overactive imagination, characters whispering to her from the shadows.

Rowena weaves romantic tales of flawed heroes who fall hard and love deeply, and strong, passionate heroines courageous enough to take a risk.

She lives on her farm with her husband, doing her best writing against the backdrop of Victoria's breathtaking South Gippsland hills, surrounded by cows, sheep, and one crazy dog.

For more information about Rowena Spark and her books visit www.rowenaspark.com and facebook.com/RowenaSparkAuthor

I0593493

COPYRIGHT

CREDENCE

BY ROWENA SPARK

NATIONAL LIBRARY OF AUSTRALIA

A catalogue record of this book is available from: www.trove.nla.gov.au

ISBN (print): 978-0-6489089-8-2
ISBN (eBook): 978-0-6489089-5-1
Editor: Sharyn Constantine
Cover Design: White Clover Creative
Cover Images: Shutterstock: zffoto
Interior Design: White Clover Creative
Print typesetting and eBook production: Adobe Indesign/MS Word

BOOK ONE OF THE SCARS OF CREDENCE SERIES

credence

ROWENA SPARK

LIME TIGER ENTERPRISES

CHAPTER 1

BEGINNINGS

*T*his could be your last one, Rain." Simone murmurs softly. I find myself cringing instinctively. She says the same thing each time, and it always ends with me in tears slipping into Simone's car in the wee hours before dawn. I insist she's jinxing me.

"Sorry." She flicks me an apologetic smile. I offer a weak one in return. Simone is a beautiful hearted woman, and I suppress the urge to ask again if I could live with her. Over the years I've asked that question a total of six times, all with the same response.

"I wish I could, Rain. I really do. But you know our home is full."

Simone is a foster carer. They give her the children with the biggest issues, the ones nobody else will take. Her boundless patience and capacity for empathy calms the most unsettled souls, and their angry inner demons find peace in her home.

I wasn't ever destined to be one of her children. I'm easy. I'm respectful, use my manners, pull my weight and obey the rules. Whatever school I drift into, I'm always at the top of my class. And always alone. As if she knows my thoughts, Simone squeezes my hand.

"You could make friends here."

I offer a thoughtful nod. That would be nice. Through the years Simone has been my only constant, the closest thing to a friend I've ever known. Our letters to each other began just after I turned eleven. Simple correspondence at first that grew over the years into detailed letters about our lives, loves and pain.

I nurse a knot in my stomach. If this place works out, it will be my last home before being sent into the big wide world to fend for myself, carving a very different future to the destructive path my mother chose.

Visions of her dilated pupils and vacant expression stab at me constantly. If that's what independence does to a person, perhaps I don't want it.

"Tell me about them again, please." I whisper. My last hope. I'm a month away from my fifteenth birthday. Once my birthday arrives, I will become a gray area in the foster system. I know the possibilities, then. Nobody wants to foster an almost-adult with "issues", but I will still be too young to be on my own. I've heard stories of kids trapped in the Grey Zone where there is a new bed for them every night, a different town every day. Their lives fit into a standard issue backpack. Often, the option of sleeping in parks was preferable to the constant shifts. No matter their stories, they were all viewed with the same disdain. They were the unwanted. Life's parasites. *The Grey Zone*. I shiver in the warm car.

"Her name is Heather Marraton. She's been widowed for twelve years and has been fostering for a little over ten, all with safe and positive outcomes. She currently has a boy, a little older than you who is also in her care. His feedback is positive, as are all the other reviews. The home is a brick two storey, warm in the winter and cool in the summer."

I felt a smile tug at my lips then. A brick house. And two storeys. I might be able to play my guitar without disturbing anyone. Hope flutters.

"What's the town like?" I probe as she turns her car towards a winding road on the side of a mountain. She tosses me a grin.

"I think you'll like it, Rain. It's not a big town, but I checked it out last week and the locals seemed lovely, if not a little curious. It's quiet, but there's a few buses passing through each day, so it's not isolated."

I allow myself to exhale and free up the tension in my shoulders. The little things are important to me. The details. Simone knows this, and I love her for it. She knows I'm terrified of Alsatians, but love dogs. She knows I like my own company, but need to know I can escape into a sea of humans if things get too overwhelming. She understands.

"Thank you, Simone." I hope my tone conveys the depths of my gratitude. Her voice deepens and grows serious.

"What's my phone number? What's my address? Do you have my envelopes? How much money are you carrying?" This drill is not part of the formal exercise. This comes from a place deeper down, of nurture set aside just for me. I rattle off the details, assure her I have the pack of twenty postage paid envelopes, and paper, and tell her I have twenty-five dollars in my wallet, and another seventy-five hidden in my suitcase.

She puffs out a breath, not taking her eyes off the road.

The car winds through the hills until the mountaintop evens out and a heavily wooded backdrop comes into view, the sun catching glints of silver from the numerous rooftops.

Welcome to Mountain Plateau, Population 528.

Simone flicks her eyes over to me and grins at my slack mouth.

"I thought you'd like it here. Are you ready?" I nod cautiously and wrap my fingers around the throat of my guitar.

When we pull into the driveway, my shoulders tighten. The house appears well-kept and welcoming but I know how deceitful first impressions can be.

Shiny chocolate eyes hang above the golden muzzle of a wagging Labrador behind the garden gate.

Simone pauses beside me, giving me a look that conveys hope and excitement.

"Okay?" She asks. I fill my trembling lungs.

"Let's do this" I say with courage I don't feel.

The rapping of her knuckles on the wooden door sounds final. The gavel dropping. The firm handshake of my final transaction. I lock my knees, resisting the urge to dive for the safety of the car and demand Simone take me away.

The woman who opens the door has kind brown eyes. I always look in their eyes. It tells the story of my future. I have stared into cold and cruel eyes before, but this time, I release my breath. Simone notices and steps backwards, understanding I feel safe enough to do this myself.

Heather Marraton is your typical middle-aged motherly sort. Shots of silver pepper her light brown hair, fixed in a relaxed bun. Casual and laid back in jeans and a t-shirt over a thick waist, and the slightest dusting of make-up on her face. I note the wrinkles forming around her eyes and the corners of her mouth and relax a little more. Laugh lines and smile creases are so very important. She takes a tentative step towards me.

"You must be Rain. I'm Heather. I'd like to welcome you to your new home, if you would like it to be?" She darts a nervous look at Simone for approval, her expression relaxing with Simone's encouraging smile.

I straighten my shoulders and offer a cautious smile, holding out a hand to shake.

"Thank you, Heather. Your home is beautiful." Heather softens and steps backwards, silently inviting us in. It's protocol for a cup of tea and biscuits to give an hour's conversation before carer and child decide to move forward together or keep searching for a better fit. It always bewilders me how blasé the system is when it comes to such an important decision. One minute you could be on the streets, and an hour later be settling into your forever home. Kind of like an animal shelter. I bite a nervous smile. I'm a rescue.

"Heather, is your dog a rescue?" I ask before I realise. Heather smiles, showing all the right valleys in the corners of her eyes.

"One of my foster sons, Lucas, fell in love with her. I decided to find him a dog because he had trouble settling in, and the moment we stepped into her row, he just gravitated towards her. Of course Lucas is grown and moved to the city for work, and can't have pets, but he comes back often to see her, and once he can buy a home himself he wants to take her."

The story tells me more about the woman than the dog. My smile widens.

"If you would like to, Rain, I'd love to know about you. You know I'll read your file, but it won't tell me who you are."

I feel my eyes widen. My breath snags in my throat at her request, and my vision blurs with relief. Simone fumbles for my hand and squeezes. I swallow.

"My name is Rain. Music is my life and I escape as often as I can into it. I like the peace and quiet of my own head, or a good book. I don't deal well with aggressive people, or injustice. I want to study psychology when I finish school."

"Well, Rain, as you know, my name is Heather. I adore my garden, and also love my books. I have a library upstairs you are welcome to enjoy anytime. I have a wide variety to choose from; Shakespeare to King and everything in between.'

My teeth show. Biting my lip for courage, I control my inhale and get out the question that determines my future here.

"What are your rules, Heather?" I feel Simone's fingers freeze. It's the only indication of her tension, otherwise her demeanour reflects the normal response to a perfectly casual conversation.

Heather seeks her answer in the air.

"Just the usual ones, I suppose. No lying, sneaking or disrespectful behaviour. I assume that being so close to becoming an adult, you will accept responsibility where required and are at a position where you can expect the same behaviour from me. My deal breaker is no skipping school. I still work full time hours in a town over, but I have the principal on speed dial if I need him. I will begin by offering you my full trust, and Simone assures me you have an excellent school history so I don't imagine I will need to have him keep an eye on you."

Her shoulders are stiff with expectation, but her expression is gentle. Simone's reassuring pressure warms my hand.

Simone glances at me, asking in the tone of standing ritual.

"What about you, Rain? Do you have any rules?"

We all know what that means. Taking the conversation to a deeper level, while pretending it's small talk. She's really asking me to air my laundry. My dirty secrets, my triggers. My issues. It's the nasty part of the interview. Of course, it *should* all be written down in my file. My darkest moments in print being passed from foster carer to foster carer. I swallow against the distasteful thought of strangers flicking through it like a novel they can't put down. I've seen my *full* file. It's big, and the pages look like they've felt a thousand fascinated fingers. But not the folder that carries my name now. That one carries but three sheets of paper. My school history, my personal details and my medical information. Everything else is gone. I flick my eyes to Simone for support, then lock my eyes on Heather's with the full gravity of my stipulation.

"I can promise you, you won't have a problem with me. I cook, clean, pull my weight and love school. I'm respectful and honest. But I have the same rule the rest of us have. Heather, please don't ask about my past."

CHAPTER 2

SETTLING IN

I swallow my tears when Heather shows me to my room. My room. I'm not sharing. I'm not shown to a couch and an empty corner for my things. I'm not squashed in beside a cradle with feeding instructions sitting on my pillow. It has white walls, a door that closes and a big window with thick curtains framing the bushland beyond. The linen is a soft, elegant grey with forest green highlights. It looks like a page from a home decor magazine. I have a dresser for my clothes, a bedside table, a work desk for my homework, and...

Breathless, I twist the handle on the door next to the window.

"Oh my!" I gush in excitement I can't hide. "I have a closet?" The silence behind me pushes me to crack the door. As it swings open, my hands find my face and cover my eyes, too overcome to choke out a sound.

"You have an ensuite, Rain." Simone's voice penetrates the dream I'm trapped in. I spin around. Heather is grinning.

"Have a look, Rain. It's all yours. I expect you to keep it clean and tidy, and I have a man coming to fit a lock next week, but a girl your age needs some privacy."

My chest rattles with gratitude. I can't stop the tears sliding from my eyes.

"Oh, Heather, this is too much! I can't believe it. Thank you."

I hear Heather's smile in her gentle voice.

"My husband, Eric and I always wanted to foster, but we were completely past entertaining dirty nappies and sleepless nights. We set up all four rooms with their own bathrooms to avoid the morning teenage gridlock and offer a little independence."

Heather stands beside me as Simone's car twists out of view.

"You okay?" She asks.

Biting my lip nervously, I drop my chin. I'm a little tentative, reflecting on just how perfect it all appears, waiting for the illusion to fracture. Until then, I'll embrace the fantasy.

"Yeah, I think I am."

My suitcase remains on the desk as a beacon of caution. That's the funny thing about being a foster. There's a routine stretch in time where the need to remain alert and ready to escape is imperative. As it begins to ebb, the suitcase empties. It's a knowing they don't teach you. Sometimes you never feel safe enough to open your case. Raphael was the perfect example. I shared a home with him the year he was exited from the system. When the time came for him to take that walk, he pulled his suitcase with him, leaving behind a rectangle of carpet that hadn't seen the light for the twelve years he'd lived there. After what had happened to him, even the greatest nurturing couldn't smooth out the furrows or soften the haunted shadows in his eyes. We all knew, of course, but we knew intrinsically never to discuss it. Never mention *Before*. Even enemies find a comforting unity in mutually respectful silence. It's an understanding and acceptance that stands us apart from the others, those who aren't familiar with the system. To them we are the unwanted, the wild, damaged filth who deserved pity and disgust. To us, though, they were the ungrateful ones, the shallow, the poison we needed to surround ourselves with to appear "normal". We are tougher than them.

We understand our limits because we've met them before in victory or defeat. Or both.

It's why most of us never make friends. Its the "others" who devour our scars like oxygen and reveal them to the world. Then the rumours start. The accusations. We are held accountable for everything they think we have done and treated with suspicion. It's a cruelty born of ignorance. How could a lapdog understand or empathise with a wolf's plight to survive. I've watched the lack of understanding transcend into fear pretty fast. And fear holds the chill hand of hate. Hate breeds malice, and they show us fangs when all we're looking for is a smile. I remember the fangs. Reaching for my guitar, I strum the chords, tuning the journey from the strings.

*   *   *

I know the drill. I sit in the comfort of predictability outside the Principal's office waiting for my name to be called. Of all the schools I've attended, this is undoubtedly the smallest. With its old clad buildings and minimal gardens, the place looks like its preparing to close at a moment's notice, holding on by the skin of its teeth and the bare minimum students required to keep it running.

"Rain Harrison?"

I swoop up with rehearsed attention, and sit square and tight before Principal Thompson. Inside, relief floods through me. Heather enrolled me using the name we'd given her. Sometimes they get my name wrong and it triggers off a panic attack, and it's usually an early indication of what my stay will be like.

"It's good to meet you. I'm Mr. Thompson. My staff and I make ourselves available to all students, and that extends to you, too. But if you ever want to speak with me, just knock."

I nod humbly. His voice rumbles around the room like distant summer thunder and the soothing sound unlocks my jaw.

"I must say, I was a little concerned with the limited information about your file at first. I like to get a bigger picture of a student's school career, and you are probably aware yours is merely a snapshot."

His eyes narrow briefly when he notes my spine stiffen, but he continues with a reassuring smile.

"Which is why the initial test you took this morning was so

important."

Principal Thompson leans back in his chair, pressing his fingertips together.

"This is obviously no surprise to you, but it seems you are an extremely bright young woman, and I'm very interested to see what you can achieve in this school with us." I nod, expression clean.

"Normally, you'd be put into a Year Ten class with the rest of students your age, but I'd like to discuss how you think you'd manage if you were to consider tackling Year Twelve classes."

Mr Thompson's eyes narrow as he watches me absorb his suggestion.

"If you would prefer to stick with classmates your own age I can leave you in Year Ten, but based on the results in front of me I think you'd become bored pretty quickly."

I pull a breath.

"I've completed Year Eleven studies already." I admit cautiously. His eyes widen.

"I don't think it will be difficult for me to adapt to the social aspects of it. As for the workload…"

I pull an image of the study area in my room to mind, and smile. I focus on him with conviction.

"Thank you, Principal Thompson, I think I'll enjoy the challenge of Year Twelve."

* * *

My tingling fingertips stroke the shell of the laptop in disbelief before shuffling it inside its protective case. It won't fit into my bag, but it wouldn't have mattered anyway. I'll be gripping it so tightly in my hands, afraid to let go in case I lose it. Heather grins at my stunned expression.

"I can't thank you enough, Heather" My voice is so small I hope she can hear it. "I've never had new stuff for school before, and a computer…"

"You're welcome." She pats my arm at my wonder. My words

don't seem enough, but I try anyway.

"This is huge, really. I feel so spoilt, just like the other girls... It will be nice to fit in. I'll put these in the room. My room." I correct with the faint stirrings of a smile.

* * *

I peel the skins off the potatoes with practised ease, chop the carrots and pumpkin and season them before slipping the tray beside the lamb. Roast lamb has got to be my favourite meal of all time. I find the stack of plates in the cupboard, setting the table for three and filling the jug with water to complete the picture.

Heather steps into the kitchen, rounding on me in surprise. A fleeting panic seizes me before I read the amazement on her face. She's pleased. I release a breath.

"Oh, Rain! This is incredible. You didn't have to do this, you know. I don't expect it, but....wow!"

"it's no trouble at all, Heather. I love cooking, and you said Archer was going to be here tonight too, so I thought it was a good way to thank you both for having me."

All I knew about the other foster was that he had completed high school and was out most nights working shifts behind the bar at the local pub. I'm strangely unconcerned about meeting him. Maybe it's that having my own room gives me security if we didn't get along, and with his work, we would rarely see each other anyway. Regardless, I will keep my head down, make no waves, and focus on studying.

My gut knots when he walks through the door.

He rests a heavy scowl on me and a kiss on Heather's forehead.

He clears Heather easily with his six-foot-something height, and she leans up into his lips with comfortable familiarity. A messy shock of dark hair contrasts with his intense green eyes and firm features. His default expression seems to be a glower, an added portion of distrust injected behind his eyes just for me.

"Archer, I'd like you to meet Rain. She's enrolled in school as of this morning. Rain, this is Archer. He works at The Broken Keg most nights if you ever need someone and I'm not home."

I mumble the required greeting, and receive a suspicious nod in return before they discuss the day's events.

"What's the school like?" I ask Archer over dinner.

His eyes flicker with emerald fire. His nostrils flare. It's not hard to read the signs he's showing me. I can stay, but he's top dog and I'll never be a friend.

The smile freezes on his lips.

"It's pretty good. Being a small school, they're able to give extra help to the students who are most in need." His tone is light but I read the meaning, swallowing the urge to react, to shove his assumptions so far up his arse that he'd smell his own shit. I lower my eyes to my plate, forcing my indignation to sound like appreciation.

"Oh, well, that's great to know. Some schools can be tough, you know?"

Heather's laughter rattles easily as she turns a soft expression to Archer. "Archer had some troubles when he started, didn't you? Before he came to me, too. He preferred to spend the day at the pub rather than pay attention in class."

I choke a gasp at Heather's open comments about his *Before*. Archer doesn't seem to be disturbed by it, though, instead, he rests a gentle smile on the woman, his lips twitching. It transforms his entire face. Someone who, in different circumstances could have been a friend. That elusive connection that I haven't experienced in… My thought escapes me.

"Yeah, and how's the irony? They now pay me to be there." The two laugh and I offer my teeth, rising to collect the dinner plates and clear the table.

"Goodnight, Heather. Thank you for today. Goodnight Archer. It was lovely to meet you."

"You're very welcome, my dear. Thanks for dinner. You're

a great cook. I hope you sleep well, and if there's anything you need, just ask Archer or myself." Heather offers. Archer's expression is cold granite.

In the privacy of my room I allow my muscles to unwind. I have no idea the reason for Archer's glacial reception. His body language was protective, but not aggressive. That meant he didn't know anything further than a new foster may be threatening whatever security he feels here. I allow a sigh to tumble from my lips, and pull my briefcase from beneath my clothes to rest on the bed. A gift from Simone. A precious possession kept safe with the four digit combination barrel. I spin them carefully. 11 11. My stomach clenches strangely as it does every time I punch in the code. The clasps spring apart and open on the papers inside. They are all in order, and I rarely dig past the top handful. My songs. Simone helped me find a way to express myself, get it out without using a diary. I'd seen too many diaries held hostage in malice to ever consider one of my own. I pull a fresh sheet from the lid pocket and one of my many pencils, then, with the caress of a lover I bring my guitar to me and lose myself among the dancing chords and birthing words.

"What's *your* story?"

Torn from my distraction by Archer's biting tone, I let my fingers loosen. He stands rigid and suspicious in the doorway, arms crossed tight, green glare full of bitter loathing.

"We don't discuss that." I defend.

"*We* do. What's your story, Rain?" His lip curls back. Without Heather between us, I send the full force of my own glower his way.

"You're clearly not an idiot. I won't tell you and you know it. We both know that whatever happens *Before* is not relevant, anyway." I snarl. He has the audacity to step into my room. It's not a threat, it's a display that I'm on his turf, and he's flexing his authority.

"I've seen your file, Rain, and I have to admit it's the thinnest damn file I've ever seen. You can't be that dumb to not at least try to pad it out with breadcrumbs."

I shrug nonchalantly and he drops his hands to tight fists by his side, daring another step towards me.

"Heather is great. What I'm saying is, don't hurt her, or ruin my chances here, or you're toast." His whispered words are icy hooks that send chills deep into my spine.

I clench my teeth.

"This is my last stop. I have no intention of doing anything other than keeping my head low and flying under the radar. I'm done with that drama. I just want to be left alone to study."

He samples the sincerity in my admission. His face relaxes uncertainly, his eyes flicking for the first time to the guitar in my hands and the open case at my side. I slam the lid down, catching his attention. He runs his eyes over to my packed suitcase, and a flicker of understanding passes between us.

I'm not settled in yet.

Archer spins around and leaves my room, pausing once in the doorway.

"Shit floats, Rain. And I'm gonna find it," he warns, before his back disappears from view.

I don't have anything to hide.

Except that in the darkest, foggiest corners of my soul there's a niggling feeling that perhaps I do.

CHAPTER 3

ROUTINE

*O*ver the next few months, my life relaxes into the most wonderfully mundane routine of all. At school I'm almost anonymous, hiding at the rear of the classroom, blending into the furniture. By being a non-event, the initial attention received for being a new face quickly ebbs. For a smaller school, they manage to offer most of the subjects I want, and I throw myself into the challenging workload with an excitement I never dared feel before. On the breaks I slip up to the library, using the time to study or read.

"It's been three months, Rain. It appears you are handling the workload just fine. In fact you are surpassing our expectations and I think it's time we started discussing what will happen once you finish this year." Principal Thompson taps his ballpoint pen on the notepad laying open on his desk. A shudder of excitement ripples through me.

"I want to be a psychologist." I say quietly, although my words run together. My lungs hold their fill of air. I spent my short life reading body language, detecting personality traits, priding myself on uncovering every character nuance and tell in everyone around me. In the beginning it was so I could find my place in new family dynamics with as little angst as possible, but it also protected me. For the most part, anyway.

"You could be a doctor, Rain, with your abilities. Your grasp of the sciences and advanced mathematics is at a level higher than

I've seen before. Your intelligence far exceeds any of the staff…"

He cuts himself off with a deep breath and a shake of his head.

"What I'm trying to say, Rain, is that I strongly urge you not to undersell yourself when considering your future."

I slump in the plastic chair, shaking my head. Of course he's excited. He sees me as a phenomenon. Someone who he can connect his name to when I find fame within the ranks of my chosen sector. I feel for him. I know the career I want isn't as glorious as he imagines for me. But here's the thing. The kids I've known in the system are all so damaged, and something inside me pulls to reach out to them. They are the children hiding behind faces that aren't connected to the scars inside them. The nightmares and memories chew them up from the inside while they keep focus on their masks, ensuring the "normal" people don't spot the cancer in them. They know on a subliminal level not to tell. I've been haunted by that specific look foster children show when they finally understand the concept of creating the illusion. We are the unwanted children, and therefore must be grateful for any handout offered. Even when the abuse accompanies it. I want to help them. I want to infiltrate the system and help weed out the few bad seeds that manage to slip through the screening process.

"I want to be a psychologist. Specifically a child psychologist." His mouth closes on my determination, but hee nods in his reluctance to entertain my dream.

"I understand. I really do, and if I can be frank, I'm sure you've seen and felt things incomprehensible to the rest of us in your life, and I respect your desire to help others in similar situations. Will you at least humour me and allow me to arm you with options in both psychology and medicine?"

I dump my bag as soon as I reach home, change clothes and prepare dinner. On the occasions Heather sends a message to me that she's working late, I seek the solitude of the trees, sometimes with guitar in hand. I call my guitar Wind. I was told once that it's good luck to name your instrument. It helps you connect with it, learn the personality of its sound; helps me understand what it's trying to tell me. Wind must be lucky. He's been through *Before* with me and come out more intact than I have.

I always wait for Heather to come home so I can share dinner with her. Archer's late shifts at the pub means he rarely joins us, so for the most part I can imagine it's just Heather and me. I enjoy her company, and I find that she fills the social void that I occasionally crave. She is also an interesting study. With her heart of gold, but an unbridled desire to watch romance throw seeds and bloom. Over dinner, I learn that Janice in the copy room has her eyes on Robbie in Printing, but Harry with the lisp in Editing is infatuated with Janice.

"I just want to see a few happily ever afters, you know?" She sighs.

I offer a weak smile.

"There's no such thing. Love is nothing more than a series of trials two people must endure that changes who they are. It binds them to one another, and if they make it out the other side intact they're reluctant to let go of the only other person who understands what they went through. Or, it disintegrates entirely when they realise the bond they share is the one thing that anchors them to an unfortunate event and they find that severing that connection is the only way for them to heal."

Heather squints at me and cocks her head.

"That's quite insightful, albeit unromantic. Are you sure you're not a 90 year old woman in the body of a teenager?"

"I feel like it, sometimes."

She studies my face sadly, then leans over the space to hug me. The warm acceptance in her embrace settles in my heart and spreads.

"I'm so glad you're here, Rain."

Outside of the routine, no hiccups, no incidents, no waves. Thanks to pub dinners, no Archer either. It's a relief not to have to contend with his suspicion and determination to dig up dirt on me. My letters to Simone are full of honest contentment. Her replies are relief and support in blue ink. She fills paragraphs with her delight about my completion of high school this year.

I begin to relax.

When I reminisce about where the *real* journey began, I always arrive back at that Monday Heather texted me to tell me she was going to be working late. I set the uncooked chicken dish in the fridge to cook later and headed for the woods with Wind. I'd found a small clearing with a wide flat rock in the centre weeks ago, perfect for me to perch at the right position for my guitar to feel comfortable. Blank sheets of paper are rolled around my pencil and jammed into my jeans pocket. My favourite place would have to be in this clearing, my fingers tensing with electricity that seems to make the notes louder. I bend my head to tune the instrument, when the sound of branches shifting roughly intrudes on my solitude.

Archer stumbles into the clearing, a girl held tightly in his arms. He doesn't see me straight away, too absorbed in dancing his tongue with the redhead. I freeze; a tendril of fear snakes through my lungs. Knowing it's too late to sneak off unnoticed, I can only sigh as I hear his tongue detangle from the girl with a wet squelch, the green flames in his glare stabbing into me.

"Rain! You're spying on me! Damn it, what the hell do you want?"

I step back with the force of his venom, trepidation stealing my voice. When I can't answer, he stalks towards me, his rage gnashing and snarling like a wild thing.

"What are you going to do, little *Rainbow*? Run off to Heather and tell her all about it, how innocent little Rain was just strolling along and there he was, naughty Archer who wasn't really too sick to be at work? How he needs to be reminded of acceptable behaviour? Well? You got me. Got what you wanted. Congratu-fucking-lations."

The redhead steps away from the path of his fury.

But I hear notes of panic filtering through his aggression. He must be treading a fine line with his conduct with the heated performance he is giving, and I now I have him by the balls.

Right now I could demand everything he owns, and he would give it to me, or risk the wrath of Heather and the system. Or better still, I could settle for a future claim so no matter how badly I screw up while I'm here, Archer will have to take the fall for me. The urge to dangle it before him buds and flowers. I could destroy him for being so cold and aggressive towards me.

Instead, I clutch the fretboard of Wind, turn my back on them and escape home.

I don't want this shit.

* * *

Archer shuffles tentatively through the front door, the fear in his eyes searching for and locking on mine when he finally returns that evening.

"Archer?" Heather questions him gently, her furrowed brow angled towards him.

Archer's neck bobs and his spine locks, and I know he's convinced I told Heather. His tight expression prepares for the fight he's sure is coming.

"Yes?" He speaks warily, his gaze shifting from me to Heather.

"You look like you've had a hard day at work with your shoulders tense like that. Do you want to tell me about it?"

His eyes flash with surprise.

No, Archer, I didn't tell her.

"No, thanks Heather. Just...uh...a busy night and ran embarrassingly low on lager on tap. I hate it when that happens."

The woman laughs sympathetically.

"Tomorrow will be better, I'm sure. It always is. Come, sit and eat. Rain always makes extra in case you're hungry after work."

I raise my eyes to find green ones boring into me. I hold his gaze as I lift another forkful to my mouth. He looks away first.

I finish the dishes and seek my room. Cross-legged on my bed with my pillow at my back, I just sit and hold my guitar with eyelids closed, enjoying the stirrings of a tune coming to life within me. The notes begin from smoke that gathers in my veins, becoming solid things pushing against the insides of my fingers. They seek counsel with my pencil. Demanding notes on paper, the lyrics dancing on the edges of every chord progression. My guitar is a living thing. Everything it feels travels through my blood and speaks to me.

"What do you want?" Archer's hiss from the doorway startles it away.

The sigh falls down my chin. *Can't he just leave me be?*

"Nothing." My monotone is exhausted. His eyes flash.

"Bullshit, Rainbow! You just hit paydirt. We both know how this works. What do you want from me in exchange for your silence?" His fury loses its sharp edge. I watch as he flicks his attention to my suitcase, still packed on the desk beside open school books. He expects me to have unpacked. After today, I should be celebrating. If one of us has to go now, it will be him. I watch confusion win him over as I attempt to show my sincerity.

"I want nothing, Archer. Nothing at all. I saw nothing, I'll say nothing. Period." My words are low, calm. Finite.

Archer shifts his weight like he is going to cross the threshold. He holds back instead, struggling to find his footing in the new set of circumstances.

I return my attention to the instrument speaking to me and pluck. An idea forms and I began scratching words into the paper. When I look up sometime later, Archer has gone.

> *Within the threat of impending betrayal*
> *A light can change our fate*
> *Don't let the ice of darkness prevail*
> *Or our anger will never abate.*

CHAPTER 4

ARCHER

*A*rcher maintains space between us which suites me fine. Seven months on I'm still trying to figure him out. He'll appear aggressive at times, suspicious, outright curious, and everything in between. As late spring stretches the days out, however, I notice changes settle over him. With summer looming, Archer disappears for days at a time without warning. Heather's face was often creased with concern, but whenever I ask, she makes a show of smoothing her features, slipping into an empty smile and tells me Archer is staying at a friend's house. The most unsettling part is that he's never made mention of friends, preferring to be alone.

Then one day I look up and he's standing silently before me as if he's been there all along, and he seems…larger than before. After his return he hovers around the house, interest flicking to me between friendly conversations with Heather. Whats more, his scowl has reset itself into a constant light frown, as if he's visualising a puzzle inside me that he's putting together. Its disconcerting, but I detect no malice in it.

"I love having both of you home." Heather's heart shows in her expression.

"I'm just so glad you're part of our family, Rain, and I'm seeing so much of you lately, Archer, that it's like my whole family is finally together, warming my heart."

I pull her into a hug. She's the only person besides Simone I feel safe enough to show affection. She's such a beautiful person. Her hugs are maternal and soothing, and I sink into the kindness. She clutches my waist hard as her happiness overflows.

Without warning, pressure lands against my back and adrenaline explodes through me. My eyes open wide and I suck air, scrambling free.

The brutal force of Willow's wide horror locks on me. Her mouth stretches in shocked pain that shudders through the air. Her agony is so great that she can't even scream, just emits low chokes and guttural grunts that echo with chilling clarity in all my nightmares. After far too long, she finds a way to breathe, her body swelling with air.

And finally, she screams.

A thin wail is torn from my lips.

"Shit, sorry, Rain. It's okay. It's Heather and Archer. You're safe. You're home." Archer's soothing voice penetrates the veil of terror like hot chocolate in winter.

My chest heaves against the instinct to fight. I latch onto the voice inside me, the comforting mantra that insists I'm safe. *Nobody is touching me. There are no threats. Nothing can hurt me.* I scratch at my throat and reassure myself that it's nothing more than panic restricting my airways.

The fog creeps in as it always does, anaesthetising the sting. It folds the images into a suitcase, snaps it closed and slips away.

My breaths even out and I note an odd expression on Archer's face. Heather wears a frown of deep concern, focused on me. A scratch running down her nose and over her lip is flowering with crimson beads. She's hurt.

"Oh, Jesus, Heather. What happened to your face? You're bleeding..." Horror wedges in my stomach. One moment the three of us are bonding, the next they're staring at me like I'm a ghostly apparition, and Heather is bleeding. They share a look.

I glance between them, bewildered. It happened again, I just know it. I lose moments sometimes, a brief blackout that fills me with dread and everyone around me with suspicion.

"What...what happened?" I whisper hoarsely.

I feel Archer's hand slide carefully over my shoulder, Instinctively, I try to pull free of his touch, but as if he knows the tingling heat that radiates from him takes the jagged edges off my nerves, he reaches out again.

"You screamed, Rain." Archer soothes as his hand rubs and I frown.

Archer clears the table and I escape to my room, barely touching my fingertips to Wind's frets. Wind's voice is low and sad tonight, and while the lyrics flash behind my eyes, it doesn't seem right to add the vocals.

I flatten out my hand across the strings to silence the tune when the shadow appears at my door. Archer leans against the frame, his long body slumped submissively towards me, hands buried deep in his jeans pockets. He turned twenty the month after I had my fifteenth birthday. We both insisted that there be there was no fuss. I reluctantly allowed an undecorated cake without candles, and the iPod wasn't wrapped in decorative paper. It's the most special thing I own, outside of Wind. When I went to bed that night, a small box of chocolates sat on my pillow. I knew they were from Archer. A careful gift.

Tonight though, as he hovers in my doorway, the air seems to still around him, as if held in thrall by the same elusive mystery that sparks my own curiosity. Since he's turned twenty, his body has suddenly begun bulking out into a firm man-shape, the edges of his face growing harder and sharper, but with a handsome wildness that catches in my throat more and more as the days pass. He no longer moves awkwardly, having adjusted to his new build with impressive grace. I used to hear him moving through the house, but almost overnight he began covering ground in silence. It's as if he chose to upgrade everything about himself in those odd absences of his, often appearing out of thin air with bruises and cuts on his face. I understand learning to speak with your fists is a rite of passage into manhood, but any time I ask about his injuries, Archer simply shrugs dismissively.

"You didn't have to stop. That was beautiful, Rain." His tone is low and open.

"Thank you." My reply hesitates.

"I don't think I've heard it before. Who were you playing?"

"I wrote it. It's not a cover."

His brows arc. "Really? I didn't know you wrote music!"

I can't stop the ironic chuckle.

"That's because you've either avoided me, or threatened me since I arrived. The only times you're close to nice to me is if Heather is here."

His lips flatten. I watch his lungs empty.

"I'm sorry, Rain. I really am. I've been a dick, and you've been nothing but good to me." He jabs his fingers through his dark crown of soft spikes, crestfallen. I get it. He's one of the good guys, but he's battling his own unspoken demons. He feels he has to protect Heather, and to do that, he needs to assume everything is a threat. Even me. I hold up a hand.

"Don't sweat it, Archer. We both have our wars. We both have our own ways of dealing." I lift Wind.

Curiosity burns green as he stares. "You write music to escape? That's beautiful. Have you been writing long?"

I gesture to the popped lid of my full briefcase. Loose pages hang over the edge. Sheets of notes and lyrics fall around it on the bed.

"As long as I've had Wind."

"Wind?"

"My guitar. The foster who gave it to me taught me to play the notes of the wind. Told me I could change the seasons with music if I found the right notes, manipulate the weather to bring the sun, no matter how dark it got." The corner of my mouth twitches on the memory.

"And your friend gave you a guitar? That's kind." My chest sinks, and I slowly meet his eyes.

"It's his guitar. I got it when he died."

"Shit, I'm sorry. You know, you look like you have it all

together, I didn't think..."

"It's okay, Archer. We don't talk about *Before*, remember. You wouldn't know. Besides, we are all fucked up in some way or another. Some are just better at hiding it than others."

"Yeah, but..." He sucks a breath. "My dad beat up on my mum. For no reason. All the time. And I just watched. I should have stepped in. Helped her. But I was too scared..." My mouth falls open.

"Jesus, Archer. How old were you?" He won't meet my eyes.

It's a trade off of our broken pieces. I pull a splinter from my past to show him, and he offers his, but this serrated fragment he's offering still has flesh clinging to it, and his eyes narrow on the pain of it. So much so that I think he won't answer.

"My memory of it starts at eight, but when it stopped, I was thirteen." He whispers at the floor.

I wince. I know by the way he locks his jaw why it stopped, and understand how he probably ended up in the system. And I know how terrifying everything is at that age. Futile. A child's body too weak to carry out what the maturing mind knows needs to happen. My own memories and pain flare up briefly then wash away as the familiar thick, calming fog descends and absorbs them.

"You were a child still, Archer. And I see in the man you're becoming that your father would have been powerful. There was nothing you could do. Your brain was giving instructions your body was not capable of implementing. I know it hurts. It won't stop hurting, but you need to find a way to forgive yourself."

Archer's face dips and reddens. I understand. He'd just opened up about *Before*, leaving him raw and vulnerable. I could either accept his apology and say nothing, leaving our relationship the way it is, or... It would be nice to have a friend.

"You... you think I look powerful?" His face softens into a light frown.

I run my eyes over his broad shoulders and wide chest that tapers perfectly to narrow hips and muscled thighs. He is long and built to break hearts. I confirm with a slight nod and a light blush. It's not like me to ogle someone so openly. When I lift my eyes to his, they are fixed on me with a strange expression that makes my breath hitch. I clear my throat in the awkward silence.

"I don't know who my dad was. My mother is a junkie. She wasn't abusive; she simply forgot she had a daughter most of the time, which led to me entering the system at nine years old. The cops were called out to an altercation in a restaurant that Mum started, and they took her off to the station to clean up. I had been looking for her for three days when I found her. The sergeant said she'd told them she had no next of kin. We were living in bushes behind the church, so they didn't have an address in their records to check. When they took me to see her, she looked shocked. "Oh" she said. "I forgot about you. Can you tell this lot to let me out now?" It was the last time I saw her, and I have no intention of seeing her again. I knew then that she was beyond help, and I didn't want that life for myself."

My tone is even and void of emotion. I'd made peace with that chapter of my life. My mother was a victim of her own weakness. It was easier to lose herself in tablets and needles than face reality. I pity her.

"What happened tonight, Rain?" He asks softly.

I furrow my brow. "What do you mean? What about tonight?"

His lips part, and that sinking feeling returns. *What happened? What did I do?*

"Something scared you, Rain, and I think it was…me…but you screamed and fought like your life depended on it. You can't remember, can you?"

I search the dark reaches of my memory, turning up nothing. But I've been here before. Archer isn't the only one who's suggested something like this happened before. Other times I met with the same confused looks with similar accusations that I lashed out. I swallow my guilt.

"The fog…" I mutter.

"The fog?"

"I never know what happens, but it's like a great curtain of fog washes over me and takes the memory of what I did away with it."

Archer shakes his head slowly, almost as if he expected the explanation I gave. The tiny twist in my stomach draws my focus to his eyes, but they're clouded over, retreated into some train of thought he's entertaining. No, I correct as I push the unease away. Probably a memory of his own.

"We're fucked up units, the two of us." My grin bares my teeth.

"Yeah. Real fucked up." His own grin flutters.

CHAPTER 5

THE PERFECT STORM

*I*n the weeks that follow, Archer reveals a softer side. The side that adores Heather and smooths out some of the sharp corners of his face. Occasionally he glances at me with a curious, resigned agony, as if he's confronted by a destiny he's compelled to defy while knowing fierce retribution awaits him. His eyes shimmer, as if heavy with some anticipation of doom, waiting quietly for the inevitable moment the earth will rebel against him. I feel it burning in my chest. Then his expression evaporates just as quickly, leaving me to wonder just what secrets linger in his thoughts.

Most often, though, the new version of Archer has become everything I've craved from another human. He's attentive to my moods, sitting quietly beside me while Wind strums my musings, and stirring me up with his cheeky grin and baited comments when I need to loosen up. It's wonderful to finally find a proper connection with someone who understands the bumps in my past. That's another thing about fosters. The survivors, the ones who refuse to be victims, they're able to communicate on a depth the others can't understand. That depth of connection is why foster parents are encouraged to open their homes to two or more kids. The bond that can form is healing to both parties, not by "fixing" the other, but by sitting in the darkness together knowing that each carries their own special kind of pain. It empowers us to understand that nobody feels our scars the way we do. There's nothing more humiliating and painful than when people who don't understand try to put a light dressing over a deep laceration.

Archer sprawls his length over the diagonal of my bed with his chin in his palm while I recline against the headboard, absently strumming Wind. The subtle notes murmur, adding a comfortable warmth to the atmosphere. Archer's gaze slips constantly between my face and my fingers stroking the strings as he speaks. Of all the homes he's lived in, Heather's has been the longest.

"For years I was so angry at the world. I blamed every person around me for not being aware of the situation with my parents. I wanted to punish them for letting it go as far as it did. It didn't help that the first house I went to was new to the system. The woman decided that she could simply fix me by insisting I call her 'Mum'. It lasted three weeks. Over the next few years I was shuttled from place to place, and I fought every one of them. I fought the other fosters, too. When I came to this town and met Heather, I was on my last warning. I didn't care. Home, Grey Zone, it was all the same to me. But there's something about her that warmed me instantly. I walked over the threshold and just…dropped my anger on the mat."

I nod. "I know what you mean. Heather is…I don't know. She doesn't pretend to understand. She doesn't try to fix us. She accepts who we are completely and expects nothing more than what we are prepared to give. Right from the beginning I wanted a home, and the first home I was placed in was like paradise. I was so blown away with having a roof to sleep under that everything else didn't seem to matter, but when I found I was placed with others, I could barely contain my excitement. They could be friends, and I'd never had friends before since people on the streets were to be treated with caution and avoided. There were four of us girls, all within a year of the same age, and we all shared a room for two years. They were all nice, though. Then…" I swallow my rising bile. "The next place was pretty awful. The foster parents had their biologicals and proceeded to plan a holiday that didn't include me. Like I was a family pet they offloaded into a kennel. I never unpacked."

Awareness shivers through me and I take in the intensity of his eyes. This conversation should be off limits, our words void of the past, but Archer's proximity is the skeleton key to everything I keep locked away from the world. Every reinforced door inside me swings open on rusty hinges and beckons him further in.

"So you've only had two before, then? You're luckier than most."

My spine goes cold. I swallow thickly.

"I've had at least eighteen homes, but I feel there's more that I can't remember. Some of them lasted a few weeks. Others lasting just days." My words are carefully selected but Archer senses something. He leans, and I watch his body tense and his eyes sharpen. He doesn't get in my space, but he's right on the edge. I feel his closeness rouse the hairs on my arm and resist the urge to lay my hand on his bicep. He's not stupid, and he knows the inside of the system enough to pick the holes in my story.

"The missing pages in your file!" His eyes widen. I allow the barest nod. I hear his swallow.

"What happened, Rain? What was so big that even the system withheld it? I looked at your file, and it tells the story of someone just entering foster care. I thought you were here to take over, or hurt Heather... but you're not, are you?"

He knows the answer, and he can see with the lift of my chin that I won't tell him. I can't go there. Partially because I'm not ready to fall into a fully-fledged panic attack in front of him, but also because of this fog that wraps itself around the open wounds in my memory that I can't seem to penetrate. He doesn't push, but he wants to know. His stiff spine tells me he's burying his urge to persuade me. I see curiosity, a shimmer of fear and...anger? His protectiveness of Heather has expanded to incorporate me.

Intuitively, Archer emotionally backs off a fraction. His emerald eyes are warm and kind.

"Wanna play cards?"

* * *

The wind's bitter chill pushes through my bones. While a

school uniform is a great idea in theory, blustery days like this convince me the dresses were designed by a man, with no thought given to modesty or protection from the elements. My arms are sore from holding the fabric down tight around my legs.

Heather has a long shift tonight, so I make risotto for Archer and me. I thought he may have been rostered on at the pub, but even if he was he could reheat it afterwards if he was hungry. He doesn't like mushrooms, so I leave them out of the meal completely. I eat alone by the window, watching darker clouds swallow up the landscape of bending trees and howling wind. The storm is building into a nasty one and I text Heather to be safe as I change into the shorts and singlet top I sleep in. The power would most likely be cut with the storm, so I figure I'd just sleep through it and leave my homework until tomorrow night, enjoying the show. I love a good storm. The utter rage and destruction of thunder tearing open the world touches me. I used to feed my anger to these storms, and they'd take it from me and unleash it on an unprepared world. I'd rejoice in the trees it ripped from the earth with the vengeance I shared with it. I'm not feeling so angry these days, and I wonder if there are other fosters feeding its fury. The crack and roll of the heavens roar outside on the edge of sleep.

I hear my bedroom door crack open. It stands slightly ajar in the flickering lightning. My stomach twists and I throw the covers back, instantly on guard. My hand flies to my bedside lamp, but the switch gives an empty *snap*.

The power is out.

The power is out and there is someone in my room! My heart thumps painfully against my ribs as I edge out of bed, scanning the room for movement, waiting for the lightning to reveal my intruder. I lean through the darkness to snatch my briefcase. The corners and weight would make a satisfactory weapon if need be. It's then I become aware of movement beneath my desk. I muffle a shriek of terror and step back, leaving enough room to wield my weapon.

The flash of lightning turns my bedroom to day, catching a sharp glint from the eyes of the huddled figure in the corner.

Jesus. It's Archer!

The dots of perspiration shine on his forehead with the next flash, the whites of his eyes impossibly large. His mouth limp in a terror so consuming that I'm amazed his body was able to function enough to bring him here. His eyes look blankly through mine in his panic, and I resist the urge to reach out and comfort him. He is wild in his fear, and he could hurt me if he felt trapped and lashed out.

Instead, I reach for Wind. I sit on the bed close to him, leaving a clear path to my door if he needs it.

I close my fingers on the frets and began to drown out the storm with some strong chords and my voice.

This storm got nothing on you, my friend

Your courage is tattooed on your roar

You drown out the thunder as you transcend

You have already won this war.

You have already won this war.

When I check on him, his lips are closed and his eyes are clear and focused. In a voice lighter than the rain he whispers:

"Again, please, will you play it again?" And I do, running through it three more times before the storm loses strength and the thunder rolls away. He shuffles out from under the desk slowly. His body less rigid than before, Archer uncurls in front of me. I watch in my periphery as his shoulders round, and he can't look at me. He's peeled open and vulnerable, forced by his terror to expose his weakness. When he reaches the door I look up at him.

"I have nightmares. Bad ones. And I have panic attacks leading up to my birthday," I admit to his back. His shoulders lift in gratitude.

For the next week I don't see him at all.

CHAPTER 6

UNPACKING

*I*n the weeks following the storm, Archer's shifts are changed to the lunchtime roster and he starts coming home every night. It feels strange that such easy conversations now bloom in place of the steely silence that had existed for almost eight months. Heather is beside herself with delight. Never being able to have children of her own, Heather is now experiencing the joy of family for the first time with Archer and me. We laugh and talk each night over dinner, often skipping dessert and launching into card games instead. Heather chases sleep soon after eight, but Archer and I recline on the couch together and talk, sometimes well into the small hours of the morning.

"I want to do a degree in child psychology. Principal Thompson has been looking into it and thinks he can get around the age thing. Mr Thompson's found a couple of Universities who might be willing to offer the course by correspondence. I can attend the lectures online, and submit any oral works the same way. It might actually work!"

Archer offers that special smile that lights up his whole face and triggers a warm wave in my belly.

"That means you can keep living here?" I guess he would miss our conversations. I would, too. Archer keeps people at arms length like us fosters tend to do.

"Yeah, but regardless, they'll only allow me to do a few subjects a year, so I'm thinking about getting a part time job somewhere. That's where I'm stumped, really. With the limited transport, my hours of work would be hard to juggle with the bus schedule."

"I could drive you…"

I smirk and shove his shoulder playfully. "And what would happen when we have shifts at the same time, silly? One of us would have to drop work. It's counter productive."

Archer flashes me a funny look. One that I haven't been able to interpret yet.

"Why don't you and Wind do a few nights in the pub? I can move a shift easily a few nights a week so I work the nights you do. I've talked to Zachary about some live music, and he seems pretty keen…"

I taste the idea, pulling my lip between my teeth. It could be a good way to bring in some money to help Heather out a bit, and I can play covers pretty easily. I know I'm trying to stay under the radar, but excitement overrides my need for caution.

'Okay, I'll zip over to the pub after school tomorrow and speak to him. I'll take Wind with me. I hope he'll like my singing."

Archer's gaze lingers on my mouth, a flare of light swirling in the vibrant depths of green, both frightening and exciting me. The meaning of it lingers in the fringes of my awareness like a secret unfurling, catching in my throat while my pulse spikes.

"Rain, you sound like an angel. He'll love you. I can see we're going to be busy on the nights you play. Rain and Wind. The perfect storm." The deep liquid of his voice makes me shiver. I choke on my confusion and jump up off the couch.

"Goodnight, Archer. See you tomorrow." I hurry away before he can respond.

Yesterday, I hit a milestone. On a deep inhale I lifted my underwear from their corner of my suitcase, and sat them in my top drawer. They appear lost and alien in all the space around them. I marvel at how so few items could stuff a suitcase past capacity so easily. Then I'd closed the drawer and walked away without the urge to retrieve them and replace them with the rest of my clothes. For the first time in a very, very long time, I almost felt like this was becoming home. I had already been stowing my pyjamas in my bedside table for weeks now.

I'd just slipped into my singlet top and shorts when the light tap sounded on my door.

"Yeah?" I invite. Archer opens the door a crack.

"I just thought, if you like, when you come to the pub tomorrow, I'll be on. Um, If you wanted to stick around for dinner, I can drive you home when I'm finished."

I reach for the brush behind me, flashing my back to him.

"Actually, that sounds great, thanks. I've never eaten out bef… what's wrong?" I turn back to meet a look of shock printed on his face. I furrow my brow at what could cause such a reaction.

"Is that…is that a *tattoo* on your back?" His timbre trembles in concern.

I feel the moment my face closes down, shutting Archer out completely. Yanking my hair out of its tie, letting my hair tumble over the offending image on my shoulder blade. I know what he saw. Panic twists my mouth.

"Get out of my room now, Archer!" His shock intensifies, and I know I sound hysterical. I can't help it. He needs to leave.

"Get out or I'll scream!' My words crash together in high pitched horror.

His head rears back, eyes wide. He sees my sincerity and retreats quickly, closing my door as I crumple into a full blown panic attack.

* * *

Zachary is in his late fifties with peppered hair and a bulbous nose.

"How about Flame Trees by Cold Chisel?"

Zachary nods sharply. It's a great pub song. I perch on a bar stool in the far corner of the pub, microphone angled between Wind and my mouth. I slow the song down into a gentle ballad, close my eyes and lose myself in the music. The lyrics weave around my skin with the incredible acoustics in the room. The sound amplified is beautiful, even to my own ears, and by the time I've strummed the last chord, I'm ready to launch into another. I open my eyes and seek a response from Zachary. He stands with his mouth open, staring at me appreciatively. I feel my smile spread. From the other side of the room, the two patrons put down their beers and start clapping. I see Archer's deep green eyes land on me, a proud smile on his face.

Zachary's silence embarrasses me, and I shift awkwardly on my stool. He finds his voice finally.

"How old are you?" He fires at me. I matured early, grew into my curves and dips like a grown woman, but I won't lie.

"Fifteen."

He eyes me curiously, hesitation crawling in.

Archer calls out from behind the bar, dishcloth poking out of a schooner.

"She's studying Year Twelve, Zack. She's mature."

My breath waits, escaping loudly when the older man blinks away his concern.

"Okay. You can call me Zack. How many nights do you want?" My heart floats. I dart a glance at Archer. He'd be driving me home, so I need to fit in with his schedule. He shrugs towards me. *Any time suits.*

"Four nights to start okay?"

Zack nods vigorously. "If you make two of those nights Fridays and Saturdays, it's a deal!"

I grin idiotically.

"Can you start this Friday? It will give me a chance to advertise it. What do you call yourself, just Rain, or do you want your surname on as well?" I don't want my name anywhere, not even in part. My eyes lock on Archer affectionately.

"The Perfect Storm."

Archer smirks and drops a wink at me. I frown at how it

makes my stomach jump.

Customers start drifting in. Archer drops a chicken parmigiana in front of me and my heart leaps to my lungs. I stare at the chips, the tiny bowl of salad arranged on the side. Archer's long body falls into the chair opposite me and lifts an eyebrow.

"I've never eaten out before. I mean, chips on a plate? And the salad……just for me? I feel like a woman of society."

Archer lands a lopsided grin.

"You can eat like this every night you work. Zack feeds everyone at the end of their shift." My shining eyes slowly narrow.

"So why do you have dinner with us after work? Surely you'd have already eaten?"

Archer blushes faintly. "I like your cooking." And with that he spins off to serve a customer.

With fifteen minutes left to kill until Archer ends his shift, I raise Wind and my eyebrows to Zack as he zips past. He slows as he passes.

"I can't pay you till Friday, but feel free to test it out if you like."

I wander nervously to the microphone and clear my throat softly. The only ones paying attention are the same two bodies from earlier, Zack and Archer. I test the sound of Wind, then fall into "Buses and Trains" by Bachelor Girl. By the time the last chord falls, cheering erupts from around the room.

A voice booms from the occupied table in the corner. "Play something else."

"She'll be back Friday. You can listen to more then." Zack calls out.

My face warms with pleasure as I reflect on my good fortune and watch Archer, bent and focused over the till.

What an incredible day. I've got myself a job. Not just any job, but one in which I can do what I love the most. And Archer likes my cooking. That feels the best of all. I stiffen suddenly with the gravity of what that implies. Zeroing in on Archer, I look past the defensive boy I met months ago and take him in as a man for the first time. How easily he became the friend I never thought I'd have. My best friend. But now…he's…more. With a naturally muscular frame, wide at the shoulders and chest, slim and firm at the hips. My throat dries as I note the outline of pecs and abs beneath his tight black shirt. The top two buttons have fallen open, and a light sprinkle of dark hair peeks out. The tight edges of his sculpted jaw, strong cheekbones, the strength of his nose. The faint silver of old scars should have detracted from his looks, but instead they seem to highlight a wild ferocity within that makes him almost glow. Archer is utterly beautiful. *Why had I not seen him as a man before now?* But when I reach his eyes I see him staring right back at me. The deep emerald darkens and simmers. And I feel it, creeping up from my stomach, tingling through my veins and heating my skin. My steep inhale catches, falters and lodges in my throat as understanding finally dawns.

I now recognise that look in his eye, that one I couldn't place before. I shiver and my breath stutters.

Oh, damn.

CHAPTER 7

WORKING GIRL

*T*he pub is packed out. Patrons filled the chairs or group in the floorspace as I play. My covers are a hit. There are more bodies in here than the population of the town, and Zack grins at me as he helps out the wait staff.

The last lyrics in "Glory Days" by Bruce Springsteen fall from my lips to thundering applause. I let the sound trickle down my spine. It always gives the sensation of owning the world when I sit here behind the microphone. I sip my water. Still well under the legal drinking age, the bar only supplies water or soft drinks to me. Not that I'd want something harder, after watching my mother's drinking progress into harder highs. I never want to repeat that pattern.

"Play something else." The echoes supporting the request burst from all over.

Before I lose my nerve, I reply. "Okay. This is one of mine... "Small Town." I hope you like it."

Wind comes alive with a light snappy riff.

> *"The sign brings me home to Mountain Plateau*
> *Population five-twenty eight*
> *The supermarket hours are nine 'til god knows*
> *And Zack serves the tenderest steak*

The townsfolk wear smiles, they all lend a hand
If you need a trailer or a ride
And if you're after an ale and an ear for your rant
The bartender's a good friend of mine.
Yeah, the barman's a good friend of mine."

I see Archer's face whip to mine, lips parted. He drops his cloth to the bar and his shoulders flex with the power of his applause. The patrons stomp their feet, and the seated ones rise from their chairs. They all love a song about their hometown, and the roar rises with requests for more. But my set is over and my throat scratches. My gratitude is so wide my cheeks ache. As always I sneak straight out the back, down the long corridor that leads to the office. I love their appreciation, but I can't deal with the touches, the crowding, the alcohol-laden breaths. They cascade over the edges of my personal space. My ears ring and my fingers are tender, but I don't think I've ever been this happy before.

"You were brilliant, Rain! And that song...they loved it!" Archer bursts in and lands a kiss on my temple. The puff of exhale on my face, the sensation of his hot, soft lips makes my lungs catch. I clench my teeth against the reaction, but the warmth spreads through my body regardless. A blush colors my face.

"I'm glad you liked it." I stutter. Archer takes my hands in his, the warmth and electric pulses drowning out all sense and reason.

"Rain, you have to know how amazing and talented you are. I...uh...everybody loves you." His voice deepens. Green eyes darken and I force myself to pull away from his touch. Eyebrows leap at my withdrawal, his soulful gaze darting between mine for answers. It's a moment where time has no place, suspended and irrelevant, while our hearts share the futility of a love that's doomed before it has a chance to begin. My skin cries out at the loss of his warmth but I ignore it.

Archer is my friend. My brother, for Christ's sake. And in

our position as fosters, we can't afford for our relationship to expand into anything more than that. Not until we're both free of the system, but even then there will be other things to consider. Like Heather's feelings. He flinches as I tuck my hands protectively around my waist, and mirrors the sadness in my own expression. We don't need to say a word. We just stare at each other with our hearts reaching out and don't move away for a long while, suspended in the chasm of fantasy. He knows now how I feel about him, it hangs in the space between us and radiates from the heat of my heart. I see his throat bob and his hands flex at his sides.

"I, uh...finish in ten. I'll come and get you when it's time to go." His smile is forced and weak. He knocks his knuckles gently on the desktop on his way out.

My breath escapes my lungs.

Heather tells me the next day that Archer's been rostered on every night, and won't be joining us for a while. I miss him already.

I throw myself into study with such force that I run out of work to complete. I begin searching online for case studies for trauma survivors. It's the area I want to get into most. Help the children trying to manage fractured nightmares, navigate triggers, fear the panic attacks that invade and shape their existence. A name hovers in the shadows of my consciousness, and on a whim, I enter Sarah Aldridge into the search bar. My heart clatters as the results spread across the screen. There's her face smeared with blood and tears. The dead, haunted eyes, the tattoo. The articles. I scroll down the page. There are no recent photos of her, so I spend the next hour scanning the article headings. And there it is. My tears fall freely. A simple death notice a couple of lines long. Her full name, birth date and date of passing. The second line simply said "At rest". There are no lines listing names of people who would miss her. Of course not. I squeeze my eyes closed and send my love and thoughts to her over space and time.

The second name I search shows the same articles, and

similar pictures. I reach out and touch the screen. I miss this girl the most. Only one more year until I can seek her out, if she wants to be found. I'd do anything to have her at my side right now. She always knew what to say, the right thing to do. I can't find any recent photos of her, but there's no death notice, either.

Hang in there, please.

I run a quick search on a third name. Amongst the clippings I see this girl's foster parents have started a foundation to fund foster children's legal fees. It's a wonderful cause, but I can't help feeling resentful. I will never contact her, or allow her to find me when the time comes, even though I loved her just as deeply as the other girls. The psychologists tell me it's normal to feel that way. I don't understand why I connect so strongly with three of these girls, but the fourth girl...for her I feel nothing. No love, no hate, no desire to reach out, nor to push her away. Its as though she's nothing but a shadow that was always there yet never really present. I never bothered running a search on her, but my fingers twitch over the keyboard. My mouth sours and dries as I tap in the first letter. C. The blood begins to hammer in my chest as my finger seeks the next letter. My hand hovers, my head throbs.

With a thin cry, I delete the letter, frowning deeper as my pounding heart evens out. I draw a shaky breath, mind whirling with confusion.

I wish Archer was here right now, but even if he wanted to, he's taken another few days off work. Zach runs the bar and tells me he doesn't know where Archer went; just that he needed time off. More than anything I need Archer here, to just sit beside me, offering me the strength he seems to exude to take some of the pain away.

But he won't.

* * *

It becomes part of my regular Friday night set. I finish my covers, and throw in one of my own. It works well for Zack too, he keeps the pub full of paying customers until my last song at midnight, when they all trickle out until my next shift. I throw a smile at a table full of young men on my left. There's five of them, and they make sure to come early to snag the closest table. They cheer the loudest, too. I let Wind find the new tune, a gentle melancholy song.

"I'm sitting on the couch wrapped tight
My smile gently fades away
Remember when we talked all night?
But now you've gone away.
Oh, now you've gone away.

Don't stay away, we'll manage this
Without you, I can't grow
We've been through more, we must persist
We're tougher than they know
Yeah, you're tougher than they know.

I know this thing can't have a place
In where we have to be
But I'm lonely and I miss your face
You're everything I need.
Yeah, you're everything I need"

The car winds through the trees as the silence stretches like acres between us. I hate this. I look over at Archer's stony face and cringe. He never takes focus from the road. In fact, he's barely said a word to me since he returned after another unexplained absence to take me to work. He barely looks at me, and when he does it's with a flash of fierce heat and an agony that he quickly buries beneath a scowl. I open the door before the car has stopped and stalk to my bedroom. Burying my face in the softness of my pillow, I sob until sleep finds me.

Sarah looks accusingly at me. "You left me alone. I needed you and you didn't come, and you promised you would." Her fingernails reach over her shoulder and slowly dig out a clump of bloody flesh, holding it out to me to see. I stare at the chunk in horror for a while, then at the hole in her shoulder. I can see the white of the bone at the bottom of the wound. Her tattoo is sharp and black and engraved into her skeleton.

"It doesn't go away, Credence, It's too deep inside." She whispers sadly. Blood trickles in crimson rivulets from her eyes.

Hands grip and shake me in the dark. I choke off the scream coming from my throat as I'm yanked from sleep and pulled against a wall of warmth. Two thick, familiar arms wrap around me, and I relax into their security.

Archer.

My breaths burn as they slow.

"Rainbow, it's okay. It's Archer. I'm here and you're safe. Nothing can hurt you here." His mantra settles over me, forcing rhythm back into my pulse. Sobs hitch my chest as he murmurs against my hair, rocking with me in the darkness.

"Is it *Before*?" He asks gently. I turn sideways in his arms so I'm sitting across his lap and nod into his chest. The heat from his body winds into my skin and sparks an ache in my throat that has nothing to do with the nightmare and everything to do with how right this feels, and its inevitable end. I flex my palm against his chest in agonised desperation. I need him.

"Want to talk about it?" I shake my head and feel him sigh under my hand. As I relax into hiccups, I'm aware of the earth and spice smell of him curling into my nostrils. and his stirring reaction nudges into me. My pulse firing erratically in response, tears of futility slide down my cheeks. It's all so useless.

"My friend, Sarah. I found out today that she died. Over a year ago, and I didn't know. She's one of three people in the world that are more important to me than anything, and she's gone. I feel like I've lost you, too, and that's worse than death, Archer, because I can see you every day but I can't talk to you." He squeezes me, inhaling my hair. His sigh cracks.

"I know, but it's best this way. Neither of us want to complicate things. Neither of us want to go into the Grey Zone."

Annoyance spikes. "*You* won't. You're twenty and independent."

"I know, but do you think I'd still be welcome here? And what if you end up back in the system with another home to get used to? Do you think I want that for you? You'd never get the opportunity to do your course, either."

He's right. If we give in to our emotions and Heather disapproves, we both suffer, and my career will be over before it's had a chance to begin. My voice wobbles.

"I've never felt so alone, Archer."

His arms tighten. "What about your other friend. You said there were three?"

I shake my head. "I can't make contact for another two years, and even then, I don't know if she'll let me back in." When I admit my fear to him, his eyes narrow. He's well aware that we are free to maintain communication between fosters, unless there's extenuating circumstances.

"It's something bad, isn't it?" His soft voice undoes me and the tears begin again. He thinks I'm such a good, wholesome person, but he doesn't know about the other side of me. The part that eludes even me but grips me with a darkness that reeks of evil. Whatever it is, I think there's a reason it hovers out of reach.

"It's connected to your tattoo, isn't it?" Archer speculates. I collapse into sobs. After a while, Archer moves me off his lap and under the sheets. My body shakes.

"Hold me?" I plead. I listen to him deliberate. He slides beside me, fully clothed, and throws an arm over me, pulling me close to his chest. The tragic perfection of lying here in his arms tears my heart to shreds.

CHAPTER 8

TRIGGERS & THINGS

*N*othing changes. Archer continues to avoid me, and I continue to study. Principal Thompson enrols me in an online degree, and I've already started reviewing the university subjects.

I'm already halfway through the module on Cognitive Development. It's even more interesting than I had imagined and I soak up every word, reflecting on my experiences to compare them with the teachings. There's an entire textbook on developmental psychology that's as thick as a dictionary. I turn to the subject that excites me most. The Psychology of Trauma. My fingers tremble on the printed notes. We get to do a case study based on a real life scenario, and apply learned techniques to achieve the possible outcomes. I scan the pages for the details. And there it is;

Case Study 1. Is separation an acceptable way to heal trauma victims and why? The trial of Sarah Aldridge, Willow Zimms, Credence Bowman and Katherine Elson.

My lungs empty out and freeze.

My sisters!

Still in a state of shock when Friday night comes, I walk in just before my set starts and Zack brings me my bottle of water. My songs flow smoothly enough, and when my time is up, I encore with another cover instead of one of my songs. Archer furrows his brow from behind the bar.

When my set concludes, I make for the familiar comfort of the office and exhale sharply. The urge to call Simone to come and get me is overwhelming. Angst jams in my lungs. I don't want to see Archer, either. I'm angry at him for deserting me when I need him. For taking away the only friend I have because he thinks it's too hard to be around me. I step out for some air, winding through the narrow hallway and through the rear entrance. The crisp air cleans out my lungs.

"I thought I'd find you here." My eyes widen on the figure in front of me. I didn't hear anybody through the fog of my thoughts. One of the guys from the fan table steps out of the shadows.

"Oh, hi. Thanks for coming to support me so often. I hope you enjoy the music." I stutter through the turmoil in my head.

"It's incredible. I'm Flynn. I was hoping I could talk with you, but you disappear after your set each night, so I hope you don't mind me seeking you out."

Flynn is tall and lean, muscles wiry and hard. His features are gentle, but magazine perfect. With gentle eyes the colour of liquid turquoise and perfectly sculptured lips, he's an extremely attractive man. If you like blondes.

"I'm not a fan of crowds. Nice to meet you, Flynn. I'm Rain."

"What a beautiful name. It suits you. More like summer Rain." He dazzles me with a smile that conveys genuine warmth and lights his eyes with sincerity that quiets my wariness.

"Thanks. Look, My ride's due so I'd better get back in. But thanks for coming. It's nice to see a friendly face in the crowd." I turn from him, but he moves between me and the door. His expression is kind, curious, but I start to panic. He doesn't notice.

"I was hoping I could take you out some time, Rain?"

I don't have the ability to give him an answer. I reign in my panic, suck in air and push past him.

"I have to go," I manage before I embarrass myself, and snap the door closed. I lean against it and regain my composure.

Archer appears at the end if the hall. His frown smooths out when he sees me.

"There you are. I couldn't find you. What's wrong?" *My life is falling apart in front of me and I'm all alone* I want to scream at him. Instead I shake my head and wrap my arms around my waist. He slides his gaze over me, and I let him pull me into a hug. My throat crawls up as I cling to him, pressing my ear to the rhythm of his heart. His-spice-and-earth smell saturates me. It's the most wonderful thing I've ever smelled. His chin rests on my head, and my scalp tingles with the soft caress of his breath. My pulse gallops at his nearness, while Archer's builds up tempo and his breath begins to shake. His firm grip bites into my arms as he fights to put air between us. I lift my eyes to his and watch him fight the flames in them. I feel their heat reaching out for me until I submit to the impulse to touch him again, but when I step forward, he staggers back as if my touch would burn him. It makes me want to cry.

"I need a friend, Archer." My monotone drifts past the tears that threaten.

"I'm sorry, Rainbow." The anguish in his expression bleeds.

* * *

Heather is working late again, and this time Archer follows me into my bedroom. Even though he's trying to keep a chaste distance from me, he's hard wired into my anguish, compelled to help while fighting to avoid getting too involved.

His eyes narrow, darting around my room as if searching for a valid reason to be here.

My breath hitches at the idea of having him in my space, but his jaw ticks with determination. He stalks to my desk and snatches a sheet of paper I haven't stowed in my briefcase. I snarl with frantic indignance, scrambling to retrieve it, but he spins out of reach.

"Don't you dare, Archer. It's private!"

My nails seek purchase, but with uncanny ease he holds me off with one hand. I've been in fights before, but never before have I felt so weak and incapable. I notice the thick corded biceps flexing and bunching, and I wonder fleetingly how he's managed to find time to work out. There's not a gym in miles, and there's no way the muscles that hold me at bay were sculptured behind the bar. And clearly they're not painted on, because I'm seething fury, and his breathing isn't even elevated. Awareness seeps in, tangling with my rage. No matter how much injustice roars through my blood, I can't seem to disconnect from the feel of his body flexing and pressing against mine, and my body betrays me with a thrilled shiver.

When I slump, exhausted, against his chest, he peels me off him, stepping aside, lips thin and brow furrowed. Eyes smoulder on me, so potent and fierce with desire that I dare him with eyes at half-mast.

Just touch me, Archer.

But his nostrils flare and he swallows thickly, sucking in a shuddering breath. *Damn him and his self-restraint!*

He unlocks his eyes from mine, tearing his attention defiantly back to the page in his hand. My lungs empty.

I know what he reads.

> *The ghosts are waking, coming closer*
> *Sharper teeth and rotting eyes*
> *Clutch your wilting four leaf clover*
> *Before each dream inside you dies*

"Play it for me." He demands. I consider fighting him, but I'm so tired of being on edge. I reach for Wind and only play the first few dark and sombre notes before he stops me. He drags a hand over his face, not able to erase the tone of pain that grips my heart.

"I'm so sorry I can't be the friend you need right now. It's shit, and I hate it more than you know, but we both know there's nothing we can do about it. It's that black and white. I need you to tell me what's going on, Rain. You're so edgy and wild, I feel like you're a stranger suddenly, and your tunes sound like death.

What is it that haunts you?"

"I'll be okay, Archer. Really. Just a few ghosts I need to kill…" I wince unintentionally. Archer pulls me down to the bed beside him, my half-formed lyrics still gripped in his fist.

"Listen, Rain, You are the most amazing person I've ever met. You're so resilient, so quietly powerful that you blow me away. You're this stunningly gorgeous, incredibly talented woman and you could have the world eating out of your hand. You're so genuine and pure it kills me. If you can't tell me, have faith that you can survive this, too." I snake my arms around his waist awkwardly. His words spread warmth through me. He murmurs into my hair.

"What are you doing to me, beautiful girl? Why do you keep invading my thoughts like you do?" His gentle words decimate me.

I feel his fingers pinch my jaw, tilting my face to him. The green in his eyes deepens, and my tongue shoots over my lip in nervous anticipation. He almost looks like he's…

I gasp at the incredible sensation of his soft, hot mouth pressing against mine. His tongue traces my lips and I open to him without hesitation. My pulse hammers lava through my veins and I melt into him, stroking his tongue with mine as he dives deeper, desperately. Uncontrollably. My grip seeks his skin.

I've never been kissed before, but it feels like an epiphany, a vision…transcendent. I dig my nails in with the urgency to have him closer and wonder at how…right…it all is. It makes sense, Archer and me. My body recognises it and presses against him. His hand crawls up my back and tangles in my hair, pressing our heads closer as his mouth burns me. The harsh rasp of his breathing hypnotises me. I quiver at the potency of his hunger. My own craving rises to meet him and I need this more than I need my next breath. His lips slide off mine and trail a path of embers along my jaw, sparks and flames erupting at the site. I groan my desire, and Archer responds with a ravenous growl. The muscles beneath his shirt ripple and clench as I finally get the chance to explore them. His flesh is hard satin fire and I shiver with excitement. I roll my fingertips towards the button on his jeans, brushing the hot bulge pushing against the zipper. Archer hisses.

Then he shoves me from him so hard my neck jars.

I cry out as I'm ripped from his touch.

"Fucking *fuck!*" He roars. He fists his hair and stares at me in horror. His chest dances the same erratic dance as mine.

Venom emanates from his glare and he growls through clenched teeth. "This can *never* happen, Rain."

I jump at the force of the slamming door.

CHAPTER 9

RELEASING FIRE

*N*ot only is the friendship over between Archer and me, but it shifts into something volatile. He keeps physical distance between us, too. For two weeks straight, I don't see him at all. Zack tells me he's taken leave, and Heather beams at me and announces he's staying with friends for a while. Zack drives me home as he always does in Archer's absences, and the atmosphere everywhere is taut with apprehension. Life seems unnatural without Archer in it.

One Saturday night Zack pulls into the driveway beside the familiar sight of Simone's car. My dark mood evaporates and I burst through the door with excitement, almost knocking her over with the force of my embrace.

"Simone, I wasn't expecting you. Are you staying?" I grin, but Simone shakes her head.

"I just dropped by to discuss something with Heather. I didn't expect to stay so late, but I'm glad I got to see you and hear how well you're settled in here. I'm sorry I can't stay longer this time, Rain, but I need to get home."

She has trouble meeting my eyes, and suspicion simmers in my belly, but her face is hard. She won't tell me anything, so I don't ask, but I watch Heather closely for any signs she is preparing to pack my bags and let me go.

The following night, I see Archer's car by the shed. A sad thrill clashes with relief to know he's home again, but he doesn't come to see me.

The next afternoon strikes, and Archer's car idles in the driveway. My heart lurches. He's waiting for me, profile stiff and locked on the screen so he doesn't have to look at me. I don't even have to see his face to feel the chill rolling off him. This is a transaction. He's only taking me to work because he said he would. Nothing more. With empty lungs I sink into the passenger seat and take my time to muster the courage to look at him. When I do, I choke on a cry.

Archer wears stitches in his eyebrow, cuts on his jaw and a crowd of dissolving inky bruises.

"What happened?"

Silence. His jaw ticks.

"Where do you go?" I whisper, the crushing futility rough in my throat.

He doesn't acknowledge me, doesn't even look at me. There's a harder air about him that's never been present before. His eyes dart, his focus sharp, and as fast as that, all the softer edges of the Archer I knew are gone.

After my sets, Zack brings my water to the office instead of Archer. The rides home are stony and uncomfortable. My teeth clench with tension whenever are in close proximity. Heather is wonderfully oblivious.

Saturday night is another full house. Flynn and his mates smile and wave. I'm about to start my set when I notice I don't have my bottle of water next to my chair. I push through the crowd to the bar, but I can't see Archer anywhere. I slip under the bar door and open the drinks fridge when I hear a noise coming from the back room. A giggle? I frown as I follow the sound. Archer comes into sight, his back towards me and head tilted downwards, and he's smiling. Warmth rushes through me.

I can't remember the last time I saw him without a scowl on his face. Maybe he'll speak to me now. I wear my friendliest smile and move closer. When he comes into full view my lungs ice over.

There's a woman in his arms.

He's pressing a redhead into the wall, his body hard against her, hands leaning on the brick wall, caging her in. My heart twists as I watch his lips dipping towards hers. The hunger burning on his face, the heat in her eyes that tells me they know each other more intimately than a mere kiss.

My water drops in numb shock, and I spin away from the decimating scene. Archer is about to kiss her. Kiss her like he'd once kissed me. I can't watch his lips on hers and feel the remnants of my heart splinter. The pub blurs as I walk away, my body betraying me with memories of how his mouth felt on mine. My stomach bottoms out and I swallow the rising bile. I know we should keep our distance from each other, but… I can't believe he moved on so fast.

On the way out, I snag another water bottle from the fridge and, with trembling limbs and my forced smile hiding my shattered heart, I begin my set. I can't help but notice when Archer returns to the bar, clutching the bottle I dropped. I stab a glare at him. When it comes time for my final song, I curl my lip at him, ensuring his attention belongs to me. Wind starts with mournful notes, my voice soft and agonised.

I sit among the pieces of my broken heart
The wound just won't stop bleeding
Your lips on hers tore my world apart
Leaving me without your touch, grieving

My fingers stiffen on the strings, and Wind vibrates with the tension I pluck into him. My voice grows deeper and richer. Angry chords resonate through the room like bloodthirsty talons. My audience goes wild.

Well you moved on so fucking quick
Never really tried to hide it
My replacement sitting on your dick
Your tender words were bullshit.

I've been through worse, my heart will heal
And you mean shit to me
Just so you're clear on our deal
Keep the fuck away from me.
Yeah, keep the fuck away from me.

Wind roars his fury, my vocals so powerful in my rage that on the last note, one of the strings snaps. And the pub is an uproar. The applause thunders around me and I shake with the strength of my pain and anger. Adrenaline rips through my lungs, and instead of withdrawing into the office, I step into the crowd. Flynn rushes over to me immediately, eyes sparkling.

"That was incredible! Listen to them all, they love it!" He catches me by my arms and presses a quick, gentle kiss to my cheek. My body stiffens with his boldness, but the adrenaline courses through me, drowning out the pain. Emptying out reason.

"Let me take you home, Rain?" He smiles his offer.

My stomach curdles, but my anger is still loud enough to drown out the warning. Defiance wins over caution, and I find myself nodding. I don't look back.

"Let's go." I reply, smiling stiffly as he pulls me to his side.

Flynn's car is newer than Archer's with fancy electric windows and leather seats. It feels luxuriously like what I imagine a limo would feel like. He grins at me as he pulls away from The Broken Keg.

"I've been dying to show you this spot I know of. Do you want to see it?"

Once the blind rage has passed, panic seizes me. It's not like me at all to take risks. Hurt breeds irrationality, and my pulse thunders with alarmed vigilance. As if he knows, Flynn gently pats my hand.

"It's okay, Rain. You're safe with me. It's a pretty spot and we can just sit and talk. I just want to get to know you, if you'll let me? We can give it a miss if you like, but it's just down here, within walking distance of your house if you feel uncomfortable."

I grit my teeth but his smile is honest and safe. I pull in a breath and scan the road to where he's pointing. He's right. I could walk home from here. My stomach loosens its knot a little.

Flynn shoots me a reassuring smile and pulls up in the shrub lined parking bay. I can see the main road clearly on the other side of the bushes, but I'm not surprised I hadn't noticed this place before. The trees form a natural hedge, just thick and tall enough to conceal a parked car.

"It's over here, Rain." He doesn't reach for my hand, just leads the way down a short, narrow track. He's giving me the space I crave with intuitive care. I hang back, ready to escape if I need to. Branches tickle me as I push through. It smells like damp earth in the warm spring evening.

I push through the trees to stop behind Flynn. The moonlight casts faint shadows through the darkness, and I see above a distant valley of thick treetops. Nestled at the bottom is a thick spattering of lights where a town stretches out within the shelter of the trees. The stars prick holes in the ebony fabric of midnight.

"Ohhhh!" Awe escapes me.

"Isn't it amazing, Rain? I thought you'd like it."

I gaze about in wonder. "Oh, Flynn, this is beautiful."

"Just like you." He says, burning his eyes on me.

I know that look now, but it doesn't snag my pulse and heat my blood the way Archer does. Did. Flynn is a lovely guy, I can feel that truth deep inside, but there's nothing between us that electrifies my soul. That expression on Flynn just makes me sad.

"Listen, Flynn, I don't want to play games. I can't be anything more than friends with you, okay?" I know how stringing people along can turn nasty. I've seen it. I don't want that kind of drama.

Flynn's smile slips, but the tenderness remains.

"I really like you, Rain. I mean, we've only just met, but I admire you, I'm attracted to you, and I want to get to know you. Can't you give it a chance?" I focus on the lights of a car moving along the floor of the valley.

"I'm so sorry, Flynn. I don't want to waste your time, but all I have room for in my fucked up life is a friend." Flynn goes silent. I feast on the stunning view as I wait. He's tasting my response. I sigh inwardly. Perhaps if I met him before Archer...

"Sure. I can be a friend." He's sadly hopeful. I let the silence hang strained and smothering for a while so he can process.

After a few moments, Flynn finds a rock flat enough to work as a seat, gesturing to another a few rocks over.

"Hey, is it true you write those songs you play at the end of your set each night?"

I exhale my tension and sink gratefully to the rock. As the night deepens and our conversation flows, my muscles unwind.

Flynn drops me off at home. We sat just talking for what seemed like hours with that gorgeous backdrop. I told him I was an only child before becoming a foster and he told me he had a younger sister. Both of us steered clear of our pasts, choosing deeper, more reflective topics. How summer makes us feel, or pondering the mysteries of our real purpose is here on Earth... just having someone to talk to fills a hole inside me. I'm lighter, emptier, in a wholesome way. I smile and make my way to bed, but it freezes on my face when I open the door to see Archer on my bed, glaring at the textbook I'd left open. My briefcase sits, still locked on the desk, but it doesn't pacify me.

Archer drops the book and glares up the moment he senses me at the door. The muscles in his neck are taut, drawing my attention to the sexy shape of him. Each time I see him now, he seems bulkier, stronger. More handsome. Good for him.

"What are you doing in here, Archer?" My tone lowers, jaw locks.

"Where did you go?" He accuses. "I looked for you, but Zack said you left with some guy already." His eyes shine with hurt.

I bristle.

"I got tired of pretending I was okay with sitting in silence with you. You closed down and moved on. You're dealing with it your way, I'm managing in my own way. I'm moving on, too."

His eyes close, and the muscles in his face twitch.

"I don't like knowing you're with another guy." He admits reluctantly.

Red explosions fill my head and paint my vision. I round on him, shaking in rage.

"Well, how about I slip into my iron chastity belt and give you the key while I watch you shove your dick into whatever you like!" I'm utterly livid. "*I* didn't kiss *you*, remember, *you* initiated that one, and at the next opportunity you move on to someone else and I'm not supposed to have a problem with that?"

"I heard your song, Rain. I'm sorry. I just kissed her, but that was all. I told her I wasn't interested."

My blood is lava through my veins, wasps rage in my tone.

"It's not my problem, Archer. You made it clear how it has to be. *Real* clear. We'll just avoid each other for the next two-and a-bit years, shall we?"

He falls silent. He doesn't like that idea, but the other option will ruin us. He runs his eyes over the textbooks resting open on my desk absently.

"Did you kiss him?"

I glare at him.

"It doesn't matter, Archer." His fingers tighten and I'm worried he'll rip the pages.

But when the silence stretches, I realise he's not reacting to my words, he's reacting to a picture under his fingers.

"Holy shit, Rain, what's a picture of your tattoo doing in here?" My gaze follows his arm to his finger. I know the body that was the canvas for that image. I could tell from the positioning of the freckle that it was an image of Sarah. I blanch and land heavily on the bed when my knees fail. I don't have the strength to snatch the book away from him. He lifts it and reads the title:

Case Study 1. Is separation an acceptable way to heal trauma victims and why? The trial of Sarah Aldridge, Willow Zimms, Credence Bowman and Katherine Elson.

Archer lands a severe look on me. "You have the same tattoo as her...that nightmare you had about your friend that died, Sarah? You were talking about Sarah Aldridge, weren't you?" He rasps in disbelief.

CHAPTER 10

FIRE & RAIN

*C*alm down, Rain, it's okay. You're safe. Nobody can hurt you." He chants the mantra in his rumbling velvet voice and strokes my back as I struggle to suck air.

"Jesus, Rain. Maybe you should drop the course. You've been so twisted in knots lately because you know that the case study you have to do is on your friends." Archer makes the connection incredulously.

I shake my head with all the strength I can muster. I need to do this. For me, for them that I left behind.

"I know this case. I read all the articles. You were his foster, weren't you?" Archer's expression tightens, as if he just realised he's crossed a line, but some heavier meaning lurks behind it, like he's pushing me to confide in him.

The problem is, I can't remember. No, I'm certain I was there, but nothing about my stay is in my head. Just confusing still-shots that flash around in my mind and don't make sense. A gentle fog filters down and takes them them away.

"Just leave me alone, Archer. Just let it go."

"You know you can talk to me, Rain." His eyes plead, his beautiful face is twisted with anguish.

The beautiful face that barely hours ago gave that red haired woman the heated look that was supposed to be for me.

The adrenaline coursing through me shudders back into burning rage.

"You have to be kidding me, Archer! For weeks I've chased you, told you how much I needed you and missed you, all but screaming at you my need for a friend, and you ignore me. And now you think you can put on a smile, pat me on the back and it's all better? Jesus, Archer! I know this is hard for you, but it's harder for me. You completely surround me until I'm utterly submerged in you, and the next moment you avoid me, and stick your tongue down the throat of the next vagina that walks past you. You tell me it upset you that I let some other man take me home? Well, at least I didn't kiss him in front of you!"

"So you *did* kiss him?" His knuckles whiten at his side.

White hot rage blisters. I've peeled open my soul and laid it at his feet, and all he can do is fixate on the possibility of me kissing another man? I don't care how possessive and jealous he is, he revoked his right to feel those things the second he kissed that girl.

"*That's* what you got out of this? You know, I think I finally agree with you on one thing. We need to keep well away from each other. Just erase what has happened between us and move forward. If us fosters excel at anything, its hiding how we really feel. Now get out, Archer. I need to be alone."

Archer slides his fingers through his hair and clutches the back of his neck. He blows a breath into the air.

"Rain, Christ! I'm shit at this. I need you to understand. Heather means the world to me, and her acceptance got me through a lot of stuff. I owe her so much. I can't hurt her. Anything between us would hurt her, Rain. But the last few months with you... there's something inside me that needs to know everything about you, like a mystery I have to solve. That's not all, though. I get riled up around you. I want to punch anyone who hurts you, touches you. Even *looks* at you. That terrifies me. This anger builds in me and threatens to explode to protect you, and I don't want to be the person my dad was. I tried to shake you out of my every thought when I kissed that girl in the pub, but I couldn't. It wasn't the same. She didn't taste like you, and I felt like I was cheating on you, how screwed up is that? You're so goddamn perfect it eats away at me to not have you, and sometimes it's all I can do not to drag you off to my bed like a wild animal. I'm so scared of the monster I turn into around you."

My heart squeezes painfully, his own pain easing some of my anger.

"You're not your father, just like I'm not my mother. You are a good person, Archer, and you know I love you for it, scars and all. But you need to understand that I can't continue on like this, either. I've made my feelings toward you clear, and it's cruel to play me like you are. You're either hot, or ice cold, and I need to know right now which one it is. I'll be honest with you. I need a friend so badly right now, and I want it to be you, but If you can't do that, can't be there for me without hurting me, then tell me right now, so I can get over you and move on."

His eyes glimmer with fear and pain, threatening to spill. But there is something else lingering on his outskirts that confuses me. Something he doesn't want to tell me, and that thought stings. We used to tell each other everything, but whatever secret he's holding forms an even stronger barrier than Heather's disapproval. Stronger than his love for me. He bites down.

"I don't want you to move on."

I grit my teeth. I lock my hands in my lap so I don't reach for him and wait. We stare at each other.

He swallows and turns away. "Who will you choose as your friend?"

My stomach bottoms out. He's made his decision. He's just torturing us both now.

"Flynn." I watch as he balks. My heart breaks a little more. I'm not telling him to hurt him. I have lived through most levels of lies in my short life, pretending my mother was fine, lying to the authorities, lying about who I am with every name change, and honesty in any form is sacred to me. Archer would find out eventually, anyway. Without another word or glance, he leaves my room.

The very next day our agreement to keep our distance is destroyed.

"Heather, I might be away for a day tomorrow. I have to go to the city for a new guitar string so I can play Thursday night, but it means I'll need to miss a day of school. I've tried to find a supplier nearer, but the city's the closest." I sigh my frustration. The bus would leave Mountain Plateau at 5.30am, and the last bus home again isn't until 9pm at night. A long day for a simple purchase.

Heather lands a smile on me. "Considering your school record, one day off wouldn't hurt. I'd offer, but I have shifts all week covering for April, so I can't switch. I know. Hey Archer, since you're not working until late tomorrow, do you mind taking Rain in to the city to get a new string?"

I ball my fists. I'm making every attempt to avoid looking at him, but I I can feel in my tingling spine that he was in the room. *Please say you're busy.*

"Um, yeah, Okay. I can do that." His velvet voice strokes my ears and I stiffen. Heather grins at me and plants a kiss on my cheek.

"Thanks Archer. That will save you a few hours, Rain. See you later, sweetheart, and Archer, have a good night at work."

I gape at him, but his gaze barely lands on me before flitting away again.

What are you playing at, Archer?

I stare at the broken string on my guitar and struggle to contain the spinning vortex in my head without it's calming tunes, so instead I read the case study to pass the time.

Three of the girls were branded with the mark of their abuser. In what ways could that impact their ability to 1.) Form a connection with each other? 2.) Accept the permanent visual reminder of their ordeal? 3.) Regain self-esteem and confidence to achieve a healthy future?

I knew the answers to two of them. Sarah and Willow shared their own bond forged from shared horror. Sarah, Willow and

Credence all bore tattoos that were etched into the scars on their souls. The familiar weight of dread collided with unease. I'd read everything I could on this case over the years. I read the articles, the online documents that went into deeper detail than the tabloids. They detailed how the girls were found when the foster father died, the mental and emotional issues they presented with, the trauma counselling and the eventual separation of them, but I could never find again that document I must have come across that detailed the cause of death for the abuser. Yet those details were some of the sharpest in my mind.

As for the rehabilitation to pave the way for a future for them? Sarah didn't have one any longer, Katherine seemed to be doing well, and the future of Willow and Credence was an unknown quantity.

* * *

Besides my initial murmur of gratitude for the ride, the drive into the city is silent. Archer's knuckles are white on the wheel, and his jaw twitches as he trains his eyes on the road. As the buildings grow taller and the traffic heavier, I press myself into the seat. This used to be my hometown for a few weeks, and I'm hoping to avoid being recognised. Archer's GPS cuts through my thoughts, giving the directions that I can't manage with my dry mouth.

"Pull up here." My voice is sharp and agitated. He frowns but does as I ask. It's an alleyway, and an empty one at that. The best sort. I fight the urge to ask Archer to go in and get the string for me so I can remain in the car, but his face is marble and I resign myself to the task.

"What are you doing?" I ask nervously when Archer climbs from behind the wheel.

"I'm coming with you." He jerks an eyebrow like it was a stupid question.

"I can do this myself. I'll only be a moment." Archer frowns and pockets his keys. He keeps pace with me and my stomach knots. I don't want to be recognised, but even more, I don't want Archer to be there if I am. My hands shake as I enter the shop.

Lunie Tunes is one of those obscure shops you can only reach through back streets and a narrow flight of stairs, but Mr. Barker has the best range at the best prices, and I've spent a great deal of time here. He likes a chat, but today I hope he's not working.

"Oh, darling, it's been a while. How's the old axe going?" My heart sinks as the balding man looks at me over the rim of his glasses.

"Hey, Mr Barker. It's good to see you again. It's good thanks. I'm just after some strings, but I'm in a hurry, please." Archer frowns in my periphery. Mr Barker rambles as he retrieves my order.

"Of course, my dear Alice. I'm so delighted to hear you're keeping it up. You still owe me a jam session, remember? I haven't seen or heard from you in a bit. Are you still around these parts?"

I'm sorry, I scream in my head as Archer's head rears back.

"Yes, Mr Barker. Still here. I've just been busy." I despise lying, but he can't know where I am now. I finish the transaction and head for the door. My head pounds when I register Archer's stiffer gait. He heard it all. These days, it seems Archer misses nothing.

My day turns into a horror movie. The door opens at the foot of the stairs and four girls plastered with make-up and designer clothes enter. I dip my head and squeeze past them, but fingers close like a vice around my arm.

"Oh, look, Chantelle, it's that slut that used to hang around with Donna. Aren't you going to say hello?" I stare into their snarling faces and narrow my eyes.

Dianna with her entitled existence and shallow mind intrudes on my view. Her false, blood red nails dig into my skin with a hatred that stems from ignorance. If she wasn't so hard and cruel looking, twisted and pushed into my own face, she could have been pretty.

"Get the fuck away from me." I growl, hoping the tremble keeps out of my voice.

"It seems the little whore can talk when there's no cock in her mouth." Chantelle sniggers. I try and yank out of her grip, but fingernails bite in, and all I do is pull her closer. Archer appears at the top of the stairs and freezes.

"Keep the fuck out of our town, you little slut. Whores like you deserve what you get." The strength of her venom makes her spit out her curse.

Her words sting. There's no truth in her aggression. Her insults come from a place of fear, sprouted from a seed of rumor and speculation, but I still feel accountable.

"Leave her alone!" Archer growls. He won't punch a girl, but I can see he wants to. The grip on my arm releases, and they round on him in unison.

"Oh, this must be her newest cock. If you don't already know she loves it. Lots of it, all the time. You'll have a great time nailing her."

"Get away from her!" Archer's roar makes me jump. Mortified, I push past them and run to the car, burying my head in my hands as Archer's footsteps approach. He grips my wrists and stares into my face, rich green clouded and darting between my eyes.

"Jesus, Rain, are you okay?"

I nod stiffly and whisper. "Can we go home now?"

My throat scratches with unshed tears. He fires the car up and I stare out the window as the city shrinks behind us.

"Talk to me Rain."

The emotion in his velvet tone is my undoing. My sobs snap loudly through the car. I hide my face in my hands and cry out my broken heart.

CHAPTER 11

KEEPING AWAY

*T*he car veers to the shoulder of the road and my door clicks open. Archer unbuckles me and sits me in his lap on the grass that lines the quiet suburban road.

"I can handle most things, Archer, but the one thing that never, ever stops hurting is the ignorant cruelty of people who judge without knowing me. I'm not any of those things they accuse me of, but no matter what I do or say, it makes no difference. I think they actually enjoy being cruel just for the sake of it." My breath shudders. "It makes my heart bleed, no matter how irrelevant they are to my life. It's why I move so often." Archer pulls me closer to his chest and I happily suffocate in the intoxicating fragrance that is solely him. I press my head into his chest and listen to the soothing song of his heart.

"I'm so sorry, Rainbow. I would do anything to make them apologise to you. I should have really given it to them, but if I stayed another moment, girl or not, I would have knocked them all to the ground."

I listen to the breath play in his chest, dancing to the beat of his heart. He's intoxicating. But he's not mine.

This time, I'm the one that pulls away.

I cradle the strings as we wind back towards Mountain Plateau.

"Did you always want to play?" Archer asks. My lips lift

slightly.

"No. Until I met David I'd never thought of it. He had leukaemia, and was the biological of the family I was with. On his good days I'd take him outside and he'd teach me to play the songs to the tune of the wind. The worse he got, the less able he was to play himself, so I started teaching myself and playing it for him. When he lost his ability to speak, I found I was able to tell him about Before through my songs, and it helped me heal a bit. He's the only one I ever spoke to about it, besides you." I sigh. "You once told me that shit floats. If only you weren't right about that. If only there was a way to keep the past in the past, I wouldn't have to live constantly wound up inside waiting for it to hit the surface. I'm so tired of living in fear, Archer. And of having to run away all the time. It makes me feel weak. It makes it feel like they're right about me, after all, and I just have to tuck tail and hide again."

Archer's fist slams hard onto the steering wheel and his handsome face contorts with pain.

"Jesus Christ, Rain! I hate it when you talk like this. You're the strongest person I know. And I hate it that you're the best thing in my life and I can't do a damn thing to change the fact that we can't be together."

He swerves the car down a dirt road and skids to a stop, cutting the engine. He turns his shoulders towards me, his eyes darkening instantly with heat. That look changes his entire face and I can't help it. I reach out and cup the prickly shadow of his jaw, watching his mouth slacken in response. He pulls my hand down with his warm hand engulfing mine and presses it against his chest. His heartbeat thunders.

His tone drifts with the hushed tones of agony and his eyes drill into mine. "There's something inside me that's rotting away because you're so far away from me all the time. I have this constant crushing ache that just won't go away, no matter how hard I try and ignore it. You're in my bloodstream, in every breath I take and every time my heart beats, it calls your name. I love you and it hurts so damn much."

His admission steals a gasp from me. There's something so

powerful and deeply breathtaking about being able to affect him that way. The same way he affects me. His gaze catches fire. I know I should insist that he drive us home, remind him he made his choice to keep away, and that he should honour it, but every fibre in my body spears against my skin and reaches for him. And that's what I do. I wind my fingers through his hair and crash my lips on his, releasing my seatbelt.

His groan reverberates through his chest as he dives his tongue between my lips, tasting, swirling, tangling deliciously with mine. He breaks the kiss and I whimper.

"Don't you dare stop..." I cut off when he unbuckles his own belt and yanks open his door, then mine. He lifts me out and wraps his arm around my waist, the other clutching a fistful of hair, pinning me to him. I feel so tiny, dwarfed by the height of him, the width of his chest. All of his body touching all of mine is an aphrodisiac in itself. I groan and cling to him. *My Archer.*

He ducks down and lifts me off the ground, carrying me to a soft patch of grass. His serrated breath chops at my neck as he slides his body over mine with unrivalled hunger. I've never felt the weight of a man on top of me like this. It's incredible. I feel his strength, the muscles in his body flexing and working as he drops nibbles down my chin and neck. My hands bunch and scrape over his body, learning the heated valleys and ridges of his landscape. He lifts his face to mine.

"You're so damn beautiful, Rainbow. You're mine. *Always*." I groan and arch my spine to him.

The shivers that spike through me as his mouth worships my neck erases thought. Large hands explore with burning, exquisite languor until I'm heavy with quivering desire. Searching fingers reach under my shirt, a wanton cry escapes me when his fingers graze the sensitive skin below my breasts. His arm lifts me slightly, enough to deftly release the catch of my bra. A certainty lodges in my chest as it falls away. This is the first note in our song. The first magnificent verse of a musical masterpiece with the drumming of breaths, the strumming of flesh, and the nonsensical lyrics of our desire. The breathless acceptance that our destination lies in each others arms.

He palms my breasts, pinching my nipples gently and fire and ice twists and spreads through every inch of me. My blood ignites and I cry out his name.

He moves his mouth to my breasts, nipping, licking, dragging more whimpers from me as he runs his hands over my hips. Instinctively I jerk my pelvis against him, and the shudders travel through his muscles.

"Jesus, you're exquisite!" He growls, and my body throbs. I gasp loudly as he slips his hand against the seam of my jeans. A craving older than time leaps to life and replaces my bones with the need to have him.

"I want-" I groan and pant into the air. I don't know what I need. I listen to what my body cries for and put my trust in Archer.

I feel him pop a button, and my zipper releases. I angle my hips towards him, and he frantically slides my jeans down my legs. I kick them off.

"I'm burning, Archer. Show me what I need." And his hand is right there, under my panties, stroking the soft hair between my legs. It feels like electricity prickling deep inside me. He strokes gently, his lips learning my skin. He moves over me in slow, deliberate movements, leaving no part of me untouched.

"I can't believe you're really here, Rain. I've dreamed about the feel of you. The taste of you. For so long."

He pulls back and burns my eyes with intense green, like he wants to make sure it's really me. I understand. I hold my breath down, frightened that any movement will break this heavenly spell we're under. His scent tangles in my nostrils and fills my lungs like he belongs there. He does. He's mine.

"Oh, God, Archer. I need you now." I whimper as the sensation coils. He swipes a finger down and feels my slick arousal and I arch my back into him on a moan.

"Jesus, Rain, you're a goddamn dream." His voice deepens. He slowly sinks a finger inside me, and it's the most consuming experience of my life. The wave erupts inside me, and I feel my muscles clench tight around his finger and I can't help the cry of ecstasy that rips out of my lungs.

"I need you, Rain. Please tell me yes. I have to have you."

The intensity of his fight for control decimates any hesitation within me.

"I need you, Archer. Please. Yes." Relief and lust rage in his expression, and he leans back to release his own arousal straining against his own jeans. He's beautiful. His jeans fall away. I've never seen a man this close before and I stare at it in a symphony of heaving breaths. The thick length juts and twitches in the miles between us. My pulse bucks and pitches, sending stars to dance with the intoxicating inevitability of us.

"Will you fit?" I breathe nervously.

Archer pauses, hovering over me, soul wide open, holding me beneath him with green sincerity. His lungs surge and strain, the inferno of his desire held in check. For me.

"I will never hurt you, Rainbow." He pledges, sealing his promise with a kiss that erases everything but the sensation of him.

Pulling back slightly, he draws my attention to where he rolls a condom over his length. A gesture of trust, I barely register, because I'm a writhing, burning mess of nerve endings. I reach out to stroke him but he groans and catches my wrist.

"If you touch me I'll lose control." Then the weight of his body pushes me deliciously into the ground. I feel his hot erection at my entrance and brace. Archer pulls back so he can watch my expressions.

"I need to see you, baby. You ready?" I bite my lip and nod. I squirm in ecstasy as he breaches my entrance. My mouth falls open as he slides in, way too slowly. His eyes flick between mine, charged with awe and something warmer while his sinews strain with careful control. I whimper when he rolls his hips slightly, almost rupturing with desperate anticipation. I'm hyper aware of his burning girth deliciously stretching me as he slides just a fraction deeper, savoring the moment. With the barest movement, a sharp sting interrupts and I cry out in shock. Archer freezes and stills inside me.

"Christ, Rain. I didn't know." I breathe through the burn as it slowly subsides. Archer hovers above me, anguish and concern focused on me.

"Are you okay?" Panic weaves through his barely restrained lust. A sheen of perspiration covers his flesh. I nod.

"Yeah, I'm okay. Don't stop." I implore.

Gently, Archer pushes further into me and I feel my insides stretch and burn. When he stops, he's buried deep inside my body. *I'm full of Archer!* My head drops back in euphoria.

"Oh my god that feels good. Oh, Jesus. You're inside my body!"

Archer swallows, and there's nothing more intoxicating than this man on me. All around me. In me.

"I'm going to move now, but I need you to tell me if it hurts." Concern swims in his eyes.

"I trust you, Archer." His eyes close on the last of his control and I whimper as he drags out of me, then pushes back in. All his tendons are knotted with barely restrained control.

"More, Archer. Faster. Please."

"You're so damn tight, Rain." He hisses through locked jaw, and he does what I ask. He moves gently at first, but then his strokes become longer, deeper, faster. Harder. His pelvis snaps against my sex, and tingles gather inside me. My hips tilt towards him, matching every plunge. Needing to feel him so deep inside me that his heartbeat merges with mine. Every muscle in my body is taut and every nerve ending is on fire. I panic, feeling my control extinguish.

"Archer? What's happening - Holy Jeeessuss!" I can't stop the scream that escapes amid the waves of crashing euphoria. My muscles clench around the huge length of him, and he pounds so deep inside me I feel him push and stretch against my boundaries with a stunning burn that takes me even higher.

"Rain!" Archer roars into the sky, and I feel him twitch against my insides. My nerve endings sizzle with awareness of everything about him. His earthy scent mingling with the spice of sweat, the huff of his sharp exhales in my hair, the utter saturation of him around me. The way his large hands grip me like he's still trying to pull me closer to him.

We're both gasping for breath when he pulls out of me. I whimper, hating the empty feeling it leaves. He takes care of the condom and lays beside me, dropping an arm over my waist, his breath in hot beats against the skin on my neck.

"I'm so sorry I hurt you, Rain. I needed you so damn bad that I didn't even think. I don't have a lick of control around you."

"It didn't hurt, Archer. Well, not after that first bit." I grin wide and warm, and I feel his lips stretch against my throat. He runs the tip of his nose up towards my ear and I shiver.

"I should have thought more, Rain. I hear so many stories about girls in the system being...used..."

"Yeah, me too. I guess I've just been lucky..." Dark images burn in my skull. They begin in shadows, but slowly their edges sharpen, features clear until I feel the odd sting of recognition and realise I'm looking at...

The fog devours and erases, leaving only the light of Archer and me. The remnant unease melts away with Archer's beautiful timbre.

"Do you have any idea just how incredible you are? I've never felt-" He swallows. "I love you, Rain."

He doesn't have to use the words. I see it in his eyes, I felt it in his touch. The erratic pulsing of his heartbeat is keeping the same rhythm as mine, reiterating. It doesn't need to be said, but I say it anyway.

"I love you, too, Archer."

CHAPTER 12

THE NEXT LEVEL

*S*ated and relaxed, I snuggle into his hard chest and let the sun warm me. I'm deliriously happy. Archer surrounds me with loving energy that soaks into me. If ever I doubted his love for me, I don't now. With each beat of his heart, the way he holds me so every inch of our bodies connect and the curl of his breath in my hair I taste it. It's the beginning of our next verse.

With our focus on the trees surrounding us, we talk about the things inside that we've never even revealed to ourselves.

Archer seems so vulnerable, stroking and tugging on my hair, and I settle in to the enchanting timbre of his voice.

"The night my mother died, when I was thirteen, the thunderstorm was so loud I thought it'd burst through the roof. I remember watching my dad hit her, over and over, and the thunder took the sound of her screams. Her blood splashed further and further up his arm, and every now and again she'd just grunt. Between the thunder those sounds filled the room. It's not that they were loud, but I marveled at the time how she could still make a sound when she had no mouth left. I registered then that this was the last time I'd see Mum, and it was then that I finally broke. I stood up and called to my dad 'finish it, please'. I thought he'd be angry, but instead he grinned at me, like he was proud of me. Like after all the years he made me watch, I'd finally passed some kind of test. He kept his eyes to me and punched her so hard his entire hand disappeared into where her face had once been. And the fucked up part? I was grateful to him for it. I never felt such relief as the moment he smiled at me and ended her. I actually ran to him and he hugged me. I fucking *thanked* him!"

The tremors coursing through his body rock me. My heart labors. Every time the sky rumbles he is hurtled back in time to relive the moment his father killed his mother.

"You just wanted an end to her pain. Even before you saw death, you knew that was the end for her. You wanted him to stop her agony. It makes sense."

I watch goosebumps raise on his arms, and stroke the hairs down.

"What if it wasn't that? I mean, what if there's a part of me that liked it? I mean, I fucking *thanked* him for killing her! And it made him happy, like we finally had something in common. And I felt…I dunno, like I'd finally been freed of some burden. What if that sick part of me enjoyed it. The violence, the power, the control over someone's life?"

I swivel my head and find his eyes wet and haunted. I cup his jaw.

"You're not like your father. If you were, it wouldn't haunt you like it does. You were little more than a child, and you might have just done the kindest, most selfless thing you could have in that situation. It sounds like she wouldn't have survived anyway. Instead of begging him to stop and potentially prolonging her death just to keep her with you a while longer, you were brave enough to let her go. The relief you felt was probably for the end of her pain."

He watches my lips, unable to meet my eyes. In silence he processes, a thousand thoughts racing through his mind.

When he does respond, it's in a desperate, tortured tone, his eyes soft with agony.

"How are you so fucking perfect? You're the purest soul I've ever met, so goddamn gorgeous that I can't get you out of my mind for one second. I can't believe you're mine. And for some incredible reason, you think I'm worth something. I never thought I could feel like this about someone, Rain. It's like my veins expanded one day and filled up with you, and every time my heart beats, blood pumps, lungs fill, I feel you through every cell in my body. I die a little every breath I take without you. I want to keep you happy and safe so much I ache, and I will, Rain. I'll give my life to protect you. I promise. "

My soul dances. My heart sings.

"I know what you mean. I feel like I've been floating through life half alive until you came along. You woke something in me that makes me feel more...real than I ever have before. There's this invisible thread anchored to you and it draws me towards you. All the time. I need you, need to touch you, hear your voice, just see you, more than I need my next breath. You are my oxygen, Archer. You're my blood and my heart."

Our breaths catch and burn together. This is us, inhale and exhale, two lungs, one heart. Archer and Rain. We sink into the moment without a word and absorb each other.

I want to give him everything, take off my skin so he can see the workings of me, rip open my own scars for him to explore. I press my head deep in his chest and choke on my revelation.

"I feel like I'm losing my mind. There's something huge going on that I can't make sense of." Archer stills and tightens his hold. I pull the spicy scent of him into my lungs and find the courage to continue.

"There's huge gaps in my past that I can't seem to find. Memories that elude me, even though sometimes I manage to touch the edge of one before it evaporates. And it's bad, Archer. I know because of the unexplainable panic attacks, the fear, the strange triggers I have that don't make sense." Archer combs his fingers through my hair slowly, easing my tangles loose. It feels nice.

"That case study in your course, it's something like that? You have the tattoo and you know the girls, but you don't know how, and you can't remember being there?"

"Yes! That's exactly it. I know they were important to me, that I knew them, but I've no idea how. And the tattoo. I don't remember it being done, but whenever I think of it I feel sick to my stomach, and this cold dread settles over me. I mean, tattoos are supposed to *hurt*. Why can't I remember it? And when I try, there's just this dark fog I come up against that won't dissipate, and it's so frustrating because I know I've studied the case in great detail. I know so much about it, but I don't know why I'm so obsessed with it, or why I can't picture myself being there long enough to get this tattoo."

Archer shuffles against my back.

"Are you sure you were even there? Maybe you studied the reports so much you just think you were there?"

I huff. "I've thought of that, too, but I can't explain the tattoo. The papers said that all the girls he'd preyed on that had a tattoo were raped and sodomised, but clearly I wasn't. I'm not sure if I was there long enough to get marked and then something interrupted the process so that I was moved on before those awful things happened to me."

Archer stiffens and draws back. He makes a sound, the beginning of a reply that chokes off and dies before real words form. He draws a laboured breath, then holds me so tight against his chest I can't tell which heartbeat is mine.

The mood darkens, and we sit in silence together. A quiet that gives permission to reveal and cradle our own pain in safety and support. It's a peaceful, accepting hush that creeps around us and strengthens the threads to knot us closer together.

The shadows begin to lengthen, and I can't hold back a moment longer. I don't want to break the mood, but I need to arm myself.

"What happens now?"

He stretches out on the ground and adjusts me so I'm lying against him, facing him. The pain burning in his gaze steals my air as he gently traces my face with a finger.

"Rain, I need you to understand. We…can't. For the first time in my life I belong somewhere, and I'm safe, and you're safe. Heather is everything to me. She keeps me grounded and as far away from the thoughts of becoming my father as I've ever been. But it's also you, Rain. You have a future here. If it wasn't for Heather, you wouldn't be able to afford to do this course. You're too young to be renting. You'd be stuck in the system god knows where until you became independent, and you would be too busy finding your feet to look at further study. You need Heather as much as I do."

"What if we just tell her? She doesn't like being deceived, and that's exactly what we're doing. Maybe if we tell her she'll support us?" My voice tightens.

Anguish deepens Archer's voice. "We can't risk it. There's too much riding on it, and you know it."

I hate this. Hate that there is still so much fear inside him, when I am prepared to put all my faith in this thing between us. There's more at risk for me than him, but he can't accept I'm willing to take the chance. My stomach bottoms out.

"Your fear is bigger and stronger than we will ever be." The truth falls from my mouth in monotone, and is reflected in his sad eyes. His lips part, but before they can form words they close again. I'm not enough for him. My love for him burns holes through me, but it doesn't ravage his heart the same way. I've just given myself to the man I love with my whole heart, who is too consumed by fear to follow his own.

I can't look at him.

As we pass the welcome sign into town, a stony expression crawls slowly over Archer. The throb between my legs is dull, but it remembers his touch and already mourns the distance he's putting between us.

I can't help the desolation that colors my voice. "So it's back to being strangers, is it?"

His thinned lips plead for understanding, but I turn away from him so he can't see my tears.

After we get home, Archer changes and leaves for work. He doesn't even say goodbye. I finally feel like the cheap whore the girls always accused me of being.

CHAPTER 13

CUTTING FREE

I hold the letter from Simone with numb fingers. It's a handwritten note with a date. Nothing more. Just a date. But it may as well have been poison. It's something buried inside the paper that makes me anxious. There are words that aren't written that I know I'm supposed to understand. I concentrate on the penmanship until the stirrings of a headache threaten. I'll have to tell Heather I'm taking another day off school.

"I know, Rain. Simone called me and told me she needed to take you into the city that day." Her eyebrows knit as she pulls me into an embrace.

"Sweetheart, you know you can talk to me, don't you? Anything at all, huge or tiny. I'm here for you, and I won't judge."

It's on the tip of my tongue to tell her about Archer. Lay it all out on the table and tell her we're in love but need her blessing. But I can't betray him. Instead, I target the other thing that's niggling at me.

"Did Simone say what it was? I feel like I should know, but I don't."

Heather gives me a funny look. "No, she didn't, but I got the same impression as you, that you'd know what it was about."

I sigh. "Now I'm going to be stressing about it through Christmas."

Next month is Christmas. Christmas is supposed to be a period of excitement and happiness, but for fosters it's different. It's about watching the day pass without celebration, or unwrapping notebooks and pens while the biologicals get motorbikes and tablets. Another day that drives home the truth that we don't belong anywhere.

As if that isn't enough, there's barely time to recover before the first of February crawls up to remind me of my birthday. Another day encompassed in dread and unease. I can't shake the anxiety that grows teeth as it moves closer, because the day after my sixteenth birthday, Simone escorts me to the city.

Bad things happen in threes, right?

Heather looks into my eyes so deeply I feel like she can see what I'm feeling.

"Just promise me that if things get too big, you'll come and talk to me?"

I pull in a breath and mull it over. She's amazing, and she has taken me in, given me space, allowed me to be me and asked for nothing but my honesty. I owe her that much. I carefully nod.

* * *

Wind gets the crowd dancing. The floor is full of sweaty bodies moving to the music. I grin at Flynn between verses, and he winks back. He's been the best friend he could be within the boundaries I set out. I know he's brought someone in from out of town tonight to see me. Someone who might be interested in my act. I should feel on top of the world, but there's this underlying tension that keeps drawing my eyes to Archer. The redhead has been hanging around, and I feel sick to my stomach even though I haven't seen him touch her. I keep telling myself it's not my place to care, but my heart bleeds anyway.

When my set finishes, I step into the arms of Flynn.

"You were great as always, Rain. Here, I'd like you to meet Aaron." I turn and land my gaze on a tall, slim man in his late thirties with jeans and shirt that look casual but ooze style and wealth. He's trying to avoid drawing attention to himself, but it doesn't work. One look at him and you can tell there's an aura of power about him.

"Hi Aaron. I hope you enjoyed the music."

Aaron nods without smiling.

"I'm not a fan of bullshit, Rain. I tell it straight and expect the same in return. I want you to play in my club in the city. The pay will be good, and accommodation is included. I want you there as soon as we can make this happen. What do you say?"

My mouth falls open. Patrons jostle against me and I can't make sense of anything right now.

"Can I think on it, Aaron? It's a lot to process, but I need to think this through before I make a decision." He squints at me, then slides a card into my hand.

"I'm a busy man, Rain. You have a week to decide before I look for someone else. Call me when you reach your decision." Aaron turns and walks away, the crowd parting around him like they feel how important he is. Flynn grins in my face and drags me into the hall.

"He loves you, Rain. Just like I knew he would. He usually demands an answer on the spot, but he's giving you a week! That's huge!"

Excitement twists in my guts. I breathe through it, and then reality kicks in.

"Oh, Flynn, I'm not even sixteen yet. Once he finds out, he won't employ me. And I have my course here, and Heather's been great…" And I don't voice the stronger reason. Archer is here. Archer who took my virginity and ignored me afterwards. Declaring his love before becoming a stranger to me. Every day it hurts, but I can't summon up the strength I need to detach from him. He made his choice, and we both have to live with it.

Flynn grabs my hand.

"Aaron knows! I told him, and he says it's legal as long as he doesn't serve you alcohol. I understand about the course though. But there's no reason why you can't keep it up and pay for it yourself. He pays well and you'll have days free to study."

Shouts ring out from the pub and cuts our conversation short. As we round the hallway, I see a pile of flying fists and two bodies locked together in tight rage.

Zack appears beside me with blood oozing from the corner of his mouth. "Rain, can you try to get control of Archer? I tried to separate them but I've never seen him this angry. I got caught in the crossfire."

I snap my eyes back to the two bodies. Archer sits astride one of Flynn's mates raining blow after blow. His face is twisted and feral.

"Archer!" I scream at him, digging my nails into his shoulder, feeling the muscles beneath my hand flex and bunch.

I push my face into his line of sight screaming so loud my voice shifts his hair. "Archer, stop it. You're hurting him!"

The wild expression on his face hurts my insides. Its rage mixed with confusion, like he's lost all control. But he suddenly stops, his fist balled and frozen in mid-air as focus returns to his eyes. They lock on me even as Zack pulls him away, bending his arm behind his back to immobilise him. The crowd swarms on Flynn's friend, dragging him off in the other direction.

I round on Archer, concern colliding with confusion.

"What was that about?"

He pulls his free arm across his face, smearing his enemy's blood over his cheek like war paint. Hostility heaves in his chest. The other guy didn't even make contact, Archer's flesh perfectly unmarred.

"He said you and Flynn were seeing each other!" He spits, then turns his glare on Flynn standing beside me. "You better not even think of touching her, arsehole. I'll get you for statutory rape if you do."

Color drains from Flynn's face, and he throws his hands up in surrender.

"I didn't...I wouldn't...*fuck*!" Flynn chokes, terror so undiluted that he looks guilty.

I gasp and stagger backwards. I don't have time to analyse Flynn's response, because Archer's volatility fills my head. His uncontainable rage is one thing, beating a guy senseless another, but the raw jealousy and possessive threat he aimed at Flynn slams into me. Archer crossed that line weeks ago, and it was okay for him, but nobody else is allowed to lay a finger on me.

In shock all I can do is walk away.

"I wouldn't, Rain. Please! You have to believe me." Flynn pleads, laying a hand on my arm.

But I shake him off, closing myself in the office. Jesus, how can I be so stupid? It's laid out before me and I was too wrapped up in Archer to notice. He wants me to be his, and only his, but on his terms.

Archer bursts through the door, adrenaline still buzzing along his wild pulse, his eyes seeking mine.

"You're fucking him, aren't you?!" His accusation chills me, and he grabs me roughly in his fists, crashing his lips on mine.

I erupt. My hand cracks across his jaw and he jerks backwards. I wipe his kiss from my mouth.

My heartbreak recognises the anguish in his expression, but my rage smothers it.

"How *dare* you, Archer? How dare you stake your claim on me like that when you have no intention of being with me? Is this what you do? Declare undying love and leave a trail of lovesick girls behind to chase after you while you treat them like strangers? You can't do that to me, Archer. I gave myself to you thinking you felt the same about me, only to have you go about as if I don't exist. You don't want me, but you're waging war on anyone else who might? Why? So you can destroy my chances of moving on or finding happiness with someone else? It was your choice to let me go, remember? Damn well deal with it." The venom in my voice widens his eyes.

"Shit, Rain, it's not like that. I love you and thought you'd understand. I didn't expect you to jump into bed with- "

"Just stop it, Archer!" Fury roughens my words. "I love you so much I gave you my heart. It's the one thing I possess that I actually own, and you took it, added it to the rest of your collection and left me empty. I've spent my entire life being called a slut and a whore and it hurt so damn much, even though I knew it wasn't true and the people saying it meant nothing to me, and you know that because you saw it. But this...*thing*... between us? Being discarded by you and hearing you say these things is the only time I've ever actually *felt* like a whore, and you will never understand how much it hurts that it's *you* who caused me to feel that way." Tears track down my face.

His stricken expression blanches as he processes. My heart screams. I love him. I'll never stop loving him, but I can't have him. I realise I can no longer stand around and wait for something that will never transpire without losing myself in the process. Cold finality surges under my skin and squeezes my breath. Archer will never be mine. All he will allow himself to be is a calamity of fear, and I won't let myself be a casualty of his private war. I brand him to memory with my eyes, the impetuous, untamable hair that felt so damned good in my fingers, his face, fierce and handsome with hard lines that I now know soften in passion. The boy who wore a man's body, hard and rippling with temptation. His eyes...oh god, his eyes. They are everything. Angry, deep emerald vortexes of agony, darkness and fear. Filled with a love he's unprepared for.

Before my rage falters and ebbs, I turn my back and walk away.

* * *

It's two in the morning and I feel a panic attack threaten as the car engine takes me hurtling past foreign buildings. The lights grow so high that I could almost mistake them for stars. I try and swallow my fear away, taking a deep breath when the hand rests on my leg and squeezes gently.

"You alright?"

It was a spontaneous decision, one that I know was the right action to take, but it still doesn't sit properly. Endings generally don't. I still smell the cigarette haze that clings to my hair, the perspiration from the stage lighting dried and itchy on my forehead. But something had to be done. Changes like these leave a queasiness in my belly that linger for weeks, but I know at the end of it all, we'll all be better for it. I will be able to pick myself up and heal. Archer will get over whatever is consuming him. Or he won't. Either way. I won't hold him back. Or myself.

My head leans back and I look at Flynn.

"Yeah. Just…sad, you know." He doesn't know, not really. He doesn't know I'm driving away from Heather, while her tears soak the note I left for her to find. He doesn't know I left the broken pieces of my heart in that town, in the careless hands of a man too full of fear to be capable of loving me. I know I wouldn't be able to stop myself from falling back into his arms, time and time again, allowing him to play me however he wanted, draw me close, push me away. I just can't.

But I'm not afraid. I'm bravely driving to the city to realise the next verse of my life; discover my new song.

CHAPTER 14

FAME

*I*t's the season of broken dreams. Right now I should be gathered around whatever decorated tree Heather found, watching her open the framed picture of Archer and me that instead lies like a nasty secret at the bottom of my suitcase. Now, all Heather has is a hurried note, my hope that it would convey the depth of gratitude for her unwavering, non judgemental security. Archer already has my heart so I left him nothing.

I just couldn't.

Christmas brings around another ending. High school. I skipped the fanfare of the graduation, ignoring the lump of disappointment in my throat. I could have been there, just like the rest of the girls, and Heather would have been cheering alongside Simone. And Archer. The thought burns my throat.

They don't know where I am, and as soon as my birthday is done, they will be informed by the authorities that I have chosen to exit the system. Once I'm sixteen, I'm considered an adult in the eyes of the law, so until then I'll lay low, hoping Heather will honour my request for space. My file will be closed and my location will not be released. It's all so final. But it has to be.

Archer.

He still creeps around the edges of my thoughts, seeps through my bloodstream and speaks to me in my dreams. He doesn't fade with time or distance.

I sigh over the books spread out before me and watch the moon shimmer over the metal rooftops. It's a room without a view, my cozy home above the club. It's three rooms in total. A kitchenette-come-living-area, my bedroom and bathroom. It's everything I need, and it's cheap. Aaron explained that the extra business I bring in more than compensates for the cheaper rent, so I bank the majority of my wage each week. I've got no time between studying and work, nor interest in functions, parties and shopping so my needs are pretty basic.

A soft knock breaks my musings.

"It's almost time." Flynn whispers from the hall. I open the door and his mouth drops. His eyes explore me, from my messy styled bun, down the sleek and hugging lines of my dress to the black thin straps of my high heels. It's an upmarket club, and fortunately for me, Aaron has been happy to supply a decent wardrobe to start me off.

"Sweet Jesus, Rain! You look positively elegant!" His loud swallow boosts my confidence. I feel awkward in fancy clothes, preferring a more subdued range, but I have to admit its pretty darn good to feel like a princess.

Flynn has been such an essential part of my escape. He can't ever know or understand my past, but the friendship built on the present is constant, dependable and smooth. I press an appreciative kiss on his cheek.

"Oh, that reminds me. I got you something to celebrate your first month as a career girl, but you'll have to wait until after the show." His eyes twinkle.

"You're so good to me, Flynn. I don't know what I did to deserve you. I wouldn't be here without you."

His eyes flash with guilt. Or shame. Something dark I haven't been able to work out yet. Just like the stony silence I met with when I asked where his friends from the pub went. One day they just stopped coming around and Flynn spent more time behind the closed door of Aaron's office. But it would be hypocritical of me to demand his secrets when I hold so tightly to mine, so I give him space.

"Don't be ridiculous, Rain. You're incredible and would have been snapped up by a place like this sooner or later. I'm just pleased I had a hand in making it sooner for you. Now, on you go."

I step onto the stage and take my seat to the hushing crowd. I'm grateful for the floodlights aimed at me drowning out the faces, but I can feel it's already another full house by the slightly claustrophobic atmosphere. Streaks of white like shooting stars through the audience shows the waiters are setting a cracking pace.

I feel alive and untouchable up here, and it's overwhelming tonight. I just wish Archer could see me. It's a moment so bittersweet that I launch into "Hallelujah' by Allison Crowe. As my voice carries and surrounds me, I think of my future, the psychology degree, and the people I've left behind. I don't realise I'm crying until the last note rolls away and Flynn slips a box of tissues next to the bottle of water at my feet.

I hear chairs scrape as the applause deafens me.

"You are positively magnificent." Aaron's usual stoic comments are absent tonight. It's the most animated he's been since we met. I smile so wide my cheeks ache.

Flynn strides into the room. He thrusts a guitar into my hand with a grin that shows his teeth. It's a Martin, the highest quality brand with a sound that's second-to-none. I breathe in awe as I stroke the strings.

My voice comes out as a whisper "Oh, my God, Flynn, I can't believe you did this."

"Rain, try it out." Aaron leans in as I run a quick tune, finding the perfect tension in each string. I play one of my own melodies to test it out. The notes ring true and clear and I play until my vision blurs. Flynn catches me as I lunge, holding him tight.

"Oh, Flynn. The sound is breathtaking! I'm so lucky to have a friend as good to me as you."

He pushes me back with a gentle smile, but not fast enough.

I caught the stiffening of his spine, his sharp exhale and note the slump in his shoulders. He's still hoping I'll find room in my heart for him. I seek his understanding but he stops me with a warning glare. He doesn't want my pity.

* * *

The bond created between the four girls was strong. Explain how this transpired.

The bond would exist naturally due to age proximity and shared sleeping situations. The bond would have been strengthened through the shared trauma experienced by them individually and as a group. In the event of nightmares and episodes of extreme anxiety resulting from the abuse, the empathy and compassion of the girls was essential to emotionally support one other for the duration of their time.

An image cut through the fog in my head. A girl with her face contorted in agony as she sought my eyes for help I couldn't offer. *Sarah.* I feel my heart squeeze and sweat burns my skin as my breath begins tightening. *Oh, god, I can see the texture of her pain!*

And then the haze returns, falling over the image and washing it away. My heart slows and my lungs gradually return to normal function.

I shake my head in confusion. It's been happening more and more in the last month or so. Random images just split open in my head and with it comes a downpour of stark terror that it's difficult to bear. Sometimes the urge to vomit from fear threatens, but I don't understand why it's happening. It means little more to me beyond an upheaval in my normal day, and it goes away again just as fast when the fog descends.

It makes me miss Simone. I just have this feeling that she'd understand. But she'd have been informed immediately when I left the system, and I just can't face her disappointment in me right now. It's the same reasoning behind not contacting Heather, either, even though I know she'll be supportive and encouraging. She's done so much for me.

I think of the money I have sitting in my account. My course wasn't cheap. While they'd made it possible for me to transfer my course from Heather's name to my own without cost, it made me aware of the outlay Heather took on to help me.

I write out a cheque for the whole amount and scrawl her details on the envelope. I can't bring myself to add in a letter yet, but I draw a heart on the back and hope that conveys my thanks. I don't put a return address on it. That will come when I'm ready too.

* * *

It's two weeks later, after the Christmas holidays are done for another year, that I see Archer again.

The crowd on a Monday is always a bit light on. It's too early in the week for the usual patrons to stay out too late, so Mondays and Tuesdays tend to be of the more elite pick of the population holding business meetings or impressing wealthy acquaintants. The Blue Night down the block a little offers the same services, but there is far more sophistication here than in a strip joint, and the atmosphere is second to none. It's a night to slow the tempo, wind the notes soothingly over the patrons. A tender serenade. I taste the melody of "Sound Of Silence" by Simon and Garfunkel, swaying to the emotion easily in my black dress. The thin straps made me reluctant to wear it; the thought of revealing my tattoo curdling my stomach. Flynn insisted I try it on anyway, then surprised me by adding a tulle flower to my shoulder that hangs low and conceals my shame. It's now my favourite dress.

I don't wait for the applause when I'm done. It's not that kind of night. Instead, the faces turn my way appreciatively, and I sweep my gaze over them to acknowledge them. That's when I see him.

He's broader than I remember, the months that stretched between us completing the process of weaving him from a boy into a powerful man. He's crouched and braced, ready to face the two security guards advancing on him slowly. Flynn stands with legs wide and hands on hips behind the guards. It's clear

Flynn has ordered his removal. Archer doesn't turn to look at me, so I can't see his face, but I know without a doubt it's him. I'd know that devastatingly handsome profile anywhere. His presence fists my lungs, everything I felt for him comes roaring back just as powerful as before. Did he always move like that? He's graceful as a cat, each movement intentional and ready as he dances with Flynn's men.

"Rain!" His voice rolls in from the back of the club with a tone of urgency that rattles my bones. His voice. If the beautiful notes weren't scored into my mind already, my body throbbing in response remembers it. Betraying me, my heart pounds, reaches, desperately seeking contact with the man it beats for, and my throat catches. I want him. I need him. I love him. I grind my teeth against the need to call for him, even as my chest fills with pain. The memory of his body on mine threatens to suffocate me, the fire in his eyes, the crushed velvet of his lips when he held me and promised to protect me. My lungs fail from the poison of his betrayal, but my fingers still ache to touch him.

How dare he!

He just couldn't leave me alone. As I watch him, he turns to look at me like he registers that my silence is for him. From the other end of the club his eyes light on me. He takes my breath, and the old wound he left before rips wide open.

I need to talk to you! He mouths frantically, expectantly, as if I was to simply forgive all the times he hurt me and invite him right back in.

The pain and anger that bears his name grows and hardens. I need it to stop from running to him and handing over my bleeding heart again. He humiliated me. Accused me of being a whore. I draw down hard on the hurt until its acid frees up my lungs and I can breathe again. I grip my rage, needing it to protect myself, because I know I've already forgiven him for what he did, just like I'm destined to forgive him anything, because he is my kryptonite. But he has to go.

I narrow my eyes at him and sing clear and strong.

I never thought I'd breathe again when I watched you turn
away

I showed you pieces of my heart, you said 'there's nothing more to say

Its a shame we couldn't work things out, but my love will never fade'

And now you're back and I'm stronger now, so watch me walk away.

I tore my world apart for you believing all your pretty lies

I've tried to stitch it up, repair the cracks, cut every single tie

Convince myself that not holding you doesn't mean I'll die

I finally found it wasn't love I saw, but chaos in your eyes

I remembered how to breathe, learned again just how to smile

The love I bled has long dried up, no longer yours to defile

You'll not have another moment of me, another touch, another mile

I'm standing strong, yeah, babe, I survived, and you are in exile.

The lyrics stiffen his posture, but his eyes flash with desperation as his mouth moves again. *You're not safe!*

What lengths will Archer go to just so he can cast his spell on me one more time? As much as my feet itch to find him, I can't. Instead I watch in cold silence as another two guards arrive.

His shoulders slump and he watches me limply, his expression crumples, pulling painfully on my lungs while I fight to keep my breath even. Even then, the microphone catches the waver in my throat when the guards grab his arms leads him from the venue. For the rest of the night my lacklustre vocals seem to mock me.

* * *

The storm roars through the night. The lightning throws flashes of daylight over the city rooftops, and the thunder rattles the glass panes. The power flicks off. *Archer!* My heart calls for him. I hope he's found shelter from the storm, somewhere he feels safe. Would he have made it back home to Heather in time?

I lay awake, watching the light jump across the walls and worrying.

CHAPTER 15

CHANGES

*M*y sixteenth birthday arrives and departs without fanfare. I made Aaron swear he wouldn't disclose it when I filled out the paperwork, and although he eyed me suspiciously, he gave his word.

Midway through February, Aaron calls me to his office.

"I need to know what your intentions are with this club. Specifically, I need to know if you plan on remaining with us and performing long term." His question startles me. I assumed it was a given that I continue working while I finish my degree. That's another three years away.

"I enjoy entertaining, Aaron. I'm not sure if I'll continue on after I'm qualified, but I don't intend on going anywhere for the next three years. It suits me to study during the day and perform at night."

Aaron nods, expression blank. He rests his elbows and presses his fingertips together.

"Let me explain, then. March is our slowest month. The cold snap keeps people from venturing out as much, and I generally drop wait staff here or there during this period. I've been watching the figures rise since you've been with us, and it pleases me greatly."

I frown, knowing there's more.

"What you don't see, and I do, Rain, is all the paying customers we are forced to turn away each night because we have no room for them. I'm a businessman, and I don't like seeing money walk away from me."

I let silence fall. Aaron has a point, but he won't be rushed to it. I watch as he studies the walls of his office.

"I'm pleased you are planning on staying on, Rain. Immensely pleased. It allows me to move forward." He spears me with his hard stare and lays it out for me.

"Rain, I want you to sign a contract of employment for a year with an option to extend it each year. You will be given a higher wage, of course, and you can either include the unit in the contract, or you will receive a little more, but will have to find your own accommodation. If you agree to sign, it will begin on the second of April this year, but I will be closing down for the month of March to renovate and make room for more seats and a kitchen upgrade. What are your thoughts?"

The first thing that comes to mind slips out. "Why not April first?"

His lip twitches and a faint blush appears.

"I'm a little…superstitious." He admits reluctantly.

I laugh. "I suppose if somebody offers me the world on April Fool's Day, I might have reservations about how sincere they are, too."

It's the first time I've heard Aaron laugh. His head tilts back and his mirth rings out over jumping shoulders and all his teeth.

"You know, I thank the Universe every day that you came to work for me. Does that mean you're happy with my offer?"

Guaranteed steady employment! I think back to when I'd been hunting through rubbish bins and begging behind restaurant kitchens for anything to make the hunger pangs go away. When I'd huddle with Mum under bridges and in parks against the winter squalls. Now I have a steady job, home guaranteed for the next year and higher education within reach. Gratitude wells up.

"Aaron, you have no idea just how happy I am with your offer, and I love my little apartment. Hand me the paperwork and I'll sign it now!"

"You don't want to know how much you'll get paid?" His eyebrows arch.

"You've been nothing generous, Aaron. I don't know what to do with the money I'm getting as it is, so as long as it sits well with you, I'm sure it will be fair for me."

A wry smile bends his mouth.

"I guess that means you're not about to turn diva on me any time soon."

Overwhelmed with my good fortune, I waggle my eyebrows dramatically and summon the airs and graces of a queen.

"Well, then it will be a big surprise when I add into the contract that I want juggling monkeys to entertain me in my dressing room for exactly twelve minutes before I start each night."

Aaron shakes his head.

* * *

Aaron announces the renovations and I find it difficult to study with the constant noise of builders and interior designers traipsing through the ground floor.

Coping mechanisms, and how they could apply to Sarah, Willow, Credence and Katherine.

Interesting. I've studied the books, but applying it to the girls comes with an ease of understanding I don't expect.

Sarah's trauma was more devastating due to her being the initial victim. Mental shut-down would have been initiated as a coping strategy to protect the organs from being damaged if she slipped into a likely state of shock. While the trauma existed, she could remove herself emotionally and disconnect to some degree from the physical pain caused. As per her current status, the trauma eventually resurfaced, never having had the chance to be attended to, and suicide was undertaken.

Willow's trauma differed in that she was fully conscious of what would be inflicted upon her. The body and mental state in this situation was a partial shut-down which allowed her to sift through a logic sequence and better adjust. Willow's different coping strategy allowed a greater opportunity for recovery by allowing the mind controlled access to the trauma. So being, the trauma could then be better managed through psychological assistance, initially and ongoing.

Credence...

I frown when nothing comes.

Like a thick curtain falling closed in my mind, a fog settles over me, removing all thoughts and stealing images from me.

Sighing, I decide it's the noise that distracts me and take my dresses to the dry-cleaners two blocks away.

The city isn't my favourite place. I much prefer the gentler pace of small towns like Mountain Plateau with the trees, the peace and the smiles. Folks don't smile here. In fact, there's no personality in city life at all. I pull to a stop in the middle of the foot traffic. I almost hope for someone to bump into me, apologise and acknowledge my existence. Just a connection. Any connection. Instead they simply veer around me as if I were inanimate, heels clacking on the concrete with empty expressions. A heavy melancholy envelops me.

* * *

"How's the study going?" Flynn inquires. My brow furrows as I chew on a chip.

"Slow. Well, faster than it should because I started earlier, but slower than I'd like. There's a case study I'm stuck on." Flynn snatches a chip from my plate and wolfs it down with an impish grin.

"What's the study on?"

"It's…" I'm strangely reluctant to reveal too many details. "It's about some foster kids who went through trauma and I have to assign coping mechanisms to them, then suggest trauma management and a probable future result."

He quirks an eyebrow. "You are a foster child, right? Do all the kids go through tough times for them to be considered for fostering?"

"Most of the time. Sometimes their parents pass away, or their home life is too abusive and the authorities place them with foster families for their own protection."

"Why did you get fostered?" His fascination leans him forward.

"My mother was a single parent and wasn't able to care for me." I brace for the tirade of innocently intrusive questions. Instead, he sighs wistfully.

"It must have been wonderful having all those different kids to play with and getting to know all those people."

I snort.

"You've got to be kidding, Flynn. We were considered little more than disobedient pets in some homes. Others drew a definite line between their biologicals and us. People like Heather are rare and special. I count myself very fortunate to have been accepted by her. How can you think it's great?"

A strange darkness gathers in his eyes. It's a side of him I'd never seen before and it gives me chills.

"My father wasn't a nice man. He'd never physically hurt us and we could never trace it back to him, but we'd often be involved in freak accidents if we disobeyed his rules. As soon as I had a job to go to, I packed a bag and crept out. I haven't seen or heard from my family in four and a half years. Sometimes, Rain, there are things worse than being a shunted from place to place."

His mood is so sombre and un-Flynn-like it rattles me. Almost afraid to ask, I lower my tone.

"What sort of freak accidents?"

He fixes his stare on another potato chip.

"Like, once I left my shoes in the doorway and he tripped over them when he came home. I thought I'd get my first hiding from him considering he'd reminded me to move them the night before. But he just stared at me and did nothing. I can't explain it, but his eyes went dead, and I felt it in my bowels. He didn't say a word and everything was as tense as always for the night. Anyway, the following day after Dad left for work I jumped on my push bike like I normally did to go to school, and the handlebars gave way on me."

Flynn lifts up his shirt and a thick silver scar hovers over his ribs. "Luckily I hadn't started pedaling at that point because I'd paused to pat the neighbours dog, but if I had been, I would have been leaning harder on the handlebars and it would have got me higher up." He points to the area over his heart.

I frown. "But that has nothing to do with shoes, Flynn. And your dad wasn't even around you."

His harsh laugh falls between his nod.

"That's exactly right. Just a freak accident. But that night when Dad came home he sought me out immediately. He gave me this…disconnected…smile, staring at the bandages where the nurses had stitched me up and said he'd noticed I'd shifted my shoes. Then he left."

"That's just odd. I don't see how you'd think-"

"Because, Rain, nobody could understand why the handle bars came loose in the first place, and couldn't explain why the exposed post was sharpened to a point."

Flynn's eyes unfocus on his memory while I attempt to summon some logical explaination that doesn't come. With a slight shake to clear his head, Flynn blinks away the thought and snaps up another chip, dropping his shirt. As it falls, I frown.

"What about that scar?" I point my chip towards the scar that interrupts the flawless flesh of his side, running a blade thin, silver line from his waist towards his spine.

His throat locks on his mouthful, and a coughing fit ensues. He smiles weakly but he refuses to meet my eyes.

"I guess Aaron has spoken to you? He officially instated me as Head of Security. He's sending me on a training course in March so I can guard as well as manage. Then, unless you have a problem with it, I'm to be your personal security guard in the hours that you work."

I blink silently at his obvious deflection, but I have no right to push him. He'll tell me when he's ready. I squeeze his arm.

"Oh, that's fantastic, Flynn! You'll be great at it. You already are." It's true. Besides that incident when Archer appeared in the club, there have been no incidents or fights break out. There's that niggling question though.

"Flynn, what was Archer doing the other week for you to kick him out?" When his eyes flick to mine finally, his expression clouds.

"I, ah, I was hoping you didn't see that." He falls silent as if seeking a suitable answer internally.

"What did he do?" I press. Flynn huffs and stabs his hair.

"He just wouldn't let up, Rain. Always making a nuisance of himself trying to get in and force his way backstage. When they stopped letting him in, he found back ways in or slipped past my men." My head snaps back and my jaw clenches. Archer had been trying to see me for a while?

"And you didn't think to tell me?" I grind out between my teeth. He has the grace to look guilty.

"Look, Rain. I knew you two left on bad terms, and I didn't want to upset you. I guess I didn't need to, though. I think he got the hint when he finally got your attention. He hasn't been back since."

My mouth is suddenly dry. He hadn't just showed up expecting a reunion. He had been chasing me for... what?

You're not safe.

"How long was he trying to see me for, Flynn?" The ice trickles from my mouth. Flynn pales. His response is almost inaudible.

"Every night for almost two months." My inhale hisses.

"Jesus, Flynn! What if it was something important? Heather might be sick. Christ. I can make up my own mind and decide who I do and do not wish to see!" I bite on my anger so he can't see how deeply the news affects me. Archer spent almost every night for eight weeks trying to see me. They sent him away, most likely by Flynn's command, and when I did see him...my eyes blur. I told him he wasn't welcome in my life any longer. An image came of him standing defeated as the guards moved towards him. The devastation in his face. The note of despair in his voice when he'd called my name. He hadn't come by since. Nothing for over a month. Another piece of my heart snaps away. I'd held onto the desperate hope that one day Archer would realise we were meant to be, and that he'd come for me. And he did. In the privacy of my own thoughts, my stomach plummets. It's done. I finished it. The end of the Archer and Rain story. Our last words were my name and the ultimate fuck-off song.

CHAPTER 16

SIMONE

*T*he Club is packed out by customers wanting their fill of the atmosphere before going cold-turkey for the next four weeks while it's closed. Excitement vibrates through me. I can focus on my course and get a head start in to next semester. If I am able to get my head through that obscure fog that interrupts my studies, I might even be able to get to a place where the answers I seek will come easily to me.

When Simone appears in the audience that night with a solemn expression beside a perplexed looking Flynn, I know something is very wrong. She lives an hour away in a home with four highly dependent kids, but here she is, alone, wanting to speak with me. Flynn sets a chair beside her, but she remains standing through my last three songs. I am halfway to her before the last note leaves the air.

"Simone? What is it?"

"Is there somewhere we can talk?" Not even a ghost of a smile. I've never seen her so serious. With trepidation cold in my belly I lead her to my apartment and fetch two bottles of water without breaking her stare.

"Simone?"

"Rain, I need you to tell me the complete truth, and leave nothing out. Why did you leave Heather and exit the system?"

No niceties, no small talk. Straight to it. The ember in my throat is too big to swallow. Her eyes are concerned. No. More than that. They are panicked.

"Can I tell you off the record?" She nods stiffly and waits. I force my mouth to form the words I couldn't even bring myself to explore.

"I fell in love. It didn't work. I couldn't stay there without it hurting, so I took this job and left the system." Her lips thin.

"With who?" I lick my lips. I test my impulse to treat this conversation with suspicion, but this is Simone. Simone who was there when...when *what?* I keep missing important things in my life. The shadows of them linger, but the events themselves are out of reach. I just know I can count on Simone.

"Archer." Even saying his name hurts.

"Do you still...?" Not even a breath between my admission and her query. I nod slowly.

"What's happened, Simone? Is everyone okay?"

Her silence crushes my lungs.

"Heather? Archer? Simone, please?"

"It's Archer. He's alive and safe, but..." Bile rises and the room lurches sideways.

My breath blows out, and the next instant I'm in Simone's tight embrace, and I can't tell if it's to reassure me or calm her. It's the first time I've ever heard Simone's voice wobble, so I brace for the worst.

"Rain, Archer...he lost his shit when you left. I suspected you were important to him, but I never guessed he was important to you, too. He spent months trying to find you, then when he did he left for the city to bring you home. I don't know exactly what happened after that, but after going missing for three weeks, he showed up at Heather's again, black, blue and bleeding, and proceeded to overdose on heroin in your old bedroom."

She pulls back and watches me, deep concern lining the corners of her eyes.

Heroin. The devil's medication.

I can barely breathe. Simone waits, slowing down her words. "I need you to explain what you know of his movements, and what you two spoke about once he'd found you."

"Jesus, Simone, how bad is it?"

"We don't know yet. Heather called the ambulance pretty quickly. She said she heard him collapse so she found him immediately. He's alive, and they're going to release him tomorrow. Heather's beside herself. She couldn't survive losing you both. But I need to know what happened so I can work out a way to get him the help he needs, otherwise this won't be his last overdose."

My tears stream down my cheeks as I fight for breath. Not Archer. Not drugs. I knew enough about drugs to know how this was likely to end. I'd watched my mother trapped in the spiralling train wreck of euphoria and agony. The weeks of pain, vomiting, cold sweats as she tried to clean up. It never lasted. The high wasn't the most addictive component of heroin. It was the constant need to avoid the agony of coming down again. The drive to take just one more hit to stop the cramps, the diarrhoea, the nausea was often way too tempting. Heroin is nasty, and it takes ownership of your soul from the first time it's invited inside you.

"How is he taking it?"

She pulls a tiny orange cap from her jeans pocket. The kind that slips over the tip of a needle and stops you pricking yourself accidentally. Shit.

I tell her what I know. Explain to her around hiccups and blinding anguish that I didn't know he was there until the night I shut him down. That Flynn said he hadn't been around since that night. That I never had a chance to speak to him at all.

Simone's expression dances with a flash of...relief? No, it couldn't be.

I ask her why she is showing such an interest in him. He's not one of her charges, and he's an independent. Archer isn't her problem, and for her to go to such lengths to seek him out just doesn't add up.

She doesn't answer, just leaves me to process while she makes a call. I hear broken conversation about psychologists, and Simone's recommendation that he be sent to Harold Elwood for assistance. I know about Harold. I know he's supposed to be the best there is. I know he will do whatever it takes to get Archer clean. But I also know Archer won't talk to him. Harold is a man. A solid, almost imposing man. Almost the same height as Archer. Just like his father was.

"No no no no." I hear myself say. Simone cuts the call.

"I understand that this is upsetting for you, Rain. I get that. But Harold is the best there is." My head is still shaking. This is all wrong. Archer won't talk to Harold. He won't talk to anyone else either. His triggers embarrass him and it would set him backwards to have to expose them. But he needs to. This is a catch 22 that he can't possibly win. Unless…the words are out before I've finished thinking them. They come from the unshakable truth deep inside me that knows his only chance is…

"I'll help him. I'm coming home."

"No, you're not, Rain! You know how volatile he will be. You know how unpredictable and aggressive he's likely to be. He might hurt you." She growls, but my spine welds.

"Yes, Simone. Actually I *do* know. I know first hand exactly what he will be like. I know how I will need to defend myself, too. I know because I've done it before. But I also know Archer. And I'm the *only one* who has any chance of getting him through this!"

Simone stands in wide eyed shock. She sees my determination, my fists curled tight and my limbs trembling with an army of certainty. She sees me in this moment as a resource, someone with an intimate understanding that even professionals like Harold Elwood lack. She falters.

"Are you sure you want to do this?"

My voice is firm and steady. "Yes."

"What happens if you can't get him through this?"

I swallow thickly. "Then nobody can."

"And what about after?"

My heart trips and the tears make my voice husky. If I succeed, Archer could grow to despise me for all the pain I'm about to cause him, but I can't leave him in the grip of that demon, even if saving him means losing him completely.

"I just want there to *be* an after for him."

✳

Aaron takes the news in his stride. I'd only be missing one night of work, then I have a month off anyway. Aaron runs a business. He has a backup plan in place for tomorrow night before I close his office door.

Flynn shakes in a rage that doesn't suit him.

"After everything you've made for yourself here you are so quick to turn your back on Aaron and me?" He snaps, then almost instantly, his expression softens.

He runs a hand across the back of his neck sheepishly and mumbles. "I didn't mean that."

I understand. He's made a good show of being happy to be in the 'Friend Zone', but he's jealous. I also know there's nothing I can do about it. I never led him on. Never hinted at a possibility of there being more than there is. But it doesn't change how he feels. I'm not responsible for that.

"I'm not leaving you, Flynn. You're going to be in training anyway, and I have March off. I've signed the contract. I'll be back by April." I ignore his agitation and hug him goodbye. He holds me to him so long it feels like he's not expecting me to come back.

CHAPTER 17

OLD HABITS

The air in the house is thick with despair. Heather lunges at me and sobs into my neck.

"Oh, Rain. We missed you so much. I'm so sorry…"

"Why are *you* sorry, Heather?" I can't understand what part she thinks she's played in this.

"I'm sorry I wasn't there for you when you needed me. That I wasn't there to talk to you before you thought you had to leave." My lip shudders and I squeeze her tighter.

"Heather, you are more of a mother to me than my own ever was. I love you so much, and it's *me* who should be sorry for letting you down. I…just had to leave straight away. The last thing I wanted to do was upset you."

Simone pours tea and we wipe our eyes around the kitchen table. Beneath the darkness that brought us all back together, my spirit lifts a fraction with the joy of being home again.

"Archer started acting erratically after you left. He blamed himself for you leaving and became quite distraught. Considering how aloof the two of you were with each other, it took me by surprise how it affected him. He searched through all the neighbouring towns for you and came up with nothing. When you sent the cheque, he saw you'd opened the account in the city, and headed out that night. He called me a couple of months back and said he'd found you, and that he would bring you home, but then I heard nothing. Until he came here."

The damn cheque. Of course it listed the branch of my account. I'm such an idiot. Simone interjects.

"I think it's important to discuss what's going to happen with Archer. Rain, are you happy to disclose the life you experienced with your biological mother to Heather?" I nod immediately and am hit by the weight of the shift in me. My mother is a part of my past that until now I've kept secret, a shame I avoided shedding light on. Now I'm explaining in detail my experiences with my mother's drugs and withdrawal symptoms without feeling vulnerable.

Heather pales and cringes as I detail what the next week or so will be like. I tell her to take any valuables she might have and put them in a safe somewhere off the property.

"Hide your keys. I suggest keeping them on a chain around your neck, but anything that means they're always on your person is good. Any saleable items need to be gone, too."

"Archer wouldn't do that, Rain." Heather defends.

"No, Heather, he wouldn't. But it's amazing the lengths a human being will go to to stop the excruciating pain he's about to experience. His skin will itch so much he'll try to dig right through it. All his nerve endings will be working overtime, his pain receptors will be buzzing. He will feel like he's slowly being turned inside out, and all the while he won't be able to stop the vomiting. He'll be so scared he won't know what to do with it. I'm not trying to make him out as a thief, but if he can just "borrow" something of value and a car, he can find another hit and the pain will go away."

I allow that to sink in.

"What do you intend to do, Rain?" She finally whispers. I soften my tone and hope Simone doesn't make this harder.

"I'm going to sit with him through it. He's going to think I'm out to get him and he'll try and avoid me, escape me so he can find a way to get another hit. But I'll be right there with him. Every minute of every night and day." Her head dips. Then snaps up.

"You can't mean you'll be *sleeping* with him, Rain! I can't allow that under my roof!"

"Heather, If I leave him for a single second he'll be gone. All night is an open invitation to his next overdose. And he will do just that. For the next few weeks he will be unable to sleep. I know it's hard to take, but I assure you I certainly don't consider overdoses or withdrawal a turn-on."

Simone's inappropriate laughter explodes, and I can't help but smirk back at her.

"I'm sorry." She breathes. "I'm pretty strung out at the moment. But she's right, Heather. Leaving him alone for any stretch of time is a recipe for disaster."

The patient transport vehicle arrives. The paramedic in attendance shuffles us into the kitchen while they walk him from the ambulance.

"Be prepared for a shock. He's just begun exhibiting initial symptoms of acute opioid withdrawal. It looks like he's in for a nasty ride, and he's strong. He's received stitches in his forehead but he's torn it open on the way here. Is there someone who will be here to help him?"

I step forward, and watch him close his expression. I can't take offence. I'm slim and young, too young to understand in his opinion, and too weak to manage his physical strength, let alone drug-induced power. I can see him picturing wheeling Archer away in a body bag within days.

"Put him in his room, please. Right down the hall there." Heather's sobs echo in the kitchen. Simone holds her when they walk Archer through, growling like an animal one moment, grunting with pain the next. I remain out of view. I'm not ready for him to see me just yet. I peek as he's led past. Wild and captured and utterly terrified. His stubble is thick on his jaw, and with his oily hair, he's in bad shape. I fill my lungs and hold it. I've been here before. I've seen worse. But this is a physical blow to my heart. Calm and placid Archer is gone, replaced by a demon of desperation and fear. My own mother was already an addict by the time I grew into awareness, so I never knew the person she used to be. But Archer…the man I knew thoroughly and loved deeply was lost in the darkest corners of this creature.

And I have to find him again.

* * *

I listen as he roars for freedom from the other side of the door. At my instance, it's dead bolted from the outside. Only to slow him down, I admit. There is every chance he'll destroy it, or attempt to at some point.

"You okay?" Simone asks.

I swallow thickly. "As okay as I can be. He's going to wish he was dead."

I stare at the floor. For the next week or so he will feel as though every bone in his body is shattered. Every movement will be world ending agony.

And that's just the beginning.

CHAPTER 18

COMING DOWN

J'm ashamed to admit I can't even tell you when it started. I mean when he found out you'd gone he just became this different person, but I didn't notice anything obvious. Not until he collapsed. I thought he'd had a seizure or something. I never thought it would be drugs."

Heather cradles her face in her hands, the laugh lines I knew giving way to cavernous furrows of despair.

"We'll find out what happened and get through this. You can't blame yourself for this. He's independent, and you have no control over what choices he happens to make. You have given him the security of a loving home life that he'd never experienced before, Heather. You changed his life." The beautiful words sting on the way out. "He loves you more than anything."

He chose Heather over me.

Her sobs splash on the table, and I harden my heart to watch it. By the end of this journey, the wood will swell and blister with the litres of heartache it will catch. From us both.

* * *

I arm myself with nail clippers and knock gently on his door. I'm not surprised by his silence. He will be completely lucid, scared and humiliated. He wants to hide. I turn the knob and Archer's shadowy form folds in around itself in the darkness. I doubt he's conscious of his fidgety feet, or how wired he is.

Oh, sweet Jesus, Archer.

My heart bleeds. This is real bad.

Archer draws himself further into the corner of the room as I slide the curtains open, and pad slowly towards him so he can hear my approach. His dark hair falls limp over his knees as he buries his head as deep as his shame.

I peel his clawed hand away with a firm grip and begin to clip his nails short, even as he attempts to pull away.

Something stirs in my heart at the simple contact and collides with the scars of Archer that never fade with time. The space between us was only ever physical. I am intrinsically welded to this man beyond all limits of time and distance. He feels me, senses me without knowing I'm here, and I see it in the way his body sags. Seeing him like this, the darkness eating at him and the tremors controlling his movements, it renders me helpless. My own fear dips into my soul and scoops out. I am compelled to carry him through this, even if he needs to leave me behind, shattering me when we're done. I need to pour the strength of my own regret into healing him, and I do the only thing I can to reach past the turmoil consuming him.

I sing.

The lyrics of 'Beautiful War' by Kings of Leon reach for him as the last of his fingernail clippings lose themselves in the carpet with my whispered melody. By the time I finish I still clasp his hands, unable to break contact.

He's crying. It's a sound of heavy repentance and sombre dread. I ignore the filth-stained shirt and the reek of nervous sweat and pull his face into my chest, wrapping my arms around his heaving back. I'm leaden with sorrow.

"Archer" I soothe without complicated sentences or promises without substance, and his hands clutch me with desperation. His grip explains how relieved he is that I'm here with him.

When he lifts his eyes to mine, his pupils have blown out over his emerald irises and I steel myself. With firm and direct words I explain to his anguished expression what is about to happen.

"...But I won't leave you, Archer. Not for a second will I leave you alone in the darkness. I'll always be closer than arms reach, so if you're scared, just reach out. I'll already be reaching out for you. Anything you want to know, just ask me. I won't lie to you."

His mouth tries to work a few times before his voice works. It's already hoarse from the beginnings of pain.

"Please...don't let me go."

I hold him in my arms, and in my heart, whispering hope into his hair for hours. Until he pushes me away urgently and scrambles for the toilet in his ensuite, emptying the contents of his stomach with tightening force. He cries out from the pain stabbing through every bone, muscle and sinew in his body, and I wince at the agonised sound drowning through his vomit when his cramps drive the pain home.

It's begun.

* * *

He stares at me with wide eyes that shine as the moonlight spills into the room to watch.

"How long until this stops?" His husky voice makes me want to tell him it's over, that everything will get better from this point. Instead, I lock on him and monotone, stroking his clammy skin.

"About four more days. Give or take." In between the vomiting, he sips on water and explains with diminishing emotion.

"I knew you were on the mark, what you said. I wasn't being fair to you, but I couldn't handle the thought of you in another man's arms. I've never hurt so much in my life, and it was all my fault because I couldn't give you what you needed."

I nod. I'd heard a similar story many times before.

"You found a way to escape."

His eyes roll back as another wave of pain sends him into madness. He attempts to answer me, and I watch his mind blink out. His voice is rough gravel.

"They made me. We fought, but there were too many and they pinned me down and injected me."

My heart sinks. His mind is in overdrive, not able to understand the difference between reality and hallucinations. But he's tensing up. He needs my voice.

"Who fought, Archer? Who was with you?" I tether him. He frowns with the power of his concentration.

"My team, of course. It was supposed to be an easy assignment, and I should have been able to take them all out on my own, but Simone was wrong. There were way more than seven…" He slams his fist into his eye socket, body taut with effort. When he drops his hands, his eyes light on something deeper, something he buries and locks away with a blink. He's back with me.

"The pain just…disappeared. Then, after a while it stopped making me feel good-" His thoughts bounce, and I struggle to follow.

"So you took more." I finish for him. My stomach sinks. I know the tune. In fact, I know every note in the entire concert of events. The euphoria of heroin strips away real life and replaces it with elation. And when it no longer took him there, he increased the dose. The buzz he experienced initially fell into dull rapture, then joy, then only happiness, so he chased the high until it no longer came. So he stopped. Or he tried to.

"It hurt so bad, Rain. It hurt like hell to not use." So he took it simply to avoid the debilitating withdrawal, and started injecting to quicken the effect.

"Who did you get it off?"

His answer is interrupted by another bout of nausea. He rides it out and gasps into the cool tiles of the bathroom floor.

Even when his lungs settle, Archer doesn't answer.

Late that night, Heather knocks hesitantly and I crack the door.

"He's asleep." Heather's eyes widen. Archer is tucked in bed, but he doesn't look like he's sleeping. His muscles spasm and he groans low in his throat with breathing rasps. His cheeks are wet with tears.

"That's good, right? That he's sleeping?" I shrug.

"It's better that he's made it through the night. He dropped off five minutes ago, but he'll wake any second." The insomnia will stretch the minutes to days in his mind.

"I'll bring up breakfast for you both, and some more electrolytes. Harold called for an update, too."

I'll call him later. He is coaching me through the parts I don't know about, the behind the scenes emotional and mental fluctuations we'll need to attend to.

∗ ∗ ∗

Archer is awake when breakfast arrives. Two full glasses of vitamised fruit juices and a few capsules.

His huge pupils freeze on Heather suspiciously.

"They're vitamins. To help replace what the toxins stripped out." I gently explain.

"How are you doing, Archer?" Heather's voice wobbles.

"I'm so, so sorry, Heather..." Archer's voice fractures. She hugs him gently. She needs to hold her son.

"Sweetheart, I'm the one who's sorry. I should have been there for you. I wanted to give you space, but you're my son, and I should have made you talk to me. Just...please stay strong for us. You can do this, Archer. I know you can, because you're the strongest person I know. And I need you in my life." Archer bends his shaggy head. Her plea knots my chest.

I force him to drink the shake. He takes a third, and all the vitamins. Then he throws it all back up again. His eyes water when he speaks through his raw throat.

"What if I just have a little? Just to stop it hurting so bad."

I cup his chin. "No. Even a little bit now will take you back to the beginning. You might feel like you can't do it, but you already are. Only a few more days and you'll be over the worst of it."

"What about Methadone? That helps, right?" He wipes his runny nose on his sleeve. He can control that no more than the tears that sneak out without warning. He touches them with confusion. They are a neural misfire, something broken that's trying to rewire itself.

"Methadone is an opiate, too, Archer. You don't need to take more drugs to get off them."

"But it works, right?" He's desperate.

"Not really. All it does is stretch the pain out over a longer period of time. I mean, it takes the edge off, sure, but you're still on opiates and only a small step away from another hit. You're not having Methadone."

His growl is savage and filled with loathing. His yearning to escape the darkness he's trapped in clashes with the restraints of his illness and he scrambles to the bathroom. Yesterday, he closed the door each time the stomach cramps became too much, but now he leaves the door open, and I slide down the wall outside and talk to him. It doesn't need to be anything important because he's unable to maintain concentration, but when I talk to him, his twitches and jitters aren't as severe. My voice reminds him that he's not alone.

"I used to talk to my friend about life afterwards. When we became independent. Sarah, Willow and I would live together in the city and every day we'd sit in the park and feed bread to the ducks and count the ducklings. Sarah would design dresses for the rich and I'd be her 'date' to her fashion shows. Willow would open a cafe and I'd be her waitress. We'd serve specialty cakes and focaccias to the wealthy in the summer, and the three of us would travel to the Caribbean in the off-season."

"I've been there. Landed, defeated the enemy and flew out the following day, but it's no different than Thailand. Why the Caribbean specifically?" Archer's voice rumbles from behind me. Even when he seems lucid, the madness leaks in. Archer has never travelled anywhere other than between foster homes. Not wanting to confuse him, I focus on my memory and disregard his ramblings.

"Because just the name of it sounds so perfect. Like it would be tropical and decadent and tranquil and we could escape our busy lives for a while."

"What about the others? Katherine and Credence?"

I frown as I explore my memory.

"Katherine was…different. We loved her and all, but those few months younger always seemed just this huge chasm between us. She was still so mentally young then. It wasn't like we didn't include her, but none of us felt like she fit in our future, I guess."

"What about Credence?" The handle of the bucket clangs as he lifts it to his knees. He cries out with every heave that rips his already raw chest. I search the corners of my memories, but all I get is a twisting of my insides followed by sweet foggy nothing.

"I…I don't know. I remember the two older ones, and Katherine a little, but I just feel a little queasy when I think of Credence, and I can't seem to picture her. It feels like she caused me pain, betrayed me. Something like that. But that's all I get before this bizarre radio silence kicks in."

He doesn't respond. Instead, he falls into a catatonic confliction of slumber and spasms on the bathroom floor.

And so I sing for him.

* * *

Over the next two days I sing for him often. The pain is turning his bones inside out and he can't find comfort. His tremors and cramping are so bad he can't sleep for more than three minutes at a time, and the soft sheets are like sandpaper on his skin. It hurts to be touched now, the slightest contact brings the sting of a swarm of fire ants to that point and he cries out. His stomach is strained and tender from being overworked by the nausea, although I've noted a slight decrease in the frequency, which is a good sign. Archer's body is wearing out. Every movement is slight and reluctant, as if any movement saps whatever energy hasn't deserted his body, leaving him lethargic and weighted. Other times, violent, spontaneous surges of adrenaline take over.

In the face of futility, Archer snaps.

"Just fucking let me out, Rain. I can't do this any more. I just need a little bit-" He verges on hysterical. He can't see another way out.

"No. If you take some now, we'll have to go back to the start again, and you're almost through the worst of it."

He looks at me with his giant ebony orbs and I'm held in place by the absence of hope that shines on me. There is no light in his world. There's only darkness, and a pain that's unbearable. It's an expression that wants to believe in me, but can't.

CHAPTER 19

TO THE BOTTOM OF DARKNESS

*A*rcher's pulse thumps in the vein bulging from his neck. His breath saws in and out through his teeth and goosebumps distort the naturally smooth texture of his arms.

"Fucking move, bitch!" His vocals thunder and distort. He's much taller than me, and his chest and shoulders fill my vision. His power expands with formidable craving. My slight figure is no physical match for Archer's, but my determination to set him free is bigger than his addiction. I plant my feet, cross my arms and jut out my chin. The same dance we've performed too many times over the last two-and a-bit weeks.

"No."

His beautiful features contort and redden. Spittle escapes his rage and lands on my cheek. But I can't move. I won't move. I won't let him destroy himself like my mother did. He means too much to me.

His talons dig me away from the door, but I snap my palm across his face. It's not hard, but Archer recoils and wails at the agony.

I hear frantic footsteps on the other side of the door.

"Don't open it, Heather." I call calm and firm. She needs to hear that I'm still in control. If she opens up now, we're done.

"Are you okay?" Her sweet concern carries.

"Open the fucking door or I'll break it!" Archer's threat amplifies. I trap his eyes with mine and call out.

"Don't, Heather. We're fine."

Archer growls. I don't see his fist until it connects, blurring my sight. On the edge of panic I slap him again. Harder. He collapses with a groan and rocks, his knees in his arms. His attempts continue. He claws me and yanks a fistful of my hair, but his exhaustion makes me immovable. Eventually he collapses onto the bed, grabbing two fistfuls of hair as he roars his frustration and agony.

Sobs shake him and I relax a little. This round is over. I have defeated the monster within this time, but there's no telling when he'll try again.

His voice rumbles, and it's the closest to his own timbre that I've heard. It's confronting.

"Just let me go, Rain. It hurts so fucking much. I just want it to stop."

"Another hit now will kill you."

"I don't care. I'm dying, and you're not going to help me." His despondent admission bites my soul.

"Listen, Archer. You're almost over the worst, just hold out for me a little more and it will stop hurting so much."

"It's been months already, and nothing is changing. I can't sleep, I can't eat, and I'm never going to get better. Why won't you just let me die."

"It's been exactly seventeen days." I'm gentle but firm. He stiffens and eyes me suspiciously.

"They put you up to this, didn't they? They disabled my team, convinced Simone to use you to destroy my mind. But I won't talk, Rain. I'll never tell them where you are. They can cut me, beat me and shoot me up all they like, but I'll still kill them. I always find them..."

He eyes me warily, piercing into me with accusation and sharp clarity before he blinks suddenly, and his nonsensical ramblings of dark fantasies fall away. I stroke his confusion away, my fingers finding their own rhythm over his cheek, jaw, and back again.

"Right now, Archer, the vomiting has almost completely finished, the pain is dropping off. You're doing this. You're almost there. Just please hold out for me. For you."

His stare is devoid of emotion. He no longer feels pleasure. This is part of the last and longest phase of recovery.

Wind weaves magic between us, the notes reaching out and strengthening the invisible threads that hold us together, tethering him to an existence he still wants to fight. I'm deeply invested in his recovery, and I wonder if I'm setting myself up for unbearable heartache. By saving him will I inadvertently be his lingering reminder of his darkest places and his deepest regrets? Would he turn away from me in a desire to put the dirty past forever behind him? Our already strained history might be irreparable once we are finished and his baggage builds.

My fingers pull tune after tune as tears fall silently. The salty liquid stings the cut Archer opened below my eye.

Archer's fingertips tenderly smear my sadness aside. Nothing but confusion lights his face, but my blood tingles at the contact.

"Why are you sad?" His aggression has subsided for now.

"I don't want to break us, Archer. We are so dysfunctional, but I can't lose you like this. I don't understand why I need to sit with you through this so badly, even knowing that you are likely to put me behind you with the rest of this experience."

He slides his hand through his greasy hair. He attempted a shower in the first week, but the water stabbing his skin like needles was too much.

His nonchalant shrug twists a dagger in my heart. He's so far away from being the man I love in this moment that I break a little more inside. Goosebumps erupt on his arms and the shivers start. Instead of draping a soft blanket around him, I slide carefully behind him and press my chest into his back. I do this because more than anything, I need to connect with him. *My Archer.* My tears continue to fall silently as he presses into my warmth, and I hope to any god that can hear me that I won't lose him.

From that night on I sleep curled gently around him, snatching moments of sleep between the twitches and spasms in his legs and stirring the moment he shifts out of my embrace.

＊　＊　＊

At the end of the third week, Archer's tears, that initially coursed without reason, become meaningful. Harold explains that Archer's dopamine levels have dropped so low that depression hovers like a dark cloud of despair at the front of his mind. The physical pain disperses and the psychological trauma grips him in its iron fist.

I finally convince him to shower, waiting patiently for him to emerge. When he does, the water hasn't reached his face. The towel hangs low around his hips, his taut muscles shining with droplets and my breath falters. He stares at me with dull melancholy. His silent war with overwhelming hopelessness chokes me, and it's evident that the simple task of bathing has snapped the very last thread of motivation.

I gently lead him back into the bathroom and strip down to my underwear. Tears splash down his face as he watches every movement. His monotone knifes me in the chest.

"You are the most stunning woman I've ever seen, Rain, and it's so strange to not feel it. The way you made me feel is a lifetime ago, and all I am now is empty."

"It will get better, babe. I promise you." I set the shower temperature and remove his towel. His head shakes and his shoulders hang.

"I can't feel anything, Rain. Nothing at all. Irony is a bitch with fangs, because all I wanted to do was to take away the hurt you left me with. Now I'd do anything to experience it again, just so I know I'm capable of feeling."

My mouth dries at his desolation. I share that cold fist of heartache as he stands before me in his naked magnificence. The body that once lit raging spotfires in my blood stands now like cold stone before me, his thick manhood hanging heavy and useless between us. Time hasn't dulled my desires, instead, heat constantly rages through me with an intensity that chokes.

I push it away, but it lingers, always hungry. His lips that were once swollen and animated with passion are flat and thinned with pain. I swallow the ball of tension in my throat, lead him into the shower and tell him to kneel. Water sluices off his head, and I massage shampoo into his scalp. He stares absently at the stretch of skin between my flat belly and my bra.

"I just want to die, Rain. I want you to let me go. I can't keep living in this suffocating darkness. Let me just have one more hit so I can feel good again before I die."

My tears mix with the water and his body shudders beneath my hands. He wants death more than his next breath. Indeed, every resented inhale in the emotional vacuum pulls him deeper down. I do the only thing I know will take the edge off it. I sing 'Toy soldier' by Martika and my soft lyrics blend with the steam and Archer's sobs.

* * *

He has not left his bedroom or my side in weeks. Between my snatched coffees with Heather and my phone calls to Harold, I've barely been able to maintain focus and sanity.

"I've given Heather something that will help balance out the endorphins that are now absent in Archer's system as a result of the detox. It's called 5HTP. In conjunction with this, you will need to get him moving, jump start his body's natural ability to produce it's own feel-good chemicals. Maintain the vitamins and the fruit shakes, even though he's likely to fight you on it."

I fill my lungs and dread settles in my stomach. In the confines of his bedroom with a lock on the door, I am confidant I can control Archer, but the thought of trying to contain him on open ground with exit points in every direction does not bode well.

His gaze never leaves me as I clasp his hand and crack the door. Fresh air blasts in and I slowly and firmly lead Archer into it. My expectation that Archer would make a run for freedom at his first opportunity is unfounded. Instead, he stands limp and meek and takes his cue from me. He doesn't quicken his steps on the earthen track, doesn't shift his head to watch the birds. He just keeps his eyes on me with an eerie, hollow curiosity.

* * *

"We're going outside again today, Archer." He straightens, and the slightest undercurrent of life and fear flickers over his face. Anxiety lingers like a dark shadow in the edges of his hope. His pupils are shrinking slowly, the stunning emerald emerging along with my memories of the old Archer. He still can't regulate his temperature or sleep for any length of time, but the nausea and diarrhoea have finally abated. So too have his episodes of delusion.

"How do you feel?"

Archer considers with an indifferent frown and a deadpan response.

"I don't."

"I understand your legs still hurt, Archer, but the more you move, the faster you will feel better, the better you will sleep, and the less time it will take to purge the remaining toxins from your body."

It's taking longer than it should for the 5HTP to lift his depression, and I can't seem to get a clear indication of how long he was using. It could be a massive buildup of heroin residue, or it could be the inability to deal with the deeper issues, the ones that sent him into the arms of heroin in the beginning, that prevents his endorphin levels from lifting.

I lace my fingers through his, needing to feel his flesh against mine. I sleep deep and dreamless against him every night because I need to feel his presence. He pushes me away when the sweats burn through him, and pulls me closer when shivers chill him. I allow him to take from me what he needs knowing there's nothing I can deny him, and privately soothe the sadness that weeps in my chest when the only emotion he shows me is empty indifference. There was a time when the lightning that sparked between us invoked an irrepressible desire in Archer that my body echoed. That same ache for him builds with his every touch. Every breath that lands on my face in the proximity of sleep.

He stares expressionless at our hands for a long time.

CHAPTER 20

HOPE

*H*eather's tears soak her sleeve. As soon as Archer falls asleep, I call Harold and put him on loudspeaker while we sip our coffee.

"He's made remarkable progress, Rain, and if you're happy with the arrangement, I don't see any reason not to go ahead. I know this is hard for you, Heather. How do you feel about it?"

"I understand that it's best for Archer, but he's my son, and I feel absolutely helpless. I'll just...I'll miss him terribly." I rub between her shoulders as her sadness falls.

"It won't be forever, Heather. He'll come back, and in the meantime, we'll visit, and you can, too. Any time you like."

Heather looks over me slowly, lines of sadness deepening in the corners of her mouth.

"It's not just Archer, Rain. I'm worried about you, too. I know how important it is for you to be there for Archer, but don't think I don't see the way your clothes hang off you lately. I'm concerned you won't look after yourself if I'm not with you."

It's such a parent comment to make that my heart expands. This time it's me who initiates the embrace, and Heather's body shakes with emotion.

Eventually, I wear her down with promises to look after myself, too, and she agrees that Archer should come home with me. He's healing, and no longer confuses reality with whatever delusional war he waged in his imagination. I can be with him through the days and afternoons, and Aaron is happy to have him sit with me during my set for a few months if needed. The 5HTP is working, but Archer still has strong episodes of depression and anxiety. The vitamins, healthy shakes and exercise have contributed greatly to his recovery, but while he still feels the absence of joy and hope, he's still a relapse risk. And a suicide risk.

✳ ✳ ✳

Simone calls as we're packing the car.

"Rain, I was hoping to come and see you in person for this, but I can't get away right now. That date I asked you to be available for before you went to the city? Look, I had to make a new date for it. This time you can not avoid it. I can't stress the importance of this enough, Rain. You *have* to attend."

"What is it?" I frown, but an odd feeling of queasiness thuds to life. Her voice lowers.

"Rain, you know what it is. I know its a lot of pressure, but you need to find a way through the fog in your head. You have two months. Maybe have a word to Harold when you speak to him."

Chewing on my lip, my frown deepens. I have no idea what she's talking about.

Archer lifts a brow at me and my heart warms. It's not much, but that little extra animation from him is monumental to me. He's beginning to function again.

"Simone made an appointment for me that I have to attend in a couple of months, but I don't know what it is about."

"So why don't you ask her?"

I puff my breath. "I *did* ask her, but she won't tell me. She says she can't elaborate, and that I already know what it is, but I have to work through the fog in my head to find it."

I don't know why she insists on secrecy, especially when she tells me it's so damn important. It's not like Simone to play head games. It makes me uneasy.

Archer steps up and tucks a loose strand of hair behind my

ear. My belly quivers at his touch as his words puff against my face.

"We'll work it out."

He accepts without emotion that his car will remain with Heather. The city is already too accessible to everything for my liking, but if Archer has access to a vehicle he wouldn't have to put time into sourcing new dealers, just return to his old ones. The noise in my head roars as I explore him from the back of the car. He's stiff and tight in the passenger seat, unfocused eyes staring straight ahead. His lips are tight, and the scowl decorating his features could be mistaken for resentment, but in his deeper waters, he's barely holding on. His fists are balled in his lap, and a muscle ticks in his locked jaw. He jerks when my fingers stroke the nape of his neck, then relaxes into it, pushing into my touch. My caress holds him in place more securely than the seatbelt. Heather and I speak around him and he softens more in the anonymity of our conversation.

"I'll call every couple of days or with any updates or changes. I really wish I was on tonight, I'd love for you to see me."

"I was thinking of coming up on the weekend for a bit to spend some time with you both. I missed you more than I expected and I don't want to lose any more time with you. Now that both my kids are here, I have twice the incentive to visit."

My other hand squeezes her shoulder.

The winding roads straighten and thicken as the city looms.

"Its, uh, pretty." Heather remarks. I snigger.

"Yeah, I prefer Mountain Plateau too, but work is here. For the next three years, anyway. By that time I should have my degree and I can work out where and what I want from there."

Depending on where I am with Archer at that point, my head corrects. He'd hurt me with his fear to commit, broke my heart with his accusations, then shattered the pieces that were left by becoming the very creature that put me in the system in the first place. Now his empty shell lingers in my life wrapped in a blanket of doomed hopelessness. But he is still carved into my bones and the thing that matters most to me in my entire world.

Heather helps bring his suitcase up, and bites her lip when she takes in the one bedroom in the small unit. It holds a queen bed, and a chest of drawers. Her small sigh is the only indication she struggles with accepting the arrangements. Her tears trickle when Archer folds stiffly in her arms. He softens slightly and wraps her in a loose embrace like he's just remembered what he's supposed to be doing.

"Archer, honey. I love you so much. Please stay strong, and come home to me when you're ready. I'm only a phone call away, no matter the time. In the meantime, make sure my daughter takes care of herself, too."

His monotone responds. "I love you, Heather."

Stowing his suitcase on the chest of drawers, I thread my fingers through his and take him through the apartment. I open all the cupboards to show him, hoping that his appetite will return soon and fill in all the hollows in his face again.

"Why are you doing this?" His measured, bewildered tone hurts me. He is more important to me than I could ever explain, more necessary than blood. He should already know this. I want to tell him just how ensuring his next breath is the only thing keeping me sane. I've spent the last month inside the dark world of Archer, watching helplessly while the demons fought him, tortured him and broke him. When he'd finally pulled himself from their claws, those demons stole his light. I'd managed to be the strength he needed, the only reprieve from the abyss that threatened to take hold, but I know what it cost me. I'm so tired I can barely keep my eyes open. The dark circles under my eyes have stained and sunk. I'm mentally and emotionally exhausted. My smooth curves have shrunk into hard, ugly angles, neglected in the greater need to heal Archer. Now the end finally feels in sight, the walls I've built around my sadness fracture and crumble. I stand in the centre of my apartment and feel the power of my desperate hope claim my body.

"Because I love you, and I need to do this for you so my

heart continues beating." I whisper. He moves faster than I've seen him and snatches me into an embrace that presses our heartbeats together. My hands splay over his chest as bittersweet sobs wrack my body. The firm muscles fit against me and I feel our connection in the ache in my belly. I can pretend, for the slightest moment, that Archer is Archer again, and that he's holding me like this because he loves me as much as I love him. Too soon he stiffens, retreating into himself. I feel the blade of every ounce of pain he blames me for, sensing his rejection even before his mouth moves.

"I..."

I cut off his words of regret with wild desperation. "Please don't say it, Archer." I hiccup.

The storm rolls through after dinner. Archer's eyes dart around the room while he paces before the first flash or peal of thunder.

"Come to bed, Archer." I invite calmly. "I want you to listen to some new songs I'm trying out." I imagine a flash of genuine gratitude interrupting his usual stoic expression. I watch with an ache in my chest as he strips down to his boxers and slips between the sheets. In my shorts and tank, I sit on the side of the bed with my new guitar and knee bent towards him and play him some covers.

"That song you sang the first time I came to your room, Rain, please play that one."

Smiling softly, I hover over the frets. And a fog creeps in and smothers every thought. My head completely empties.

"What is it?" Archer frowns.

"I...I'm not sure. I've forgotten it."

He sits up against the pillows, the covers falling away from the tantalising flesh on his chest, the light sprinkle of hair inviting my touch. "You don't forget your songs, Rain. What is going on?"

I can't swallow through the desert in my mouth.

"Come here." He frowns, opening his arms. I fall onto him, pressing my ear against the warm satin dip between his pectorals.

My fingers splay over the hard plains of his chest, finally able to remember the warmth of him. I breathe him in. He still smells like Archer. My lips yearn to feel him, but I focus on the steady beat of his heart, feeling my pulse relax into the rhythm he sets.

"Now tell me what just happened."

I pinch my eyes closed. "I pictured the song, Archer. Just like every other time I play. The notes and lyrics were right there, but the moment I touched the strings it's like something came over me and took it all away."

"You had the strangest look on your face just now. What was that all about?"

I frown at his concern.

What look? I search the cavities of my memory.

"I don't know. I don't think I felt anything at all."

Archer shuffles higher in the bed, shifting my face off his chest.

"Nonsense, Rain. It was absolutely something. You looked like you were in pain. You went white as a ghost and looked like you were going to be sick. It can't be nothing. Think harder."

"I remembered the song. I remembered playing it for you and then…" Memories gather at the edge of my consciousness and then fall away and out of reach.

"You did it again, Rain. It's this fog you and Simone are talking about. Think hard. Focus." Archer's voice is hard and sure. It's a snippet of the old Archer. It's as if, for a second, he's again the boy who crept into my room during the storm and gave me a glimpse of his soul. When I'd sung acceptance into his beautiful heart laid out at my feet.

"Oh my God!"

"What is it, Rain. What were you thinking just now?"

My heart races. "I thought about how concerned you sounded just now, and how you sounded like the Archer I remembered in my room that night, before the…" It flees my mind again.

Archer zeroes in on my face, holding my arms tight as he holds my focus.

"Before the what, Rain? Before…?" He prompts. I search for the rest, hidden deep in the forest green of his eyes. It plays out again behind my forehead. Before he was stolen away by the heroin. Pain explodes in my chest at the difference between the Archer I knew and the shadow of a man he is now. The pain of my loss is so strong it takes my breath and…

Blissful emptiness crawls in, smothering the hurt.

"Rain?"

My eyes widen and blur.

"Archer." I say in wonder. "I think It's how I cope. How I handle my pain. I just, bury it and my head takes it away…"

"What do you mean? What kind of coping mechanism is that?"

"It's one that works. I remembered the song, clear as day, but the pain of facing how different you are now to the Archer I met in that storm was just too painful. So it was taken away."

Archer's face falls.

"I'm so sorry, Rain. I shouldn't…"

"Don't say it. It doesn't matter any more. It's behind us and you're doing so well. You won't feel like this forever. Every minute that goes by is better than the last."

He strokes his fingers lightly over the puckered scar that's fading on my cheekbone. Its the only blow he landed on me, but authentic guilt makes a subtle appearance. Emotions are beginning to bleed through slowly and it fills me with hope, even if the positive ones aren't surfacing yet.

"You've helped me, Rain. Now I want to help you."

CHAPTER 21

FIGHTING THE FOG

*P*lay it, Rain." The thunderstorm rips open the night sky, and the rumbles travel through his body.

The images remain steady in my mind's eye, but my fingers falter. Nothing comes.

"I…can't. I can see it, but it won't come."

His scowl deepens. I think for a moment he's giving up, because he throws the covers back and walks from the bedroom.

"Try this." He hands me Wind. I run my fingers over the wood, stunned at the warmth it invokes inside me. The weight feels natural, like the embrace of a lover.

A blast of warm air hits me, the smell of rain and electricity inviting and familiar in my lungs. Archer has opened the window to the storm. Light flickers determined in his stare.

"Play it to the wind, Rain." His velvet timbre was strong and deep. Lightning flashes from the open window, silhouetting Archer's frame. The wide shoulders, broad chest tapering down over the rapids of his stomach to narrow hips and powerful legs. My Archer, taking my breath away, standing with me against the storm like a broken angel. My head clears.

I find the breath he stole and let my fingers move.

This storm got nothing on you, my friend

Your courage is tattooed on your roar
You drown out the thunder as you transcend
You have already won this war.
You have already won this war.

Archer grins his victory with all his teeth. It chases his pain away and transforms his face. It's the first time in months I've seen him smile. Time unwinds and closes on the miles of emptiness that has laid between us. Wind falls softly to the bed and I leap at Archer, wrapping my arms around his neck and my legs around his waist. I pull as much of my body to as much of his that I can, and it's still not enough. I bury my face in his neck and weep against the spicy musk of his skin. His fingers dig into my thighs and he holds me through my tears.

* * *

He's sleeping better; often through the night again. He drapes a heavy arm in the dip of my waist and my palm runs the length of it while the thunder rumbles on the horizon. Anticipation expands in my ribcage as I snuggle under the covers. Archer rolls towards me and presses his chest into my back on a sigh. I've become used to the feel of his body against mine in sleep, and the first tendrils of fear chill my thoughts. Archer is numb. He's going through the motions of the routine I've set out for him without hesitation. Healthy diet, exercise through the day and lay in each other's arms through the night. With equal possibility, Archer might love being here or hate it, and I'm forced to wait it out until he works out how he feels about it.

* * *

In the week he's been with me, Archer's improvement has been remarkable. Fewer tears and more conversation. Softer posture and stronger focus. Most of all, Archer's unwavering attention on me is showing hints of the old intensity. With crisp determination, Archer has been pushing the boundaries of my brain fog each afternoon. He forces me to unpack my boxes of pain discovered every time he helps me clear the fog.

Sometimes, the memories are bitter, sometimes sad, but always painful. The greater the pain, the more resistant the fog is to our efforts. I've detailed the life I'd forgotten with my mother, the terror I'd experienced when my mother's hand bit into my shoulder as she dragged me through the streets seeking drugs or money in return for some time with me. Her nine year old daughter. The cops had arrived just before she could complete her transaction with a drunk who smelled like a public restroom and cigarettes. Archer holds me as I remember the betrayal. He kisses the crown of my head as I bring life to the ugly parts of me.

* * *

Archer looks around him at the gray towers lining the city blocks as we make our way towards the park.

"I don't think I'll ever get used to how big these buildings are."

My smile adores him.

"I know. Give me Mountain Plateau any day. This place has no soul."

He nods as his eyes light over the concrete landscape.

"I think when I'm done with the city, I'll never come back here." He says it with light reflection but it hits me like a physical blow. He's already thinking of leaving me. I understand he needs to move forward, but the ease at which he's overlooking me burns.

"What will you do?" I force a neutral tone.

My stomach feels Archer's shrug. He's become so essential in my day to day routine and I've simply assumed our living arrangements suited him, too.

"You want to go."

It's a statement, a death knell. Archer slips his hand around mine and squeezes.

"Eventually. I don't want to be a burden, and I don't want to be that guy who needs looking after."

Nothing about how he feels about me. Our silence lengthens,

the seed of distance sprouting branches between us.

We reach the park for our run, and I push in front of him, refusing to stop until my lungs give out and my secret tears dry.

* * *

"I felt so guilty, Rain. I waited in your bedroom to apologise and you never came home. You were right, and I was so angry that I lost control and took it out on you."

He stares at his flexing hand, and I press my palm against it.

"I was hurting, too. I kept getting mixed signals from you and it was so confusing and frustrating. I couldn't keep up with the push and pull. I had to give you space."

He nods.

"You knew how I felt about you. But in the back of my mind the thoughts of you just merged with the image of my father beating Mum, and I was so scared that the depth of passion I felt for you would eventually drive me to lose control. And it happened that night at Zack's."

Felt. Past tense. I wince. I take two full breaths before I can respond.

"You are *not* your father, Archer. You are intense and passionate, but you are nothing like him."

He avoids my gaze. Long, thick eyelashes hide his thoughts.

"No" He murmurs, an odd lilt to his voice. "I'm your mother."

Regret shines in his eyes. A real emotion.

"I'm so sorry, Rain. I didn't think about it until recently, but I just seem to find all your scars and rip them open without thinking. I don't understand why you're fighting for me after the way I've treated you."

"I fight for you, *with* you, because you're a good person, and I love you."

"I don't deserve your love." There's a brittle edge to his tone that invites me deeper.

"You don't get to choose who you love." It's barely a whisper but it bleeds from my heart.

"I know. I can't get the image of my father covered in Mum's blood out of my mind, so I don't understand how I can still love someone who broke me so bad."

I shuffle closer and wrap my arm around his broad shoulders.

"It's a child's natural instinct to love a parent, no matter what they do. It's all documented in the course material I've been studying. A child needs a sense of being cared for by their parents to feel safe and protected, and to accept that they are bad people damages that critical security. They naturally transfer all the negative traits onto others. That way their parent is still perfect and it's everyone else who is the problem. Like believing your mother drove him to it. It's natural to feel that way, Archer."

"So why do I hate him for what he did at the same time?"

"At a certain stage in a child's life, they begin to break away from their parents, and to do that they begin to see their parents as having flaws. It naturally progresses that the child will eventually see their parent as a normal person with human weaknesses. During that time, though, the child views the parent as two separate people. Either all good, or all bad. You were at that point when it happened. Your all-bad father killed your mother, but the all-good father showed the pride and acceptance that you needed."

Archer tastes the information, absently brushing his lips against my temple.

"I can't bring myself to visit him, you know, in jail. Part of me wants to, but I can't. Do you feel the same about your mum?"

I sigh reluctantly. "To be honest, she's rarely in my mind. I can't remember most of my time with her. Snippets here and there, and a general feeling of cold, hunger and fear."

The warm body moves away.

"It's this damn fog again, Rain. It's your heroin."

He's hit a raw spot. "It is not, Archer. It's completely different."

His tone is clipped and sure.

"How is it different? It takes away the pain like heroin does, numbs the bad bits so you don't have to deal with them. And you're doing it all the time. You know damn well you need to deal with the trauma to be able to move past it, but it's your coping mechanism, and you're addicted."

Rocks crash in my chest. Am I addicted? The pain I felt in the thunderstorm the other night when I was faced with the heartbreaking difference between the old Archer, and the damaged one was deep. So deep that my body anaesthetised me. Like a drug.

Archer traps me in his green scrutiny. His face has begun filling out again as his appetite grows, replacing his hard angles with a more subtle power. A light dusting of stubble shadows his jaw, and his full lips are relaxed and sensuous. So close to but still a world away from who he used to be. But he's no longer that boy. Heroin waged a war on him and stole all but his last breath, and it was in that dying breath that a new Archer rose. From my cruel vantage point, I lay witness to it all. The man that grew from those final moments did so from pain, sculptured by the cuts of insanity, his grit forged in his blood stained armour. The pain of the boy that was lost gathers in my stomach and... disappears. I feel it happen this time. My mouth slackens and eyes widen.

"Oh, Jesus, Archer." I breathe.

Repressed memories. Memories that drift away into the shadows of my mind and never come out. The memory Archer helped me recall, the one of a green-eyed boy who lay his fears before me that night, it was more precious than painful. I need to remember that, as hurtful as it was because it is part of the beautiful dance that is Archer and me. To lose that again...

Wide eyed and lost, my terror whispers. "What other memories have been taken away?"

CHAPTER 22

CHANGING THE SEASONS

*M*y fingers spin the discs so that 11 11 line-up, and the clasps release.

"My stomach knots every time I open this. I wish I knew why."

Archer's forehead creases. He stares at the pages inside. This is my version of a diary, my thoughts and feelings scrawled within the staves, quavers, and lyrics. He jams his hand into the stack and pulls out a random sheet, resting it on the bed between us.

"Play this one, then tell me about it."

I lift Wind against me and find the first note. The mournful sound floated heavily in the room.

> *There's nothing left to hide behind*
> *When their weapons are their words*
> *I can't undo, I can't rewind*
> *So their hate is undeterred*

> *I won't retreat from them this time*
> *I'll not surrender to false claim*
> *I'm a reluctant captive of my crime*
> *Though I regret, I'm not to blame*

My hand drops to my lap and I try and keep the haze at bay. It hurts, my entire body seemingly screaming its reluctance.

"Feel it, Rain!" Archer's voice connects with the pain and pins it, dulling it a little. "Now talk to me." He commands.

Pointing fingers, sneering faces. Cruel words, they all wait for me. The fog slides in like a poison compelled to do my bidding. It waits for my order to swallow the scene. Not today. Today, I have Archer, and the green eyes that help hold the fog at bay. I fill my lungs and step into the memory.

"I'm hurting, Archer. They're calling me names, and they're so vicious. I just want to get away."

"Who is it, Rain? Is it kids at school?" I feel my head shake but I'm no longer sitting with Archer. I'm standing next to a sink in a vaguely familiar kitchen.

"It's...it's my foster parents, and they're looking at me like they loathe me. They told the other fosters to keep away from me. They...they told me to wait for Simone outside. Why do they hate me, Archer?"

Archer's relentless. "What are they calling you?"

"They're calling me...whore. They're saying I'm a filthy slut, and they won't house a m..." It's gone. There's something bigger in the stolen memory.

"What else, Rain?"

I bury my head in my shaking hands. Archer notices that I'm on the edge of an anxiety attack and pulls me against his chest.

"Just concentrate on my heartbeat, babe. Listen to it beating."

My breaths rasp shallow and hard as I seek the rhythm over the noise of my panic.

"Who is holding you now?" His voice demands, reassures and calms.

"Archer." I whimper.

"What does my heartbeat sound like?"

"Steady, calm, strong." He's grounding me. He's shifting my thoughts to a safer platform, and I feel my own heart slow to match his. I curl my fingers against his chest.

"Now, can you play the song again?"

Reluctantly, the lyrics fall from my lips and the memories return with a little less severity. Archer asks me to explain again, and this time more images emerge. The look of fear in their eyes, mistrust and an overwhelming feeling of desolation and injustice, mixed with the relief that Simone would come and take me away.

"They didn't even let me pack my things. They made me wait outside, threw my things on the path and locked the door. I thought they'd damaged Wind. Simone helped me pack my things in the car."

We're lying on the bed as we always do, facing each other with our legs tangled, but something new and light fills us both. Over the last few days, Archer stopped existing and began breathing again, and its a quiet thrill that now vibrates stronger every moment that glides by. Archer holds my attention as he reaches behind him. The scrape of paper as he selects another song to unravel no longer makes my pulse hammer, although I continue to tense at the sound. Whatever he finds, we discuss. There are lyrics I come across where my memories flow freely. Archer insists I play and remember those chapters in my life, too. They play their essential part in balancing out the darker moments.

It becomes our new routine. We talk; Archer pushes me to the edge of discomfort, forces me over it and brings me out the other side with his soothing timbre and steady heartbeat. I fall into an exhausted sleep in his arms. Every time I'd awaken a little more renewed, lighter, clearer.

After Heather's visit last week, Archer's progress seems to have sprouted wings and taken flight. She'd gathered him firmly into an embrace that forgave both of them, the guilt and disappointment blinked out, and they'd slipped back into the easy conversation they used to have.

I see it now, that vibration of energy around him that seems to shake off the parts of him that were fractured, leaving tantalising glimpses of the old Archer. It wreaks havoc with my senses and I'm hyper aware of his every movement. Even when the idea of dragging up painful memories is overwhelming, I'm compelled to keep going just so I can have an excuse to stare at his handsome face.

When his eyebrow lifts in the arc that brings butterflies to life in my stomach, I roll to my back and pluck the strings of Wind.

Karma wrapped in fuzzy grey descending from the tree
Tired of climbing down the trunk she instead leapt free
Landing in the pond hidden underneath the rosemary
And using all her claws she then climbed up his knee

I can't finish the song and the lively tune breaks apart. My laughter interrupts as I recount the day one of my foster brothers chased Maggot, the family cat, up a tree and was victim to the feline's revenge on him as he stood laughing beside the fish pond. The laughter made me feel lighter and my ribs strain with something other than tension.

I am suddenly aware of another sound, a beautiful clear note just as powerful as my mirth. My eyes snap open on the miracle before me as Archer laughs, his gorgeous head thrown backwards, his throat bobbing. It softens his sadness and transforms his features to a beautiful masterpiece of flesh and vibrant joy, offering a heartbreaking glimpse of the boy I knew a year ago. My heart expands and reaches for him, and so do I, silencing his laughter with the press of my lips on his.

He stills against me, and rejection bruises me. He's not kissing me back. But as I'm about to pull away in shame, long fingers capture the back of my head and take control, deepening it with a savage passion that has my veins humming with pleasure.

My body quakes with the unexpected ferocity of an erupting volcano from months of restrained desire.

He moves closer so our knees rest together, but my impatience tugs him closer still. Heat surges from my chest to my stomach, sending knives of fire into every cell inside me. I'm euphoric.

His lips move against my own and I reacquaint myself with his taste.

It doesn't add up. From emotionally unobtainable to fiery desire in seconds is something I couldn't have seen coming. I've wanted this so deeply, but his dead eyes haven't lit with anything but depression for so long. And now, emerald burns with sizzling liquid that I feel between my legs. The hunger I've fought, the urges I thought I mastered, they all rupture and are lost in the taste of him. His pulse thunders in his chest to the same beat as mine, and I stop caring why.

"I starved without you, Rain." He growls into my mouth, then stops any possibility of a reply with his diving tongue and heavy breaths. I shudder and squirm as he lays me backwards against the bed, and moan when his burning body presses me into the mattress.

"Yes!" My gasp answers any question he has.

My man, in my arms, in my bed. Just as it should have been all along. Tears slip into my hair in bliss and I dig my nails into his shoulders for fear he'll stop.

He sits back and devours me with dark green lightning and dilated pupils. His mouth sags swollen and sensual. His chest pulses beneath his shirt, and I ruck it up, watching as he pulls it over his head with one hand. His body has thickened and bulked with our runs through the city gardens, his muscles reformed and toned with it. The breadth of his shoulders is wide and hard, and my body shudders in response.

"You are breathtaking, Archer." I whisper.

"I don't deserve you, Rain. You are exquisite." His voice deepens. His mouth crashes on mine again, more urgent and wild that before, and I am trapped in thrall. I cling to him, relearning his hard edges, the satin over steel physique that drives me crazy. He breaks away and nibbles on my jaw, raining tiny nips down my throat to the swell of my breasts. His arms move me just enough to peel away my shirt and bra. He stares at me, a swarm of emotions crashing into his gaze, everything that has been cold and empty now explodes to life. The ache in my heart burns. How could I have ever thought to keep from touching him? He's…he's mine.

Cupping my breasts with firm hands and a gravelly growl.

"Mine."

"Please!" I gasp.

Archer answers with his lips on my breasts, worshipping them with kisses, and bites that make my body arch up against him. His tongue teases my nipples, sending shock waves into my core. A long moan of desire falls from me, and I bite into his shoulder, taking in the salty tang of his skin, his incredible ambrosia expanding my lungs. The world falls away, leaving only me, and him, and everything we feel.

I run my palms in awe from his shoulders, down the taper of his waist, and knead his firm round buttocks. They flex beneath the denim, and I growl my frustration, tugging impatiently on the waistband of his jeans.

"Are you sure?" His eyebrow lifts as he straightens, but he already knows my answer. I take advantage of the space and free the button, dragging the zipper down over the huge bulge beneath them. His erection tents his black underwear, so I slip them down over his hips, too. He just watches my face, his intense focus darkening when I gasp. It's been six months since I've seen him naked. I reach out and stroke it's silky length, sliding my finger over the bead of arousal that forms at the tip. I bring my wet finger to my tongue, and sample the saltiness.

Archer's groan strangles. "You're killing me, Rainbow."

I hood my eyes and give him a sultry pout, daring him to stop me, and as he growls his delight, I grip a smooth buttock in one hand, and wrap my hand around his length with the other.

"Mine," I tell him and push him backwards until he's leaning against the bed head. Another bead forms on the head of his hard length, and I give in to my urge to taste it again. His gasp and moan set me on fire as I swirl my tongue around his tip. He fills my mouth, but I need more. I slide my lips down his length languorously, running the surface of my tongue around him until he presses against the opening of my throat. His length twitches in my mouth and I hold him there, loving the feel of him, the musky scent of him so potently masculine and overwhelming. So completely Archer. I pull back and sink down again as Archer's breath hisses. I feel one hand fist my hair, the other finding my nipple and rolling it gently. When he pinches it hard, my moan of ecstasy vibrates along his shaft and he yanks me back, slipping wetly from my mouth.

"My turn." He grunts and flips me on my back with ease. He keeps pinching and tugging my nipples while his lips move down my body, his hot breath curling onto my stomach. Just above my hip, he brushes a ticklish area and my whole body clenches. I writhe beneath him and he smirks down at me, like he knows it sends me wild. He does it again and my body bucks involuntarily, the soft fuzz between my legs pressing against his chin. His smirk darkens, and his head ducks down.

I whimper. I feel his feather light kisses push into my sex, and can't contain the groan when his tongue darts out and stabs between my folds.

Panting shallow and ravenous, he groans deeply.

"You're so goddamn slick for me, Rain. I love that you do this for me."

My reply is an unintelligible mutation of groans and gasps. He holds my hips in place with splayed hands as he ravages my burning centre with his relentless mouth, his hair twisting in my fingers. He licks my wet slit, plunging into my depths before lifting again to tease my swollen nub. My head whips from side to side, chasing my pleasure. He brings me to the brink, the edge of euphoria, before slowing his movements. He knows what he's doing to me. I see it in the way his eyes burn on me as he continues his tender torture.

"I need...need you." My body shimmers with perspiration, and I'm a crazed wanton mess.

Shameless desperation drives me to buck my hips into his face and hold his head firmly against my sex. All thoughts but the need to climax drains away, and I grind against his mouth, whimpering my hunger.

He brings me to the edge fast, the electrical pulses flickering to life in my veins, and I'm so, so close.

He bites down gently on my sensitive nub and raw fire roars under my skin. I orgasm with a scream, my body convulsing in rapturous release.

I had no idea my body was capable of feeling so incredible. My fingers lock in his hair as I fight for breath, and I drag him upwards, needing to see the emotions on his face.

"You're stunning when you come apart." He murmurs. I'm still gasping when he captures my mouth again, tenderly running his tongue over my lips. I taste my arousal in his mouth and I groan.

"Archer, please baby, I need you."

His smile is victorious and smug, and he kisses me into silence. Then his head jerks with reality.

"Rain, I don't have condoms."

I dig my nails into his back. "I'm on the pill, and clean."

"I'm clean too, babe. It's been only you since last time." Tendrils of thrill flicker inside me at the gravity of his admission. Then I feel the huge head of his erection pressing against me, driving all thought from my mind.

The wonderment as Archer pushes inside me steals my breath. My mouth drops open and moves soundlessly as he stretches me, the beautiful burn that grows as he buries himself deeper inside me. He groans when his hips drive his length to the hilt, filling me completely. I struggle to pull air as the divine sensation sends electricity raging through my centre, and I come again with him lodged inside me and an awed expression on his beautiful face.

Archer curses softly as I gaze wide-eyed at him, the muscle in his jaw twitching and hard.

He slowly moves his hips, and I whimper at his retreat. My fingers bite into his back and my legs circle and cross around his waist. When he pushes in again I moan and tilt my hips into him, grinding against him. His strokes are long and slow, his intense gaze never once shifting from mine. Every few thrusts he dips down to kiss me, or drag his nose up my neck in that possessive way that makes my lungs vibrate.

I want to stay in this moment, where my body blazes for him

and his eyes telling me everything I want to hear from him. I want to feel this perfect forever.

My hips strain to meet every thrust of Archer's. His pace quickens and our dance begins, the beautiful choreography of sweat and primal desire, moving to the symphony of our hearts.

My hands slide, smearing the beads of perspiration on his shoulders, dragging my nails down his back. He growls, wild and primal above me, his pupils blown. I am his drug, and he is mine.

A carnal look overtakes him, his nostrils flaring and his jaw twitching, and he plunges fast and hard into me. He grabs a handful of my hair, and I press my breasts against his chest, holding on tight for the ride. The tingles build and spread. His breaths rasp in my face.

I come apart with a thrust of my pelvis and his name on my lips. He's right behind me, his roar resonating through my bones and his body convulsing with mine.

CHAPTER 23

TRANSCENDENCE

*W*e kiss until our pulses steady.

"Christ, Rain, I didn't think it could get any better with you." I kiss the curve between his shoulder and throat. He rests his arm possessively over my stomach.

"Mmmmmnn, can't talk. In heaven." My entire body is sated and relaxed.

I shiver at his soft chuckle.

"I've wanted you so badly for so long it was killing me."

I frown. "Why didn't you do anything about it? You know how I feel about you."

He shakes his gorgeous shaggy hair.

"I didn't, Rainbow, not really. After you saw the ugliness inside me, I thought you considered me as nothing more than your charge. You never reached out to me, and although I am grateful for your help, I would have traded it all if it meant I kept your heart." Anguish bleeds into his face.

"You needed me to reach out to you so you knew it wasn't charity." I understand, but all this lost time...

He nods, the stubble scratching the fabric on the pillow as his fingers start stroking the valley of my waist.

"You intoxicate me, Rain. No matter how I try and distract

myself, how I try and stop these feelings, all it seems to do is make me thirst for you even more. I would kill to get another moment with my hands on your perfect body, my lips on yours, or to lose myself in you." As if driving the point home, I feel him twitch against my thigh and smirk.

"I was worried it wouldn't work."

His low chuckle lifts the corners of my mouth.

"Not a chance with you around." His smile stiffens and he searches my face. "You're on the pill?"

I laugh at his expression. "I'm performing for six hours every night. The last thing I wanted was an ill timed surprise on stage."

His expression remains and his eyebrows raise. I kiss the tip of his nose and flatten my hand on his bare chest.

"There is only you. There only ever *was* you."

His face softens. "Me too. It can only ever be you for me, Rainbow."

I sprinkle kisses on the scattering of dark hair on his chest and saturate my senses with him.

"It's the first time I've heard you laugh in months. It's the most incredible sound…I'm hoping that means you are beginning to feel better?"

His nod scratches my head, and the warmth in my belly lifts a smile to my face.

"I still have bad days. Sometimes its an effort not to chase that high, and there are days when I'm right back in my bedroom, feeling like my stomach lining has been ripped out." His tone is weighted with the exhaustion of his war, the fear hovering on the edges of his victory, because he knows how unpredictable the enemy is.

My fingertips trace the newer scars on his face. The ones he's never really given me a direct answer for. Were they part of his descent into drugs, or were they the results of his attempts to be free?

"I'm so proud of you, Archer. You've come so far and fought so hard."

I shiver when he brushes his lips against my ear.

"I felt like I was dying, Rainbow. I wanted to die. But its still a part of me. It changed my blood, I can still feel it."

My mouth dries. I've watched it, felt its claws as I sat by its side, but I don't know how it feels to be invaded by heroin. Mum never made it to the place Archer is now, and now it's a waiting game to see if it will draw him back into its grip.

"When it was bad…why did you keep going? You could have broken the door and escaped. I couldn't have stopped you."

His emerald eyes dart to the small scar he left on me.

"It was you, Rainbow. I fought harder because when I stopped wanting to get through it for me, I still wanted to do it for you. Every second you were beside me, I was reminded that I had something to fight for. More than I wanted to feel the high, I wanted to taste your sweet lips again. I was determined to keep striving, even if it killed me. I had to try. I promised you once I'd protect you. I'd die for you, and I couldn't do that if I was a slave to drugs."

Raw emotion flows from him, the green shadows of torture stark and lingering in his gaze. As the deep timbre of his voice heals us, I'm aware of the slow, languid tangling of our souls, reconnecting the threads that had snapped when we parted. I sigh into the warm flesh where his neck and shoulder meet.

"I couldn't have done it without you at my side. I came so close to giving up, Rain, so many times. And you, babe, you never let me. Never stopped believing in me. You amaze me. You're working, helping me get through my shit, dealing with your own and still finding time to study." He pulls me tighter against him.

I wriggle closer.

"Actually, I've made good headway with the assignment I've been working on. I'll be ready to submit it next week!"

It's been a gruelling task, trying to analyse the minds of the four girls. Sarah's and Willow's theories came easily, Katherine's a little less so, and Credence's was extremely difficult. Based on the limited information I have of her, and how there seems to be no trace of her current life to theorise about, I've made the assumption that she could have Dissociative Amnesia.

My speculation is based on her being unable to recall autobiographical information which would allow her to effectively lead a normal, although somewhat confusing life. That type of amnesia can be localised to a specific event or period of time when hyper-aroused. The police reports I managed to locate on an obscure website indicated she was reluctant to give information, appearing confused and less cooperative at each interview. Considering her reactions it seems the logical coping strategy.

Archer goes still. His voice tightens.

"It's not even close to due, yet. Just sit on it for a while before you submit it."

I seek his face.

"Why?"

"There's...plenty of time, is all. If you hand it in too soon you're likely to forget what you wrote, and you might need it on hand to use in your next assignment."

My frown deepens. "You do know in this day and age, technology allows me to keep a copy right there on my laptop, regardless of whether I hand it in or not, right?"

His lips move to form words, then falter. I can't place his expression and before I can give more thought to it, he's kissing me again and my mind clears of everything but him.

* * *

May chases away April with cooler nights and misty rain.

An uneasy truce simmers between Archer and Flynn, their hard looks colliding across the club as I play. Flynn knows about Archer's battle. He watched quietly as the husk of Archer gradually filled up with life, but never once used it as a weapon against him.

The air is palpable. Archer sits guarded beside me, and Flynn unfurls his height in the chair opposite, his legs stretching out so his feet rest beside mine.

"So, are you guys a thing, or what?" Flynn's eyebrows lift with loaded curiosity. I crunch the napkin in my fist and wait for Archer's response.

"Why the interest?" Archer snaps defensively.

"Oh, I'm just curious." He remarks with a feigned innocence.

"Yes, Flynn. We are a *thing*."

Butterflies swoop in my belly. I've been reluctant to ask. His track record for commitment doesn't fill me with confidence, but this is an undeniable admission to me, to Flynn, and above all, himself. My pulse jumps in joy. Archer is mine, and I am his. Finally.

Flynn smothers a wince.

"Please, the two of you, can you just try and be pleasant to each other? For me?" Archer owns my heart, but Flynn is my constant. He's a wonderful, steady friend who never once wavered during the peaks and troughs of my journey with Archer. He's aware that I consider him only as a friend, but it's not lost on me that he hopes for more. It's probably selfish of me to keep him so close, but I need his gentle stability, and an easy person I can withhold my past from and just feel normal for a while. He doesn't push me for more details. He accepts what I offer without question or judgement. It's Archer who stretches the boundaries of comfort, diving into my pain and heaving it into the light. It's he who reaches into my darkest places and plucks out my nightmares. It's he who strips me back to the scars and bruises of who I am and still thinks I'm beautiful.

Archer squares his shoulders and stares at Flynn.

"How did you find the security course?"

I hold my breath. He's trying.

Flynn tenses, searches Archer's face, then shrugs stiffly.

"It was pretty slow-paced, but simple enough. There are more intensive courses, including ones with more focus on physical combat, but they're expensive and obviously not required here. Why?"

"I was considering staying on here for a while, and thought about exploring something like that to stay close to Rain if you have a requirement for more security here?"

Archer wants to stay!

Flynn drops his eyes, and his voice lowers.

"I'll be honest, mate. This close to coming off drugs, I don't think you'd have a chance. You're still too much of a risk. Maybe in a couple of months I can approach Aaron for you, but you understand, right?"

Archer flexes his fists, but is forced to agree. He hasn't had the chance before now to contemplate how his addiction will affect his future prospects. He falls silent and his hand remains slack when I squeeze it.

The tension in their conversations flow and ebb for a couple of weeks, gradually developing into a careful friendship. Archer gets a job interview at a nearby bar as a barman working similar hours to mine, and I hope he gets the job. He doesn't say it, but I'm aware it hurts him to see me pay for his food and clothes. I don't mind, but it doesn't matter to a proud man like him. It will do him good to find himself again in a space away from me.

* * *

He gently strokes my face.

"I would starve without you, Rain. You're so deeply ingrained in me that it would kill me to be away from you."

I know what he means. As my pulse steadies and my lungs slow I see him stretched naked at my side and understand that he is where my heartbeat starts and finishes, too. I glide my hand hungrily over his still-heaving torso. I'm so consumed by him, this beautiful man who wants me with uncontrollable passion.

"You're my everything. You get that I'm messed up and it doesn't scare you."

"That's because I'm more messed up than you, Archer." I grin.

CHAPTER 24

BETRAYAL

*E*very move Archer makes, every word that falls from him has purpose, so I'm completely stunned when I'm suddenly faced with the awkward rambling man who can't meet Heather's eyes as he thrusts his hands into the bottom of his pockets.

Shuffling nervously as he reveals our news, his tongue darts over his lips as his words dry his mouth. He's been terrified of this, but Heather's forgiveness for something as monumental as his addiction lends him courage. That, and knowing she can't eject him from her home if he's not living there.

She diverts her narrowed attention to me.

"How long?"

I cringe inwardly and swallow hard. I respect her need for honesty.

"The last week or so."

"I hear a 'but' in there." She prompts me, but Archer's monotone interjects.

"We've fought feelings for each other since September last year."

Her scrutiny flicks between us and we hold our exhales, my pulse thundering.

"When you were…uh…helping him…staying in his room…

did you…?"

Embarrassment colors his face.

"Good God, no, Heather! There were more urgent matters at hand then."

Heather's features soften and lift, and she gathers us both in her arms.

"I can't believe I never saw it, but it makes perfect sense. I'm so happy for you two."

It's the anticlimax I was hoping for. Archer's fears were neither as big or as impacting as he'd thought. Heather's a romantic, bless her, and she embraces the news with unrestrained delight. With her support, Archer uncoils the last of his fears, and I allow myself finally to step into our future.

* * *

I wake up to Archer's chest pinning me to the mattress and his soft kisses on my neck. I smile into the warm flesh of his shoulder and hum. Most days begin with his mouth on me, his erection buried inside me and his name ripped from my throat before breakfast. It's a regime that binds us closer and heals our scars.

I smile when he falls back into a doze, and slip from the bed quietly, drinking him in as I pull on shorts and a shirt. He's a golden skinned god with the thick dark lashes of an angel sleeping on his cheeks. His lips are parted slightly, relaxed and plump, enticing me back into bed. I shake my head.

If this is a dream, I never want to wake. Not for a second.

The pop and hiss of the pan and the homely sound of a cutlery striking breakfast plates is a melody that brings a smile to my face and Archer from the bedroom. Leaning against the door frame wearing only jeans and a sleepy grin, he watches me with those piercing emerald eyes as I slide eggs beside bacon and hand him the plate. I follow him with my own breakfast and wait for him to pour the orange juice. The scene is so domesticated and natural that my heart binds a little more to him. He passes the salt.

"To no more shakes." Archer raises his glass and I mirror him with a smirk.

After three months of liquid fruits in the morning, he was glad to eradicate them from his diet with the leveling out of his moods.

"What's on for today?" He tilts his head, and a shaggy lock of hair flops lazily over one eye. Desire surges through me. Everything Archer does has my heart racing.

"Hmm. Simone sent me a message this morning; I think its about my appointment with her next week. I'll give her a call before lunch, then…more study, I guess."

Archer's forehead pinches.

"*More* study? I thought you'd finished that assignment? Don't they only release more units when you've handed one in?"

I shrug, but my stomach squeezes. Archer had suggested that I hold off handing in my assignment, which was strange in itself, but he hadn't given me a reason why. Not that I pushed him. I assumed he wanted to spend time with me without having school work between us, but having the completed assignment sitting in my outbox without being sent made me anxious. It was no big deal.

"I sent it in last week. I just…what's wrong?"

Archer stills mid-chew and glares at me.

"I thought I asked you to hold off." His deep rumble is dangerously chill.

"It was a suggestion, Archer, and you gave no reason why. I don't know why it's important to you. It's *my* schooling, and I can study and submit assignments how and when I like. Besides, the university called me almost immediately to thank me for the early submission."

Archer swallows, his lips pulling tight.

"What did they say, Rain?" His jaw twitches.

I frown. "Not that it matters, but they said it was very

insightful, asked me to elaborate on a couple of sources, advised they'd send through the next unit immediately, then confirmed my personal details. Why?"

"You said this was last week. Did they send the units through to you?" His terse tone shrinks my lungs.

"No, but I'm sure it will be there now."

Archer jerks from the table and snags my laptop. He powers it up wordlessly and spins it to face me. Suddenly losing my appetite I push my plate aside and log on. I refresh the screen but nothing new appears.

"I might give them a call today. It should be here, but there's nothing from them as yet."

Archer growls, and my concern shifts to dread.

"What's going on, Archer. Why, after all your support is it suddenly a crime for me to study? I don't understand."

A shadow crosses his expression, then guilt fills his face.

"Rain, I can't…I can't tell you. I, uh, I need to step out for a while. I'll be back soon." He grabs my chin and kisses me hard. He snatches a shirt from the floor and slips it over his head as he pokes his long feet into runners.

"Archer? You can tell me anything. No secrets, remember?" My heart clenches and reaches for him, but he's already out the door.

I fall back in the wooden kitchen chair, baffled. There's no reason for Archer to be so upset. He's known about my passion and drive to be a psychologist since he's known me, and I can't understand why it's now suddenly an issue. He's angry at me, for what I don't know, but his fear is the loudest emotion I heard. He picked up on something that frightened him, but there is nothing here that could be a problem. I think about the phone call from the university and recall nothing unusual about the conversation, other than they'd called me specifically to thank me.

Frowning, I make a call.

"It's Rain Harrison here. I recently handed in a completed

unit, can you please confirm you have received it?"

The receptionists tone was abrupt and impatient.

"Um, yes. Here it is. We received it last week. Is there a problem?"

"The teacher who called me about it said the next unit would be sent through for me to work on, but I haven't had anything come through yet. Can you check you have the right email address."

The woman sighs heavily and confirms my email address.

"But you won't be receiving anything for another month. The next unit hasn't been released to us yet, so you will have to wait until then. The lecturers are well aware of this, so I doubt you would have been told to expect it."

The cold knot tightens in my stomach.

"But he did. He called the day after I submitted, and said he'd send it through immediately. I'm not lying."

The woman is rude, and her attitude has my spine stiffening. I hear her sniff disdainfully.

"We have no record on the system of any contact with you. Listen, I appreciate your drive to get through this course, but you will have to wait like everybody else."

Words fail me. Long after she disconnects the call I hold the phone to my ear and feel the churning weight in my belly grow.

I call Simone. When I feel unsettled, she's my grounding, but her phone rings back in my ear to indicate she's on another call.

* * *

Archer drifts into the apartment an hour later. He wraps his arms around me from behind and buries his lips in my neck for a long time. I hold his arms, unsure if he's reassuring me, or the other way around, but we both relax a little.

"What is it, Archer? I don't understand what's going on. You're scaring me."

His eyes have a gleam to them, shiny with sadness, but his

expression is locked. He won't tell me.

"There's nothing to be scared of, babe." He murmurs.

"I don't believe you. You're acting so strange. And I called the University. They have no record of the call from the lecturer, and she said there was no way I would have been told to expect the next unit."

Archer stiffens. "Rain, you shouldn't have called them."

"And what was I supposed to do, Archer? I have no idea why you're behaving so strange, and you're telling me what I should and shouldn't do without giving me any information. You seemed to think the phone call was odd, so I followed it up. What should I have done, pray tell?"

My teeth clench.

Archer stabs a hand through his hair and rubs the nape of his neck.

"I'm sorry, Rain, I can't tell you. I shouldn't even be here."

I round on him, snarling.

"Don't you *dare* start this again, Archer! Why can't you be here? Heather knows about us, I'm old enough, so what exactly is your problem? What are you hiding from me?"

He pulls me against him so hard he takes my breath for a moment. His heart thumps harder than it should. Something has frightened him.

"It hurts that you are keeping something from me, when I've been nothing but honest with you. I thought we had something exceptional, but now I find you're holding out on me."

His breath shudders out and his fingers pinch my chin and lift my eyes to his.

"Rainbow, you're the best thing that's happened to me. There is nothing I wouldn't do for you, and we *do* have something exceptional, but…I can't tell you right now. I promise I'll tell you everything when the time is right, but its important that you not know right now. Please, babe. I need you to trust me."

His iridescent orbs drag me in.

"I...don't know if I can-"

His mouth crashes to mine. He doesn't want to hear the words. His kiss is desperate and hungry, and his tongue against mine gives and takes until we both forget.

* * *

Simone's arrival brings a kaleidoscope of emotions to life inside me. I love the woman. I kiss her cheek and drag her into my apartment to show her the life I made for myself, but my usual excited reaction is more subdued by the constant awareness that Archer's keeping something from me. Something that frightens him. The other niggling feeling stems from the fact that Simone has gone to great effort to leave her children for a conversation that could have been had over the phone.

"I tried to call you earlier, but I guess you were already on your way over by then. Why didn't you tell me you were coming?"

I glance up from the cups of coffee at Simone's pause. She seems suddenly neutral, but carefully so. Archer's focus rests on me.

Archer already knows why Simone is here.

"Um, Rain...I'm staying in town tonight, but tomorrow I need to take you to an appointment in the city. I've already arranged it all with Aaron."

I lick my lips. "What is the appointment for?"

Simone strides towards me and clutches at my hands, her eyes dancing with urgency.

"Rain, I need you to remember some things for me. This fog you're working your way through with Archer? I really need you to lift it tomorrow."

I stiffen, clench my fists and turn away to shut off the sarcastic retort that hovers around the tip of my tongue. Archer has been helping me through it every day for months. Its been a painful, drawn out process filled with tears and exhaustion to reach any kind of progress, and Simone wants me to just...'lift it' as if I haven't already been trying.

CHAPTER 25

SHATTERED

*T*he fog. More frequently now it recedes. Sometimes I feel it withdrawing; other times, like now, an image slams into me like a physical blow.

A man with an oily grin walks towards me, the scent of sour sweat mixing with harsh ammonia burns my throat. The sound of sobs and breaths sharp with terror remind me I'm not alone. Every muscle I have is taut with effort, in nauseous anticipation. I brace for the pain when I feel the weight against my back…

I can't breathe. I know I'm standing in my kitchen, but I can still smell his foul breath on my face. I try and fill my lungs but they won't work.

"Rainbow, I have you. You're safe. Whose arms are around you?" Demanding, soothing tones.

"Archer's arms," I croak out, and my chest starts freeing up.

"That's right. And where are you standing?"

"In my…my…apartment."

My vision returns gradually while Simone stands to the side watching Archer bring me down.

"Yes. Can you hear my heart beat?"

I press against him and the steady beat of his heart grounds me again. He holds me until my breath evens out.

"Can you do this tomorrow, Archer?" Simone's words are clipped.

* * *

I'm still out of sorts when I start my set at the club. I seek Archer's empty chair and my heart sinks. Simone said she would sit with him tonight, but Archer hasn't needed supervising for a long time and she knows it. The moment I'm done, I head straight upstairs. I tiptoe the last few metres and strain my ears. There's something going on. Archer's behaviour with my study, the University having no record of my call and Simone's sudden arrival; it all sets me on edge.

Simone's voice is too low to distinguish any words. I crack the door open. They sit opposite each other with biscuits opened up but untouched between them. Simone has a hand resting on Archer's closed fist. He leans on his elbow, holding his forehead in his other hand and staring down at the table. Like he's thinking hard or...?

I curse silently as the door creaks and Simone jerks away from Archer. Archer snatches up the coffee mugs and turns his back to me. But I see him wipe his eyes.

"Rain, I'm going to my hotel now to get some sleep. Rest up and be ready at nine, okay?"

I can only nod. I flick my gaze between them, but they both refuse to look at me.

The door snaps closed.

"What was that all about?"

His eyes still shimmer. "We were just talking about tomorrow, babe."

"Do you know what tomorrow's about?" I know the answer. I just need to see if he'll lie to my face.

"Yes." Deadpan.

"But you can't tell me." Its not a question.

"No."

"Why?"

His exhale explodes and his fist crashes on the table. "Because you need to remember on your own."

My mouth drops open. "That's all this is? I just have to remember something?"

His anguished expression brightens with hope.

"Yes, Rainbow. That's it. You just need to remember for us. I'll be there with you, but you can do this. It's what we've been doing for the last couple of months. You've got this, babe. Then things can all go back to normal."

* * *

His name is torn ragged from my mouth as we climax together. Our chests reach for each other as we catch our breaths, and he gazes down at me with hooded eyes and parted lips. I'll never tire of looking at him.

"You're beautiful." I whisper.

"And you're incredible. I don't deserve you."

I glide my hands over his torso. Just to touch him. Because I can.

"Honestly, Rain. I'll love you with my last breath. I am yours. You're my reason for being. You make me want to be a better man for you. A man who can give you your heart's desire. And I will go to the ends of the earth for you." His features darken and intensify.

I run my fingertips over his jaw and brush his lips until he shudders.

"I love you, Archer. You are all I need. All your scars, your dark parts. Your doubts and your fears. I love it all, and I wouldn't change a thing."

He kisses me tenderly, deeply. He shifts to his side and lifts me with him so he's still inside me.

"One day, Rain, I want a family with you."

Sleep is claiming me, but I'm sure I detect his voice thicken. Sated, I sigh happily. "Children with your beautiful eyes..."

* * *

It's still dark when I open my eyes. The alarm will go off soon, and I need to be ready. I turn my head. Archer is pressed against me, his cheek cupped in his hand and his eyes on me. He dips and kisses my forehead reverently.

"Did you sleep?"

He shakes his head. He looks exhausted.

"Do you know you smile in your sleep?"

"Do you know you fart in your sleep?" I retort and he huffs a tight laugh.

"Are you ready for today?"

I press my cheek on his chest to feel his deep rumble.

"Mmmmmmnnnn."

He doesn't take his eyes off me while I dress, dish up breakfast and open the door to Simone. She scrutinises Archer's shadowed eyes, and his skin, pale from fatigue but makes no comment.

The car ride is silent, and Simone keeps flicking her attention between Archer and me.

* * *

An older man greets us at the door of an unmarked office. My focus is drawn to the tiny cluster of wiry hairs sprouting from a mole above his top lip. It skates off into a smile crease when his eyes graze me, but I'm left with a sensation of queasiness at the sight of it as he leads us up to an old house that's been renovated into office spaces with high security fencing and a concrete pathway to the front door.

"Simone, thanks for coming in. Hello, Archer. And you must be Rain."

He spoke to Archer as if he's met him before. Archer avoids my stare.

"Yes. Rain Harrison. And you are?" I'm generally not so direct, but I'm agitated that everyone seems to know what's happening except for me.

"Detective Senior Sergeant Robert Anderson, but you can call me Rob." He grins like I'm a child as he leads us into a room. I've seen rooms like this in the crime shows on television, and my anxiety climbs. I don't have any reason to be here, but I'm being treated like I do. Perhaps I'm missing something. I can't see Archer and that makes my lungs ache. I search around the white washed walls and squint at a long dark mirror stretching along one wall. It's not a mirror, though. It's one way glass.

With trepidation seeping into my bones like ice forming, I scan the room. Blood thumps loudly in my head. I try and take my cues from Simone, the reassuring glances she sends me and the years of trust between us, but I'm zeroing in on Archer. I can feel him on the other side of the glass, sense his agitation, taste his reluctance. It doesn't sit right at all. But everything Archer has said in the last few months, the support he's shown me, that should tell me I'm safe. I put my faith in him and suck a shuddering breath.

"Rain, you're here for an interview. It's important that you tell me everything you remember. Every detail no matter how big or small. Your friend will be on the other side of that mirror, so you don't have to feel afraid. If you're thirsty or hungry, just let me know. Do you understand?"

Simone interjects with a snort. "Really, Rob, the girl has an IQ of 148. I think she understands."

I quirk my eyebrows at Simone. *How does she know that?*

Rob reddens and squirms. "Okay then. Shall we get started?"

I nod, reluctantly.

"Please state your full name"

"Rain Harrison"

"Is that your full name?"

"As far as I'm aware."

He clears his throat. After establishing my particulars, he

heads down a different path.

"Do you know Sarah Aldridge, Willow Zimms, Credence Bowman and Katherine Elson?"

What?

"No." But then an image of Sarah comes to me. My hand is on her face. "Wait. Yes. I mean I *think* so."

"Explain what you mean."

"I mean, I don't remember knowing them, but I did. I remember reaching out and touching her."

"Please explain what you mean."

Rob's voice is hard and irritating, but I focus on the table in front of me.

"I mean, I have images, memories of Sarah. Just snippets, like the memory has been fractured. I remember Willow the same way, and Katherine a little, too. But I don't have any memories or fragments of Credence." I frown. I feel the fog hovering in my periphery like a hawk. I can do this. Not that I understand what this is, quite yet.

"Okay, we'll try another way. What do you know about Sarah Aldridge?"

"Sarah was gentle. She was like a mother to them, always so caring and intuitive. She was raped and brutalised, and wasn't able to process the trauma, and committed suicide."

"And how do you know this?"

"Over the years I have been keeping updated on them via news stories. I read months ago that Sarah had died. I guess I assumed it was suicide. The death notice didn't specify, but I know how shaken up she was."

"Explain what you mean by shaken up."

I sigh heavily. "When it happened, I remember her going into shock. She disconnected from what happened to her, and never recovered."

Rob's monotone voice. "Explain what happened and how you think she went into shock."

I grind my teeth. "You know what happened!"

I pause, but Rob blinks at me with his controlled, blank expression. With a heavy sigh, I continue.

"Fine. Sarah had turned eleven that day, and…someone raped and brutalised her in front of her sisters."

The fog thickens, taking all identifying features from the gruesome vision playing out in my head. I frown with the effort of my mental shove, but it works. The fog retreats a little, revealing the familiar face of a man.

"Kurt. Kurt attacked her."

"And what did she do?"

"She was too shocked to fight him off, but the sounds she made…" I choke. Her screams echo around my head. I feel the fog descending, reaching out for the pain soaking my memories.

"Rain! Listen to me. Who is Kurt?"

I struggle to part the haze, but my heart and lungs slam together and the tears fall.

Then the fog dips down and takes the horror away.

CHAPTER 26

CREDENCE

*R*ob presses my hands around the glass, and I lift heavy arms to sip the water.

"You okay?"

I nod weakly.

"I'm going to tell you something, Rain, and I need you to pay close attention. You've done well, but we need to go a bit deeper. Do you think you can do it?"

My gaze falls to the window that Archer stands behind. I can't see him, but it's comforting to know he's there.

"Yes. Let's try again."

"Okay, this time, I'm going to disclose something that might help your memories surface. I need you to understand that all the information released regarding the girls and their ordeal was brief and vague. Nowhere on public record will you find any information alluding to what happened to the girls. The details you provided of rapes and brutalising taking place in that period is purely your recall. And those memories are what we need from you."

I gasp. My stomach turns to cold lead. That would mean I was there. "Are you sure?"

"Yes, Rain. There are only a handful of us who know besides the girls, and they are all in this room or behind that glass."

The water spills in my shaking hand and I set the glass down carefully on the table. I feel so fragile, made up of nothing more substantial than brittle memories and airless fog. I'm afraid to move, so still in case I break apart, trying to calm my straining heartbeat to make sense of Rob's revelation. The moment I heard it, I knew it to be true, but there are still fragments missing that I can't reach. How is it that I was privy to something that has nothing to do with me, other than that I knew the girls once?

"Are you ready, Rain?"

I nod and mentally fight the fog that hovers. Rob lays pen and paper before me.

"In the scenario you just disclosed, describe, with images, where in the room everybody was."

I draw two circles close together. Sarah and Kurt. On the other side of the drawn square I make another circle; Willow. Another; Katherine. The last circle, me.

"Where was Credence standing?"

Was she even there? I don't remember seeing her.

The fog threatens to swamp me. It reaches into my pain and grips. My shallow breaths saw loudly, my pulse racing to match the rhythm. I reach out blindly, struggling to stand to make room in my lungs, but the haze has stripped me of muscle control and I crumple to the floor.

I'm suddenly surrounded by a warm embrace. It gathers me and helps me stand. The steady surface rumbles, and through the darkness I concentrate on its vibration.

"...safe. Nothing can hurt you. I'm holding you, Rain. Whose arms are around you?"

"Archer?" I croak in relief.

"That's right. It's me. Listen to my heart beat, Rain. Can you hear it?" His calm timbre steadies my breathing and I press my ear to his chest. The voices talk around me.

"Can we try something different?" Archer. My eyes are closed and I breathe in his familiar scent, his elevated heartbeat both calming and concerning.

Archer's scared.

He slowly peels me away and bends so his face is level with mine. I blink at him and notice his red rimmed eyes.

"Archer, are you-" He snatches the hand that reaches for him and cuts me off.

"Rain, we're going to try another way. I need you to close your eyes again and focus on keeping that fog away, okay?"

I nod. My stomach churns, but I know Archer is within reach. If it gets too much, he can pull me out.

"Rain, I want you to remember when we were talking about David, how he gave you his guitar. You told me that when he was too ill to talk, you used to play Wind for him, and sing about *Before* to him. Now, I want you to sing one of those songs. Like how we practised."

My teeth attempt to still my quivering lip. I nod and feel something press into my hands, and finger the familiar frets and strings of my guitar. *He brought Wind.*

"Remember, Rain. Keep your eyes closed and play about before like David is listening."

I search the corners of my awareness, dive a little deeper into the dark, and find the wall of fog. I mentally push it, and become aware of a softening. A flexing, made possible by the deep green of Archer's eyes that never leave me alone.

"You can do this, Rain. Find a song."

The conviction in his voice gives me strength. Something shifts. My fingers begin their dance, the crisp notes parting the haze, breaking it up. My voice shakes.

> *Connected by our hearts, us four*
> *We laughed and loved together*
> *We'd never break apart, we swore*
> *Our childhoods were tethered*
> *My sisters, they saw the trust in me*

Darkness, it fell over us
Your shelter leaving scars
Too naive to rescue us
Our tears drowned the stars
My sisters, they saw the pain in me

My song strengthens, but the fog thickens. The lyrics light up before my mind's eye, the words stamped in my memories more real than the fog. Like a tattoo. I falter, and darkness threatens. Tattoo. My tattoo. Their tattoos. I fill my lungs and keep singing.

Now you think to own me
Your possession and your whim
You stretch your fingers out to me
You love it when we cringe.

You knew that we could never say
Heroes don't come for our sort
So when my turn came round one day
I was helpless in your sport
My sisters, they saw the fear in me

Bile threatens to launch. I straighten my spine to keep it down. Beads of perspiration prickle, and I shiver. Dread constricts my chest, but Archer is here. I can still smell him. I lean into him, and sing. For him.

Now you think to own me
Your possession and your whim
You stretch your fingers out to me

You love it when we cringe.

You never know just who you'll be
From one case to the next
Instinct said to fight for me
The honour in me flexed...

The song is interrupted by a strangled wail coming from my throat, and I open my eyes. Wind falls to my lap as the images, the sounds stampede behind my eyes. Sarah, Willow, Katherine. My sisters.

Kurt.

Kurt and Credence.

Kurt and me.

Stricken, I seek Archer's beautiful face overflowing with concern. I tell him everything he means to me in the expression I give him. My eyes tell him he is my world, my heart. And they reflect my regret as, trembling, I lift Wind and finish my song.

You never know just who you'll be
From one case to the next
Instinct said to fight for me
The honour in me flexed...
And you, you saw the killer in me.

"Archer." I choke out a broken whisper. "I'm Credence. I'm Credence Bowman, and I killed a man."

CHAPTER 27

MISSING PIECES

*A*rcher's face crumples. But there is something brighter in his expression.

"You knew!"

He cringes his response.

"How long have you known?"

He doesn't meet my glare. The emotions raging inside me blend and aim at the man who held the answers this whole time.

"You knew who I was, and you didn't think it important enough to tell me?"

Archer's jaw locks. When he doesn't respond, I detonate.

"How is it right that you know more about me than I do? While I was fighting the fog, you watched, knowing what was behind it, and you didn't think to help me?"

Rob interjects.

"Rain, it was imperative that he not disclose it to you. It was important that you work it out alone. Archer has been trained-"

"*What?*" Archer has been in training with these people, *strangers* I'd just met, all of whom knew about the dark secrets I had stored in a place I couldn't even access. They already knew. Simone. Archer. The people who meant most to me kept this vital information from me. Simone appears at the door but I ignore her, zeroing in on Archer. I shake with the treachery in his eyes. I'm open and vulnerable before a one way panel of strangers, and the only two people who held my trust have just revealed their hand to them all. I have nothing left that hasn't already been taken from me.

"Get out, Archer. Get out of this room." My words drip like venom, and I stand over his hunched frame, still kneeling before me on the floor. His submissive gesture of guilt escalates my outrage. I lower my voice.

"Get out of my house. Then get the hell out of my life."

The room screams in silence as Archer stands and looks into my face with a stricken expression and wet eyes, and turns away. Simone passes him and reaches for me but I lift my hands.

"You, too, Simone."

* * *

The rage has a calming effect.

"Okay, Rob. Let's keep going and get this done."

I barely recognise my own voice. It's strong and controlled. I feed on its vigour.

"I need you to tell me who you are, what happened that day, and the events leading up to it."

"My name is Credence Rain Bowman." I begin. My name fits now like an old friend and it takes me into my memories. I tell Rob how Kurt cared for us girls well until the day before Sarah's eleventh birthday. He called her to a room in the house we weren't ever allowed to enter before, the *forbidden* room, and closed the door. We'd been terrified of the screams that came from behind it's door, and had cuddled together in our bedroom, wondering what was wrong with Sarah. She'd come out pale and shaking, and shown us her tattoo. The afternoon was strange, because outside of the tattoo, Kurt played board games with us and made us dinner as though nothing was wrong. By the following day it was all but an unsettling memory as we decorated the kitchen for Sarah's birthday. The chocolate cake was ordered from the bakery and we were excited for the treat. Then we went into the forbidden room where Kurt said he had a special game ready.

"He had Sarah help tie Willow, Katherine and me to chairs, and we were all giggling like idiots at this new and exciting game." I recall. Then he called Sarah over to the desk in front of us all and proceeded to rape and brutalise her in front of us.

"We couldn't get out of the ropes, Rob, but I don't think we'd have done anything if we weren't tied. None of us had known a terror so deep, or witnessed this level of depravity before, and Kurt had always shown us nothing but care and kindness."

I shake my head and sip my water, tears never stopping.

"What happened next?" Rob's tone was gentler, compassionate.

"I remember the care he took afterwards to shower and dress Sarah. She lost her voice from screaming, and when she got it back she refused to utter a word. She slept from that night on in a nest of blankets in the corner of our room.

Willow was next to turn eleven. Kurt took her into the forbidden room and her screams reminded us of Sarah. Kurt knew we were scared, so he drugged our dinner, and restrained Sarah, Katherine and me the same way as last time. Willow's birthday present was the same agony and abuse as Sarah's."

"Your birthday came next. What happened then?"

"The same as Sarah and Willow. The day before he grabbed me and dragged me to the forbidden room. I knew what was coming, so I fought back. He twisted my arm behind my back to get me there. He sat on my back on a table in the middle of the room, and I could hardly breathe. There was a man there, covered in tattoos, and he pulled my shirt off my shoulder and gave me the tattoo. It stung and the pain went deep. I screamed for what felt like hours before he was done."

"Do you think you could identify the tattooist if you saw him?"

An image dances behind my eyes and I dip my head. "Yes, he had a distinctive tattoo of a black dragon on his bicep."

"What happened on the day of your eleventh birthday, Rain?"

I drag a deep breath. To say the words make it real. I take a moment and a big swallow of water.

"The day of my birthday I had my first panic attack. Willow hugged me tight all day and wouldn't let me go. Kurt drugged them; Sarah, Willow and Katherine, during dinner. None of us ate the food because we remembered, but Kurt gave us fizzy drink that the girls drank. I didn't realise until later that Kurt poured mine from a different bottle. He grabbed my arm as I was clearing the table and dragged me upstairs to the forbidden room. He had a friend to help this time. About the same age as Kurt, blonde cropped hair and blue eyes that looked like hard ice. That was the man who brought the girls up and sat them in the chairs."

Rob pressed his fingertips together. "But this time was different. What happened?"

"His friend and he were leaning over his laptop. It felt like my arm was breaking because Kurt held me so hard. They were arguing about the program they had on the computer, trying to get access. I was almost relieved when they got the password right, because Kurt relaxed his hold on me a little. But when he pushed me over the desk like he did with Sarah and Willow, I...I freaked out. Something snapped inside me the second he lifted my dress." My knuckles whiten on the edge of the table as I fight to steady my breath.

"He stank of rotten body odour and bad breath. He was breathing heavy and I wanted to be sick. Kurt pushed me over the desk and pressed his chest into my back and I just couldn't do it. I kicked out. Most of the kicks missed, but some connected. I tried to spin around to face him and swing a punch at him but he pressed harder against me. I don't know how I happened on it, but I became aware of a pen in my hand. It must have been lying on the desk, but I don't remember seeing it there before. I held it so tight in my fist and swung around with all my strength."

"Were you able to turn around? What was on your mind at that point?"

"I just wanted him off me. I wanted to stab him so he'd hurt enough to let me go. I figured if I could be free, I could run for help. Eventually I was able to turn." The fog that had cleared now descended thick and relentless.

"I'm losing you, Rain. Fight it. Tell me what happened."

Darkness closes in as I reach for the memories swallowed by the shadows.

"I stabbed him in the face. The pen sank so deep in his eye that I couldn't pull it out again…"

And the fog took my memories away.

* * *

Rob rubs my back gently. My panic attack gradually abates, and the emotional exhaustion hauls me into sleep. The nightmares would rip me awake and I barely have time to shake them off before my eyes closed again. The detectives leave me in a room with a couch, and my shivers are slow to abate, even under the jackets they pile on me.

The faint neon from the next room is the only light I can see.

"I brought you some food." Simone's whisper startles me.

"What are *you* doing here? I thought I asked you to go."

Simone shoves the plate in my arms and scoots my legs up. She falls into the couch and her tired face ages before me.

"Rain, I'm sorry. I understand how you must feel-"

"Do you?" I hiss. "Do you really? So the only two people you've ever bared your soul to have betrayed you, too?"

Her sigh flattens out.

"Fair enough, I deserve that. But I need you to understand that we had no choice."

"Spare me your martyr act. What gave you the right to hide my life from me?" I snarl.

"The right of the law, Rain. The legal documents of disclosure I was made to sign before I met you."

"You seem pretty happy to discuss it now, Simone. Would you care to elaborate?"

My icy sarcasm crinkles her brow.

"I can tell you now, Rain, because you gave us some of what we needed. Where do I begin…?"

I level my glare, refusing to soften.

"At the beginning is a pretty common place." I bite.

"Rain, I am Detective Simone Robertson. I worked in Child Protection in the years before an early retirement, but my specialty is in assaults involving children, and sexual crimes. When I was told about your case, I came out of retirement. What happened with you four girls brought to light a deeper concern. Kurt was one supplier of many in a child trafficking ring, and you four were being primed to fill an order he had. We tried for years to find answers without luck. Sarah couldn't make a statement, Willow helped greatly but Katherine couldn't give us any extra information. But there's something locked inside your head that we need to be able access to help us find who else is part of this ring. We know it's huge, but we have nothing concrete to go on. Until you. But we couldn't remind you or disclose anything to you for fear that any evidence you'd give us would be memories planted or influenced by others. When Archer started getting too close to the facts, I had to intervene. The more he searched, the greater the likelihood of people finding out who you were. Every question he sought had the potential to tip off the very people we were hiding you from and alert them to your location. I had to stop him somehow. He was relentless, so we gave him a job."

"Oh, this just gets better. I'm Archer's job. Well, I hope it was worth it for him." I remember. *Shit floats, Rain, and I'm going to find it.* Well, I guess he found it.

Her eyes squeeze closed. "It's not like that. The problem now is that between the assignment you submitted, and the information you gave us today, the wrong people know you're accessing your memories. I don't know if you remember the times I'd have to pick you up from different homes because someone found out who you were? Well, when you couldn't recall, they forgot about you. Now you're once again a threat, and I regret to tell you that you need to be very careful of possible hostilities. You need to lay low, Rain. And I suggest you return to Heather and stay there."

"You can suggest all you like, *Detective*, but I have a home, and a job, and I'm done with whatever *you* think is good for me." I sneer at her.

I'm unconcerned with the gravity of my contemptuousness. She deserves this. She deserves to pay penance by watching me become the version of me I've never shown her. This me that bubbles to the surface in vengeful rage is not a girl she's met before. She is the version of me that nobody can know more than I do.

"And Simone?" I stare her dead in the eyes with bitter loathing. "My name is Credence."

CHAPTER 28

FLYNN

I hold onto my rage like a shield against the world and take a taxi home. My ire threatens to shatter when I see the key Archer left on the table. He's been. He's gone. I gather my fury to me and growl, ripping the sheets from my bed.

I need to wash the smell of Archer out of my life. To hell with it. I have money. Aaron pays me generously and I have never been one for opulent things. I head downstairs and bump into Flynn.

"Rain? I didn't know you're back. Where are you off to?" I face him squarely and my shoulders relax a little. Flynn may not know the depths of me, but he's not betrayed my trust, either. I find a tiny smile for him.

"I need new bed linen. Do you want to join me?" The smile that glows on his face softens me. He wants to spend time with me, not caring what it entails. No ulterior motive.

The shop assistant suggests cream flannelette sheets to 'soften my sleeping experience'. I buy grey Egyptian cotton sheets because they match my mood. The old Rain would have taken the cream.

"You're different, Rain. You seem…more *together* today. I like it."

My smile widens but doesn't reach my eyes.

"I like it too."

Flynn helps me make the bed in the way only a man can. He spreads out the covers sideways and I throw a pillow at him. His delight in my playful side is obvious. I shouldn't feel playful. It's not natural for me to chuckle and smile when my heart lies in shattered pieces in my bowels. I learned a valuable lesson to rely on nobody but myself and the victorious sensation of surviving such deviousness lightens my head. In the same manner that I shielded myself from memories, I push away the pain left by Archer and Simone.

"Where's Archer?" Flynn notices the absence of Archer's clothes suddenly. His deodorant bottle missing from the bedside table.

"Gone. I sent him away."

He lifts an eyebrow at my flippancy.

"For how long?" His words are careful. And hopeful.

"For good. I told him to get out of my life." My strength amazes me. I've erased him. Made him irrelevant.

"Are you okay?"

I falter. It's on the tip of my tongue to brush him off with a casual 'I'm fine' but I'm not about to become a liar.

"I will be."

He crosses the room and swoops on me, his strong arms holding me to him. My initial response was to push him away. He's not Archer. But I find myself relaxing into him, so very grateful for his soothing embrace.

"It'll take time, Rain, but I'm here for you." His promise rings with truth. I could always find consistency in Flynn. Stability. He was always there on the periphery of my existence, finding Aaron and the club and offering only unwavering faith.

"Thanks, Flynn. I know you are, and I'm so thankful for it."

* * *

My new found strength disintegrates by the end of the first week, and while I don't miss a night of work, I am so drained and tired that I exist in half-life, unable to find sleep. I instinctively reach out for Archer's body and wake when I can't find him. Otherwise it's the nightmares keeping me from rest. When the haze clears, the memories that I haven't attended to before play out as vivid as yesterday, and force me to deal with the deluge of emotions they bring with them without pause. Alone.

Flynn grips my hand as I step down from my stage.

"Oh, Rain, you look exhausted. I'll take you upstairs. I have something I need to tell you, too."

The concern on his face almost opens the floodgates to the deluge of tears that constantly waits. My jaw clenches until the feeling passes and the floodgates remain intact.

What now? I think as I follow Flynn's retreating figure upstairs.

I sit on the bed with Flynn beside me. It still seems out of place for a man who isn't Archer to be at my side. He pulls my hand into his lap, playing with my fingers.

"Simone said you blocked her on your phone?" He registers my firm nod. "She sent me a message asking me to pass on some information. She said you need to remember what the password was urgently, and that she's sending out security to protect you until you do."

My lungs deflate.

"I know you don't want to tell me about it, and that's okay, but I worry about you. This new you is just as incredible as the old you, but even I know you need to look after the you in between. The one who still needs to deal with the residual from the old you. I'm here if you want to talk, Rain."

His tone is so gentle it twists and drags the raw parts of me. With no sleep, and the fallout from nuclear memories his sympathy finally breaks open the dam and I fall to pieces beside him.

"Hey, beautiful girl. It's okay, I'm here. Just tell me what you need."

His embrace is comforting. I hold tight to him and soak his shirt with despair until I'm empty.

"Hold me, Flynn. Just hold me."

He pushes back a little. "You're wrecked. Please, I'm going to help you out of your dress and into your pyjamas, and then I'll lie beside you, okay?"

I snuffle as I offer him my back. He slides the zipper down almost sensually and I hear his breath stutter. I sob louder, but can't summon the energy to help him. *This is a bad idea.* I know he loves me and this is sending the wrong signals, but I'm too absorbed in my own needs. I feel his eyes devour me as he slips my shorts on, but lets me wrestle with my bra under the cover of my tank top. I sense him shift as he removes his pants and slides my body under the covers with his, but leaves his shirt on.

He swallows loudly and his erection nudges my back through his underwear, but fatigue and a warm body beside me takes me from consciousness and into the arms of sleep.

* * *

It's close to lunchtime when I finally stir. Flynn sits at the kitchen table with shadows beneath his eyes and a coffee in hand.

"I'm sorry, Flynn. You didn't sleep?" He's pulled on his pants, but he discarded his shirt, using it to wipe away the water he'd splashed on his face when he woke.

He's a work of art, flawless and sculptured in all the right places. I wish I could feel something for him.

"Is it too creepy to tell you that I spent the whole night watching you sleep?"

A laugh falls surprised from my lips. There's a knock on the door and I snatch a sip of coffee before I move to answer. My security is here.

"It's pitch black in there, Flynn. I don't believe you for a moment."

I smirk at him as I open the door a crack. His grin is lopsided. "Honestly, it's been so long since I've slept with someone that I couldn't sleep a wink. Besides, you snore."

I chuckle, turning to greet the new body guard who would have overheard our conversation and already formed an opinion about Flynn and me.

When my eyes land on him, recognition stops my heart from beating and I'm frozen.

A man of broad shoulders and thick muscles stands tall and intimidating in a tailored suit and sunglasses. His jaw is locked and twitching. His olive skin pales when he sees Flynn.

"Archer." I choke. He doesn't look at me. He's staring at the topless man at my kitchen table sipping coffee with bed hair commenting on his night with me.

Flynn launches from the chair.

"You weren't supposed to come back." Flynn's voice deepens in guilty defence.

Archer's throat bobs. I know the design of him. I see past the cold marble of his expression and know his heart breaks. I know by the way he takes a double inhale that he's hurting. I watch him bleed and I want to explain. But then I remember his deception and steel myself instead.

"Why are you here, Archer?" I snap, and I see the skin around his glasses pinch at my tone.

He swallows again.

"I'm your security." His voice is brittle and fragile, and I force myself to resist falling in his arms.

"I don't need security. You can go and tell Simone I'm fine and I don't need you." Even I cringe inwardly at my callousness as the door snaps shut on him.

I smile weakly at Flynn. "I do not snore!"

But the mood is broken. Flynn jabs a sympathetic stare at me.

"It's okay, Rain."

I bite my lip.

* * *

"Do you want to catch a movie?"

"Oh, Flynn, it's sweet of you to try and distract me, and I really appreciate it, but I think I need to be alone."

"You've been spending too much time alone, Rain. Did you think getting out and into the world might help clear your mind?" His head tilts. It makes me realise how, until this point, I have been singing other people's tune instead of tightening those strings and making my own music. Floating from place to place wherever Simone planted me, waiting for the yo-yo of Archer to spin his way back to me. It's time I find whatever strength is left in me and nurture it. I stare at Flynn. His body is athletic. His attractive features enhanced by his grey eyes, offering to support me like a fledgling, encouraging me to spread my wings. I teeter on the precipice of indecision. His eyes darken on me, and I know his motivation comes from a place of love. A pure love that holds me with open hands. I don't want his love but I need his support.

"Flynn...I'm sorry. I don't want to hurt you, too. You've been so perfect to me, always been there when I needed you. You never pushed, even though I know you want to. I wish I could love you the way you deserve, but...I can't."

"Archer." His statement flattens his lips.

"Yeah." I whisper, and he flinches.

"But you sent him away."

"Yeah. He hurt me, and I don't know if I can forgive him. But that's irrelevant. Even if we never patch things up, I just don't have the space to love someone else when my heart is already full of him. I don't want to lie to you, or offer false hope. There's enough pain in my life without yours on my conscience. You mean way too much to me for that."

I watch him feel it. He fractures before me, tasting the bitter rejection I've left inside him, then bravely comes up for air.

"I should go. But, Rain, it's a beautiful sunny June day out there. The sunshine will do you good. Get out in it."

He retrieves his shirt and kisses my temple.

* * *

I take Flynn's advice. I find a pair of shorts and a modest shirt worthy of a warm afternoon and head outside. Archer falls in behind me with a silence that reverberates around us. He thinks I slept with Flynn. Of course he does. So jealous and possessive and quick to leap to the worst conclusion.

I would have made the same assumption. I shove away my automatic defence of him. I must cling to the injustice so I can remain resilient to my unwavering, burning attraction to him.

He tails me a few metres behind. Through my misery I feel my lips lift. It's just like in the movies, wearing that stereotypical suit to follow me about the city. He looks so ill at ease that I eventually take pity on him. He follows me into a clothing store where I select a pair of torn jeans and a green shirt, taking them to the register, Archer hovering awkwardly some distance away.

Two blocks away, I turn to Archer. He pulls up short in confusion as I push the bag into his stomach.

"You look ridiculously obvious. Put these on."

He glances between the bag and me. I gesture towards a public restroom.

"Go change."

His eyebrows sink behind his sunglasses. "I can't let you out of my sight."

I huff my exasperation. "Well you're not following me looking like some mobster."

I ignore the tic of his jaw.

"You'll have to come in with me." He deliberately empties his tone, but his nostrils flare.

"Fine" I mutter, roll my eyes, and enter the door Archer opens to the disabled booth. He dumps the bag on the toilet seat and shrugs off his jacket. I barely catch it. He faces me boldly, slowly unbuttoning his shirt, baring his torso to me. He's wasted no time since he left weeks ago, his muscles just that little more defined, his hips the slightest bit firmer. I'm well aware he's putting on a show for me, but I can't look away. He scoops up the new shirt. I lick my lips when his biceps flex to snap the tag.

I hate that I love this body. I reach his knowing smirk and turn my back on him, my fists clenched.

When he's dressed, he stabs his fingers through his hair and it forms a sexy, tousled mess. He grins maliciously and bites down hard on his lip so it swells and glows, then opens the door. My mouth drops when I meet the disapproving glare of an elderly couple outside, and I shoot a glare at Archer.

"You knew they were out there!" I accuse. Their scandalous expressions when they noted a dishevelled Archer and his crooked grin with me emerging from the booth behind him makes me glower. The ferocity of judgement in strangers has always been a sore point with me. And Archer knows it.

His shrug pulls his shirt tighter. "I might as well enjoy myself a little. I can't let *you* have all the fun."

The urge to thread my fingers through his thick ones decomposes and snaps as I snarl at him.

"Don't make the mistake of thinking you know me, Archer. When I sent you away, I killed off the girl I was, too. I'm not somebody you can make a fool of again, so don't even try."

"You're still you, Rain, and you're stuck with me following you. *Every day.*" He emphasises with wide eyes shifting his sunglasses.

"I'll ask for someone else." I growl.

"There *is* nobody else. This is what I'm trained to do."

That's right. I'm his job.

"How can I get rid of you?" Outrage roughens my voice.

But he's done with toying with me for the moment.

"Remember the password." He bites, and the ice settles in again.

My afternoon ends with me seething and tense. I go to the zoo, the only place I can think of where having someone follow me isn't too apparent, and where I can silence the noise in my head. I spend a long time staring at the tigers. So regal and sleek, exuding majestic arrogance, they're fascinating.

"They're incredible, aren't they? They're so…hypnotic."

I turn and notice a man beside me. He's a little taller than me with a slender build and a soft, kind face.

"Yeah," I breathe. "I could spend hours just watching them sleep. What is it about them that sets them apart from everything else?"

"I know what you mean. They're almost spirit animals. Something better than us, from another world, that fell through the cracks into ours and aren't changed by it."

"Yes. They're ethereal, but at the same time that silent power…"

"Yes!" He chuckles. "But I still want to steal one of the cubs and take it home."

I laugh and smile at him. "Me too!"

"I brought you your drink, babe. Oh, hello!" Archer's leans his body between us, possessively looping an arm around my waist. My spine welds and the other man backs up.

"I'm sorry, I was just making conversation. I meant nothing by it. Have a lovely afternoon." The man mutters and moves quickly away.

"What are you doing?" I hiss. He twists the top off the water he'd pretended was for me and gulps it down.

"Just scanning for possible threats." He says lightly.

"For Christ's sake, Archer. I can look after myself! I don't need you. And I don't need you sabotaging my opportunity to make friends."

"He was flirting with you, and I'm not here as your wing-man" His expression hardens.

"I don't care! It doesn't matter! That is for me to deal with. Not you!"

"Perhaps I was ensuring you don't cheat on Flynn."

I see red. My hand swings to strike his face but he catches my wrist and squeezes, his face cold marble.

"I think it's wise for *you* not to underestimate *me*, Rain."

CHAPTER 29

AND THEN THE WOLVES CAME

I move through the city with stubborn intent. Archer fights the crowd to keep up, but I don't care. I'm determined to make his life as tedious as possible.

The hairdresser trims my hair. I re-stock my make up and experiment with darker shades of lipstick. I window shop for handbags I have no intention of buying, and throughout it all, my bodyguard stands alert and solemn too close to me. I resent that he won't leave me alone. I can't move on with his scent and heat saturating me all day, and I can't forgive him when his face portrays that stony judgement that I stubbornly refuse to clarify for him.

His phone rings as I leave the shop and he falls back into the crowd. I tolerate the city crowds with reluctant acceptance. The hot bodies crashing through my personal space stifles me. They close in around me in the lunchtime rush and I weave my way towards the shop fronts where the crowd thins out a little.

I catch my breath outside a tiny cafe beside a narrow alley and scan the sea of people for Archer. He's taller than most, so it should be easy to spot him, but I can't, and I let my annoyance simmer. Because there's one thing that's more exasperating than having him follow me, and that's not being able to see him. The ball of anxiety inside betrays me. I'm disappointed that he's not within reach. And-

Fingers lock around my upper arm and and a palm clamps my mouth so hard I feel my teeth split my lip. Blood coats my tongue.

I yank backwards but the grip tightens and drags me into the alley. The bustle on the street is a world away from the desolation of this damp concrete canyon.

"I got her. Come help me."

In shock I can only think that they don't look how I expected. One is older with greying hair and a wiry figure in a faded high visibility shirt and faded jeans, and the younger is plump with tight jeans and loose shirt. The older man reaches for my other arm and the two lift me off the ground and carry me behind a dumpster, my kicks swinging uselessly.

My vision shakes with the violence of my pounding heartbeat. Every move I make, the twists, the resistance…each attempt to break loose from their hold is utterly futile.

Archer? I scan the alleyway for him desperately. I walked too far ahead. I wanted to lose him, and now I need him.

I'm sorry.

My scream gurgles when the back of my head slams into the concrete wall. Stars blur my vision. My muscles burn with my urgency to escape, all the while terror invades my senses. It drowns my hope. They may as well be an army with all the good my resistance is doing. The hand mashes harder on my face and partially covers my nose. I fight to breathe, a panting, terrified mess.

"Do it, man. Do it now."

The younger voice commands, at the same instant releasing one hand to secure my neck to hold me still. I scratch at it with my free hand and scream into my throat. My lungs burn and I cast aside my struggle for freedom and instead fight for breath. Its useless; my airways are completely compromised. A peaceful emptiness creeps inside me and builds and I turn my attention from the men.

If this is my last moment on the earth, I need to find something beautiful to remember. In the diminishing light of consciousness

I see it. Something so ultimately arresting that I relax into the warm embrace of death, finding comfort that I can take such a magnificent vision with me.

Archer...

"Fuck" The younger man's voice explodes and suddenly my lungs are free. I gasp on the air and slide down the wall. The heavy damp air of an alley has never felt so exquisite. I drag it into my chest over and over until I'm reassured that I'm still alive.

Archer moves like a tiger. His muscles buck and ripple as his knuckles connect with flesh. The older man drops. Archer swings on the younger man and lands his fist in the soft stomach. Winded, my assailant collapses to his knees, but the man behind Archer bounces to his feet. I try to warn him, but he already knows, the expression cold on his twisting face. His long leg swipes out low and long, knocking the older man's legs from underneath him, dropping him to the ground. His head makes a hollow sound as it strikes the damp concrete. Archer moves with lethal speed, dragging the bodies side by side while they flail weakly. Archer flips them both to their stomachs, pulling their arms behind their backs with angry force. He retrieves a handful of cable ties from the back pocket of his jeans and zips them tight around their wrists, the thin plastic biting into their flesh.

Only when they are secure does Archer eventually lift his wild gaze to me, his nostrils flaring and his neck corded with tension.

"You okay?" His bite is reprimanding.

I nod, unable to make my mouth work. His shoulders soften and he flicks out his phone. He doesn't shift his eyes from mine.

"Yeah, Al. I have two in the alley between Margot's Cafe and the boutique. Yes. She's okay."

He's a savage warrior of prowling muscles and deadly movements standing over his enemies. I lose my senses in his glare.

He breathes in the silence, ready to pounce, his mouth

twisting.

"You think it's a big game, Rain. Keep me as far away from you as you can. Try and lose me in the crowd. But what would you have done if I hadn't come? Huh?" His words are sharpened blades.

I swallow the metallic flavour in my mouth.

"I would have kept fighting." My words break. I already know my efforts would be useless.

"Bullshit! Just look around you, Rain. There's only one entrance to this alleyway." He rummages roughly over the bodies on the ground. He pulls out a knife from the waist of the older man and holds it up. A sliver of sun finds it and blinds me as if reiterating his words. Archer steps towards me with the dagger in his fist and holds it inches from my face.

"You weren't meant to come out of here." He enunciates with snarls I feel in my spine.

The world tips and I clutch at my chest. He's right. I'd be dead right now. They'd have slipped back into the street unnoticed in their work clothes, long gone before anyone found my body.

Archer lingers in my face, eyes flashing with fierce rage. I've never seen him so angry, so utterly torn and…terrified?

I could have been killed without touching him one last time. The truth burns the air I breathe.

My arms react like things separate to me. They reach for him, yanking him to me so my mouth crashes on his, making him taste the blood on my tongue and diving past it with a hunger bigger than both of us. He grunts in surprise, hesitating only briefly before releasing his own heat. And he's kissing me back. Deeply, savagely. Desperate. His chest that surged with adrenaline now heaves against my breasts with desperate passion. This is Archer. This is the other half of my heart. With one taste the distrust and the anger that raged through my body drops away. Nothing is more important than his lips against mine. He meets my strokes with a burning thirst of his own, my nails pulling him into me. Oh, Lord, his spice and earth scent surrounding me and his mouth feasting on me is rapturous. I whimper, and he groans his response. His hand runs up my back and I shiver as he strokes the back of my neck. He slides his fingers into my hair.

The moment the cry leaves my mouth, he stiffens and jerks away, his hooded eyes narrowing quizzically. He pulls the offending fingers from my hair, and smears the blood covering the tips with his thumb.

He spins me around so he can see where my head hit the wall. I feel a wet trickle make it's way through my hair.

"Damn it, Rain, you said you were okay. I need to get you to hospital."

"I *am* okay. I'm not…dead." I stare at the men secured on the ground. They were trying to kill me. It's hard to wrap my head around, but all I can think about is how trivial a bump on the head is, and how Archer is reacting like it's of monumental importance. Hysterical laughter falls uninvited from me, and Archer's beautiful, luminous eyes narrow.

"What the hell were you doing?" He means the kiss. The ardour that coloured his features is now smouldering disgust.

My body spoke louder than my fear, and I needed to feel you, because it suddenly occurred to me that I may have never felt your lips on mine again.

"Adrenaline?" I feign nonchalance.

Malevolence darkens his eyes and his lip twist like my words are poison.

"Adrenaline? A little bit of danger and you throw yourself at whatever guy is closest?"

I freeze at his glacial tone.

"What? No, it's not like that…."

He looks at me like I was the spilled contents of someone's stomach and my explanation trails off.

"It's not like what, exactly, Rain? Because it looks to me like you've just cheated on Flynn with a flippancy that turns my blood cold. Did you do the same when you were supposed to be mine?"

My chin drops as I struggle to process his allegation.

"You were right before, Rain. I might not know who you were, but I sure as hell know the type of person you are now."

* * *

The alley floods with men in suits. They haul the two men to their feet and herd them into black sedans with tinted windows. A suit is conversing with Archer while another man with a black medical bag checks over me.

"There's so many of you. What do you all do?" I frown.

"We're effectively all the same. We are all bodyguards. I just happen to also be a doctor." He smiles with coffee stained teeth. I frown, even though it opens the wound on my skull.

"I thought Archer was the only one. I said I wanted a replacement and he said there was only him."

His grin widens. "He's right. He's better than the best. He hasn't been with us long, but I've never seen someone with such single-minded focus and determination as him. He trained harder than we thought possible, persisted when he was supposed to meet his limits, and drove the trainers mad with his resolve to be the best. He's become our most valued asset with a good future with us. Word is that our superiors are willing to do whatever it takes to keep hold of him, which is partly why he's here, protecting you."

"What do you mean? What has looking out for me got to do with keeping Archer?" I narrow my eyes.

He jolts, as if he's revealed more than he intended, and flicks his eyes to the sky for a moment. Instead of answering, he stabs a sympathetic glance at me, then gathers the blood soaked cloths from the ground with a sigh.

"I've cleaned you up, but you need to go home and rest for a while with some pain killers. You should probably get stitches in that, but they'd have to shave around the wound, and I think losing that beautiful hair of yours would hurt more than the injury."

With a wink he walks away, then pauses.

"Listen, Rain. This won't be the last attempt to keep you from remembering. But we're all rooting for you. A lot of us have kids, so this is particularly frighteningly close to home for us. We know you can do this. Just…don't give up. Please."

I'm still sitting against the wall when the last of the men leave. The medic gave me food for thought. He made me aware that it's more than just me involved in the mystery locked in my brain. There are mothers and fathers out there who are missing children to people like Kurt, children who understand too well just what Sarah and Willow experienced. Knowing that their torture can be stopped, that many other children can be prevented from sharing the same fate simply by accessing a fading memory of a conversation in my head makes my chest tighten. So much more than I thought is riding behind the fog.

I watch cautiously as Archer approaches. The proverbial hero who saved the day has slipped off his cape and lay down his sword. Now he's just Archer. The man who cuts me open with the shards of my pain, then holds me through the aftermath with an understanding that accepts and heals.

No, I correct. Not anymore. Now he's the stone-hearted judgemental jerk who turned his assumption into a brutal weapon. After everything we have faced together, he still thinks I'm capable of such deceit. I feel the heaviness like bricks stacking up around my heart.

He freezes at something in my eyes.

"What?" …suspicion.

I swallow heavily. I could tell him. I *should* tell him.

Nothing ever happened between Flynn and me. There's only ever been you.

On the tip of my tongue I take him in, and my heart falls. Contempt drips off his entire demeanour and I turn away, unable to withstand his judgement. He'd reacted with desire that rivaled my own when I'd kissed him. I felt his fear in the frantic strokes of his tongue, and how anguished his body was when it called to mine, How can he still be so critical to me when its the choices he makes that have always left me raw and alone?

"I may have been enchanted by you before, Rain, but for the very first time I see who you have been all along. I was only ever there to feed your ego. I fawned over you like a complete fool, and when you felt I betrayed you, you sought revenge in the arms of another. You cast me aside and moved on like you and I were nothing." He spits the words with a loathing that incinerates me.

"Well, I'm done, Rain. I won't forget how you helped me come clean, or that you were everything to me once, and I'll pay the debt back until you find that password, but after that I'm gone." I hear the sound of his heart turn to ice, and force my tears away. He's so far from touching truth that I want to shake him until he understands I need him more than air.

But my words don't come, and he walks away.

CHAPTER 30

THE SHIFT

*U*ghh! Its not working!" I slam my fists down on the table and tear my eyelids open.

Flynn rubs my back. He's been coming to see me most days, where before he'd only catch up before my act sometimes for a drink. It's a little odd considering our relationship should be weakening after I emphasised that he would only ever be my friend. He hasn't tried to push me, simply stood beside me with sturdy support and encouragement. Like now, when I'm replaying my uncovered memories, trying to find a door into the elusive layer just beneath that holds the holy grail. It doesn't seem to help. I recall the man arguing with Kurt about the password, but not what they're actually saying to each other. I remember the feel of their impatience and the smell of their wired urgency, but the words remain shrouded in an unintelligible darkness that I can't illuminate no matter what I try.

"Perhaps a little distraction is in order?" Flynn suggests.

"What are you thinking?" I huff my frustration. It might do me some good to distance myself from these constricting walls just to step out of my head space and reboot.

"Cafe?"

I frown. "The park."

Flynn's teeth flash. He knows that I find solace in walking barefoot beneath the trees, digging my toes into the cool soil beneath.

With my ever present shadow at a distance, Flynn and I wind our way to the duck pond, where we watch the birds scamper through the water in frantic efforts to win our bread. Five ducklings float like fuzzy foam on the edges of the reeds. Five hungry mouths for mother duck to feed. I wonder how different my childhood would have been if I hadn't been an only child. Would more mouths mean the difference between hunger and starvation, or would mum have sobered up for two children? I glance curiously at Flynn.

"Tell me more about your family."

His shaggy smile reminds me how much he's been supporting me lately, though admittedly, a dusting of dark blond stubble suits him.

"I told you my father wasn't a nice man. My mother was great. She always made chocolate fudge cookies because she knew they were my favourite, and she'd sing while she baked. I knew it would be a great day when I heard her in the kitchen, because when she'd slid the cookie tray into the oven she'd pull out a deck of cards and we'd play Go Fish until the timer went off ." He shrugs.

"No brothers or sisters?" I poke. He flops on a wooden bench and I land beside him.

"I, uh, had a sister. A little sister. Amelia." He drifts into silence but my ears sharpen.

"Had? Where is she now?"

"Um, I don't really know. I was sent off to boarding school, and when I returned for the holidays she...she was just gone." His brow crumples.

"What? That's a little weird?"

He laughs coldly. "Oh, it was weird alright. Mum stood there with black circles under her eyes and shook her head when I looked for Amelia. She was warning me not to ask, so I didn't."

"What do you think happened to her? Have you seen her since?"

His head rocks slowly. "I think my dad had something to do with her disappearance. I should have asked him but I was only a kid and too afraid of him. Instead I spent the entire holidays in the shed with him handing him tools to repair the mower."

Flynn's head drops into his hands. "I'm terrified of my father, and I hate him, but I still crave his acceptance. It's pretty screwed up, but it's the truth."

I squeeze his leg. "It's not screwed up. It's survival. You know, I think if Mum showed up out of the blue, I just know I'd let her back into my life, even though logic tells me it would be a terrible move."

He lands a strange look at me.

"So what would you do if she called you tomorrow, promising you everything you wanted for just a tiny favour?"

I mull it over. If my mother called and told me she was sober, that we could be a family again if only I'd grant a small favour? Honestly, I'd love to know who my mother was without the distortion of the drugs inside her. Flynn is right. It's screwed up.

Reluctantly, I sigh. "I'd probably do it."

Flynn looks at me thoughtfully for a long time.

* * *

Archer is like moving stone as he tails me wherever I go, void of all emotion. Everything I do and say is lined with the hopelessness of him. I can't escape the agonising ache of existing so close to him without being able to touch him. But it goes deeper. I'm watching him shut off more with every sunrise; the thread that used to hold us so close together fraying and weakening as it's stretched apart. A part of me wants it to snap so I can finally disentangle from the hold he has over me, and begin to repair. But the other part of me that starves without him craves the moment every morning when I open the door and see his vacant expression waiting for me. I need that, just to know he's with me no matter how broken we both are.

There are nights where Flynn doesn't go home. Sometimes we

just talk. Other times its because I don't sleep well and I need to know another body is close by. He sleeps on the couch, of course. I don't think its fair to him to have him lie beside me and imply false hope to fulfil my own needs. Archer doesn't say anything. In fact, he's barely spoken a word in the last month. I watch that thread between us fray a little more every morning Flynn emerges looking dishevelled from what he believes to be a night in my bed.

Sometimes I want him to retaliate, yell and scream at me, even with his accusations, just so he will speak to me again. I hate that I miss the smoky velvet of his voice.

So when the storm shakes the building with the roar of thunder, I hesitate. He's full of aloof ice, and the hate permeates off his demeanour. But he's still Archer, and he's outside my door in a storm. Alone. I slide out of bed and tiptoe quietly through my apartment, careful not to wake Flynn. He's deep asleep with his forearm resting on his cheek, jaw slack and his long frame sprawled out haphazardly over the length of the couch.

I crack the door. Archer's body leans against the wall with his head turned towards the staircase that leads down to the street below, and at first glance he appears tranquil, albeit vigilant. I move to close the door, then I pause. It's the false posture of confidence he's retreated into of late. The throbbing of his jaw tells me he's terrified, and the pulse thunders in his neck so fast I can't tell one beat from the next.

"Archer." I whisper so as not to frighten him. His head whips to mine, his eyes huge and wild landing on me. His lips part and my breath hitches.

"Archer. Come inside." His inhale stutters but he shakes his head and presses his lips. He'd prefer to ride out the night in terror than come inside with me. The thunder rattles the windows and the lightning makes his gaze dart and lurch. I pull back the hand that shoots out instinctively to reassure him. It's not my place any more, but I'm compelled to do something. We share a history. A dark, living pile of crimson passion and black fury kind of history that ties me to him with a damaged knot that persists. And I can't stand by and watch his fear eat him.

In the shadows of the night, I sigh and slide my back down the wall, pulling my knees against my chest.

"We need to talk."

CHAPTER 31

THE SAME OLD SONG

*H*e stabs me a glare diluted by fear.

"I have nothing to say to you." His gruff tone is swallowed by a roar of thunder.

"Okay, but I have something to say to you." I fill my lungs. "I hate that you betrayed me. I hate that you had the key to my identity and didn't tell me. I don't trust people, Archer, but I trusted you and Simone."

"What about Flynn?" He sneers.

"Well, yes. Okay. I trust Flynn, but he doesn't know me, and he doesn't know about *Before*. He can't hurt me if I don't show him my wounds."

"Does he know his girlfriend isn't letting him in?" A sudden flash from outside highlights his disgust.

I fuse my teeth.

"I thought you said you had nothing to say to me." I hiss.

His jaw locks, but he still won't look at me. It's probably a good thing, too, because I didn't plan this conversation, and it's making me uncomfortable. I tug my hair uncertainly, and my toes twitch with indecision, but as the words fall, I realise I need to give them a voice.

"I loved my mum. I loved her the way any child would. Even now, I remember the way she smelled when she hugged me.

And she crushed me. I forgave her over and over again. Even when she tried to sell me for drugs I ran straight back into her arms. It broke me to walk away from her, but I knew it needed to happen. It was the hardest choice of my life."

"And I loved Kurt. I was happy there with my sisters. It was the childhood I'd always dreamed about. Until the day it wasn't. What he did to my sisters, and what he was intending to do to Katherine and I was - and still is - beyond my comprehension. To go from such innocence to…what I did…I think I'll spend the rest of my life trying to make sense of it. But then I had Simone to help, and she was there for me during the fallout. She helped me find a semblance of peace in what I had left. And then she too held the key to the void inside me and didn't reveal it. And then there was *you*."

Emeralds shimmer from the dark as Archer focuses on me, the storm raging behind him. I open up the wounds in my heart.

"I never had a friend before. Or maybe you were always going to be something more than a friend. The connection I felt with you came from inside my veins from the beginning, and I'm sure you felt it too. Simone was my confidante and I didn't need or want anyone else to meet my private demons, but every wall I built came crashing to the ground every time your eyes lit on me. I couldn't keep you out if I tried. And I tried so hard."

My eyes closed and my throat burned. I hear Archer's swallow in the dark.

"You know me better than anybody, Archer. I've told you things I couldn't even admit to myself, and you tread all over my triggers and nightmares to pull my buried memories from me. To know you've dipped your fingers right into my soul, and still believe me capable of betraying you decimates me, especially since you've betrayed me over and over. I thought I had nothing left to break until I tasted your judgement"

"Betrayed you over and over?" His anger has dissipated slightly, making way for confusion.

"You kissed me then backed away with silence. You made love to me then acted like it never happened. You kissed that girl behind the bar like I meant nothing to you. Then you accused me of sleeping with Flynn like you thought I would be capable of that. Each time, Archer, you tore another piece from my heart. Time and time again I've waited for you, fought for you and laid my heart at your feet, and every time I end up with one more wound from you that just won't heal. I'm so exhausted from trying to get your footprints off my heart when I never deserved this treatment in the first place."

The silence fills with his thoughts.

My voice crushes, so I whisper.

"I'm so tired of you leaving me to try to learn to breathe without you, because when I finally manage to function again, you find your way back, and that same excruciating song begins all over again." Tears slide down my cheeks and I swipe at them.

His eyes shimmer in the sliver of light trapped in them. He faces me then with the softness and compassion of the man I remember who fills my heart.

"Why are you doing this, Rain?" The velvet returns to his tone sending waves of awareness down my spine.

I bark out a snort.

"Because as much as I hate you right now, I couldn't bear the idea of you sitting though this storm on your own. How screwed up is that? I'm trying so hard to be strong, letting my anger strengthen my resolve to keep the world out, but even that's not working out."

Archer huffs through his nose, trains his focus on me and slides down the opposite wall, leaving a chaste gap between us.

"Don't change who you are. Not for anybody. Don't let bad experiences take away the light in you. Bad things happen, but the strongest people refuse to be crippled by them. You are you because you're the strongest person I know and nothing breaks you. You say you're damaged, but your resilience shines brighter than anything the world dares to inflict on you. It's what I..."

He chokes off, drawing a shaky breath before continuing.

"It's what I *love* about you, Rain, and I hate that I can't stop loving you. I hate that I've hurt you more than I'll ever know, but

I thought I was doing the right thing-"

I cut him off with venom.

"*The right thing?* How is messing with my head the right thing?"

His soft sigh is almost lost in the sudden deluge of rain that roars outside.

"It was so easy to forget how young you were at first, before anything happened between us. You had the body and face of a goddess, and you had this maturity far beyond your years. You just understood how life worked. But more than that, you understood me, and that was terrifying. I never bothered with anyone, fancied myself as a bit of a loner, and people in turn avoided me. Until Heather I never had the slightest desire to try to connect with someone else. When you showed up my instinct to fight just…evaporated. I remember just how damn haunted you looked that night you told me Heather's was your last stop and all you wanted was to be left alone to fly under the radar. I hadn't experienced until then the desire, no, *primal need* to protect someone. Not just protect, but I wanted nothing more than to be the man who kept you safe and own your heart. And suddenly your age became *extremely relevant*. I wanted things from you I had no right wanting. So I backed off. I thought I was doing you a favour by keeping away but it just made it harder for me when I was close to you. I changed my shifts to avoid you. I kept my mouth closed so I wouldn't frighten you. I…uh…kissed Emily to try and stop that damn ache in my chest every time I thought of you."

My blood aches. That depth of desire - I understand. Only it seems like too little, given too late.

"Did it work?"

"You know damn well it didn't. I tried twice… All it did was fan the inferno already raging in your name. I knew as soon as I kissed her it was a mistake because everything else was inferior to you. You ruined me. But I knew if I stayed near you I'd cross that line and hurt Heather, or end up in jail because I couldn't keep my hands off a minor. So to keep busy I gave in to a safer obsession and dug around in your past. The day after you fell apart when we were hugging Heather I found something placing you in the house with your sisters. Simone found my number and told me to stop my investigation. I told her I couldn't. She drove down to speak with me the following day."

What? Simone was working with Archer behind my back for over a year? My head throbs.

"She spent days trying to persuading me to back off, but the harder she pushed, the more frightened for you I became. When she revealed she was a detective, I demanded she tell me everything she knew. By the end of the interrogation, Simone could see I was determined, so she agreed to train me to protect you. In return I'd stop trying to probe deeper."

He stabs his fingers through his hair. I clench my thighs together and wet my lips. I hate that he has this effect on me when I need to hate him for what he's revealing.

"I knew enough about you from the research I did that Simone reluctantly filled in some blanks for me. I had to sign a non-disclosure and agree to withhold it from you. I was in awe of your strength, and committed to keeping you safe no matter what the cost, so Simone offered me intensive combat training and a paid position in the special forces on the condition I keep away from you. If I let slip anything to you, the entire operation would collapse."

"So you kept away."

Anguish flashes across his handsome face.

"I was trying to *protect* you!" He snarls.

"You weren't protecting my heart!" I snap.

"I didn't know you felt the same way! At least, I wasn't sure. When I kissed you, I realised I'd made a huge mistake."

My snort makes his nostrils flare.

"It's true, Rain. I couldn't have screwed up more. Don't mistake me. I didn't regret it for a second, but it made keeping away from you so damn difficult. That was where it got messy. If I'd just stayed away, you wouldn't be hurting right now, and neither would I."

"You're sure about that?" I growl back. Loving him grew before the kiss, and bloomed regardless of it. Within it the thread that held us together strengthened despite the war zone of secrets and confusion we fought to survive in. I feel my rage melting. I can see now why everything unravelled the way it did. It had to. The only choice Archer had was to…do exactly what he did.

"No. But I needed to convince myself it was the only way."

"You followed me to the club. That's not keeping away."

Archer's nod was barely visible.

"We'd had security tailing you. Others. Not me. I'd just finished my training but hadn't yet been signed off. The assignment you were researching was triggering off all kinds of alarms put in place by all the wrong people. The people we were trying to protect you from were suddenly aware that your memory was stirred and they were no longer safe. I was supposed to find out if you were ready for another interview."

"But why the heroin?" Something clicks into place. "You lied about that, didn't you? You lied to me!"

Archer lunges for my hands but I tear them away.

"I had to, Rain. I couldn't very well tell you that someone intercepted me and locked me in a damn box of a room for weeks forcing heroin into me because if I was desperately chasing my next hit, I wouldn't be capable of protecting you. It was a perfect way to eliminate me as a threat and not have to hide a body."

His venom rumbles and its my turn to sink into guilt. The drug induced ramblings were flashbacks, not fantasy.

"Oh, Jesus, Archer, who did that to you?" The remains of my fury evaporate, and his sigh crosses the space between us and curls against my cheek. I shudder.

Through clenched teeth his contempt hisses. "Your enemies."

CHAPTER 32

PLAIN SPEAKING

*J*s this why you can't speak to me without contempt? Because you wouldn't have been forced into that position if it weren't for me?"

The flash of lightning illuminates the green in his eyes as he scowls at me through the night. The gentleness is suddenly gone.

"No, Rain. Jesus, you're not an idiot. You *are* aware that since you slept with Flynn you've kissed me, right? I'll bet you would have spread your pretty legs for me too if I'd wanted it. Thank Christ I had the morality to put a stop to it." Bitterness laced with abhorrence cuts through the night and I wince.

He's still clinging to the conviction that I was the type of girl that would do that. Deep inside I understand he needs to project his rage. It's easier than showing hurt. I've explained what he means to me, and he refuses to understand, delving instead into the depths of my imaginary betrayal. It's on the tip of my tongue to reassure him there's nothing between Flynn and me, but he needs to manage his inclination to jump to conclusions without considering who I really am. It doesn't help that I'm stubborn and indignant. I climb to my feet and crack the door.

"Well then. Glad we had this chat." Sarcasm drips. It doesn't suit me, but I can't stop myself. "Best I be getting back to my *boyfriend,* then."

His handsome face shutters, and he turns his stony attention back to the stairwell.

* * *

I close the door quietly behind me and lean against it, blowing out a breath.

"Rain, we need to talk."

I startle as his silhouette lifts from the couch. Flynn lopes sleepily to the kitchen table and gestures for me to join him.

"Why do you keep doing this to him? To yourself?"

I huff into my hands. "I'm so angry that he thinks me capable of cheating on someone. He should know me better than that. He *does* know me better than that."

"Yes, he does. And so do I." He agrees firmly. "But even you have to admit the conversation he walked in on sounded pretty condemning."

I sigh my agreement. "I just hate my life right now. I just want everything to go back to normal."

"What is normal, Rain? Explain it to me, please, because there has never seemed to be a *normal* in your life since I met you."

I catch his eyes in the darkness. He's right.

His steady tone rocks me.

"I think we're missing the biggest issue, Rain. What would you *like* your 'normal' to be?"

What I want? The only things I was certain of to date is to be a psychologist, but nothing else in my dream was solid. Then I was placed with Heather and suddenly there were images growing wings of new things I wanted.

"I want..." I falter. Flynn holds my gaze expectantly, lifting his eyebrows to encourage me.

"I want...I want stability. Security. I want to know that I will never have to carry that damned suitcase to another place unless I choose to. I want to live peacefully, and I want to help children..."

My gasp catches me by surprise. I want to help children, and although I'm not a psychologist, I already have the power to help hundreds, apparently, locked away securely in my head.

The password! It must have something to do with the children!

"I have to remember the password." I whisper underneath my breath.

Flynn shuffles in his chair.

"I know you don't want to talk to me about it, Rain, but I'll try to help. Can you tell me anything?"

I'm hesitant, but if there's a chance he can help, I have to try. I select my words.

"I was in a room where two people were arguing about a password. The one at the computer kept getting it wrong, so the other man had to tell him a few times, but I can't remember what they said."

The thunder had rumbled away long ago but the flashes of light persisted spasmodically. One catches Flynn in a pensive frown.

"Okay, and you obviously tried to remember unsuccessfully in the interview. Do you remember how were you feeling when the men were arguing about it?"

I pull air into my diaphragm.

"I was...terrified. I was on the edge of a panic attack. I was in pain, too, and I was frantic about my...some friends that were there with me."

Flynn looks confused. "What about your friends, do they remember?"

I shake my head and picture a still-shot. They're all bound to their chairs on the other side of the room.

"They were too far away." The picture in my head begins to move. There is no sound, but I see the tattooed man mouth the password. Twice. His lips barely move. *Heaven?* No. That's not right. I lean back in the chair and dig at my eye with the heel of my hand.

"It's gone again."

Flynn rests his chin on his hand, his tone thoughtful.

"I wonder if you'd remember if we could recreate that same atmosphere. You know, another traumatic experience to trigger the memories."

My derisive laughter snaps.

"That couldn't be done, Flynn. I'll just have to keep trying. I feel that every time I do this I get a little closer."

Poor Flynn looks defeated.

"It upsets me that you can't trust me, Rain." His words whisper in the approaching dawn.

"I'm sorry, Flynn. It's not you, really. I just don't trust anyone. And I do trust you in my own way, it's just that some chapters of my life I'm better off guarding from everyone. Not just you."

His blue eyes deepen with a flash of understanding, but he blinks it away.

"You trust Simone and Archer."

"I *used* to, yes. I trusted Simone for years, and both she and Archer betrayed me. I'm so humiliated that I let them do that to me, and they seem to think they're exonerated because they believe it was for my own good."

"And *was* it for your own good?"

That handful of words suck the air from me. *Was it for my own good?* No. It wasn't. But it was for the good of so many more than me. What would I have done in their situation? Would I have honoured the trust of a friend, or like them, would I have withheld a secret that could potentially save hundreds? I swallow hard. They knew the secret would surface eventually; in fact they marched towards that goal with open determination. And I pushed them both away because that's what Rain Harrison does. The fight that has burned in my stomach is replaced now by heavy realisation, and Flynn's gentle smile reaches for me.

"Sometimes, Rain, what we imagine is treachery is really a window into the people they are. Sometimes it's exactly what it looks like, and we are given that opportunity to discard them from our lives. But others can be capable of bad things for good reasons, and deserve to be forgiven. We just have to hear them out and decide for ourselves."

I move behind him and wrap my arms around his shoulders, resting my head on the bare skin between his shoulder blades.

"Thanks for everything, Flynn. You're a good man and a treasured friend."

His spine straightens.

"Hey, I have something to ask you, Rain. I…I got a text from my fa…father, and I'm a little nervous about it."

"Oh my god, Flynn. That's come from nowhere. What does he want?"

"He, uh, wants me to go and see him. Apparently he's in town for a few days on business…"

I watch his expressions crash. He's excited, hopeful, tentative and downright scared. We've discussed this, and I know Flynn needs closure. He's hoping to find acceptance in the heart of his father.

"I'll go with you, if you like. A bit of moral support?" It's the least I could do for all the support he's given me.

His body unwinds. I boil the kettle for our coffee.

"Thanks, Rain. I was hoping you'd come. He's around today and the next two days. When suits you?"

"The day after next?" It's the wee hours of the morning, and tomorrow we'll all be tired.

Flynn nods.

* * *

For the first time in months I feel rescued from the ropes of anger I've wrapped myself in. Flynn's clarity on the intention behind Simone and Archer's deceit allows me to shrug off the cloud of self-pity, and I once again feel in control of my life. I slip into a black strapless evening gown that clings and shimmers under the stage lighting. I pull my hair into an elegant bun, leaving curled tendrils stroking my shoulders. My make up is always modestly done, simply highlighting my features instead of painting my face. My signature look. But tonight? Tonight I felt like a bold smear of red across my lips. I apply the crimson and study the results. I love how a simple line of charcoal over my lashes enhances my appearance, and the dresses I wear add another two years onto me. Closer to Archer's age. Tonight I feel like a stunning woman preparing for the performance of her life. I fasten a necklace, a tiny teardrop diamond nestled into the hollow at the base of my neck. It highlights the smooth skin pulled tight over my collarbones, and draws the eyes to my cleavage. My first instinct is to find a silk scarf to cover myself, but then I square my shoulders and lift my chin. I want to show Archer I'm not a girl anymore, that I'm old enough to know what I want, and I shouldn't be ashamed of being a woman. I find a pair of black heels with rhinestones decorating the straps to complement my necklace.

The familiar shape of Archer snags my heart from the shadows as I step through the door. His eyes feast on me, and I relish it. He's angry at me, but he can't fight the crackle that connects us. I hear him swallow hard as he falls in behind me.

Archer's intensity fixes on me for my entire set, devouring me with his heated thoughts. He almost stumbles where he stands when I sing "Stay" by Rihanna to him. He is breathtaking in the suit he dons for my performances. I don't know where or when he changes from the street clothes I make him wear, but the visions of Archer's thick shoulders and powerful chest in a suit are lodged firmly in my memory. Nobody but Archer can set my blood on fire just by breathing.

In the middle of my set, spotlight warming the crown of my head and Archer standing like a beacon in the crowd, I watch him as my guitar speaks. He betrayed me, but he didn't do it to hurt me. He did it because it was the right thing to do. He fits me, his scars nestled perfectly beside mine. Flynn asked me what I wanted, and the answer is in a tailored suit protecting me with carnal hunger and simmering ferocity. When he thought he couldn't have me in his arms he became my armour against evil, even though the thought of me with another man broke his heart. He chose to wear his fury to defend himself from the pain. In that moment, I allow myself to forgive him. I step from the stage towards him as my guitar finds a new set of chords. He holds himself rigid as I stand before him.

"I can hear your broken thoughts no longer
They're silenced by your wall of stone
That grows between us ever stronger
'til we stand here together, but all alone
But I'll fall straight back into your arms again

I need your heart, because you have mine
There was never another in my bed
Sweet darling our love was always blind
You judged me wrong, and I saw red
But I'll fall straight back into your arms again

Baby, in your eyes I can see it bleed
Those golden threads that never sever
It will only ever be you I need
Just you and me, and our forever
And I free fall straight into your arms again"

He doesn't move but I see it in his eyes. They are alight with hope. Applause reaches deafening tones and I switch off the microphone clipped to my dress. Archer's gaze follows my fingers then dips to my chest, with a hunger I can almost feel against my skin. I groan softly, but he hears me, emerald fire blazing into me.

"Flynn sleeps on the couch." I explain over the cheers. "Except for the morning you came, when he simply held me so I could fall asleep." He darts a look at Flynn who sits and watches us, a confirming sadness weighing down his mouth.

Archer's nostrils flare as he processes my admission while the crowd fills in the spaces between us.

"Rainbow." He rasps, and across the expanse of months and pain, Archer returns to me. The strong jaw that has locked me out for so long softens. I touch it. Because I can.

"I love you." I smile, and let the crowd sweep me away, because tonight, Archer will be back in my arms.

The patrons loved my song. I smile with my heart at Archer as I'm dragged into the centre of the room with hands reaching out to pat me on the back, seeking to clasp my hand in theirs.

I laugh and catch a glimpse of Archer through the sea of faces, but his expression has changed. Eyes wide, muscles bursting with fear, he's straining towards me, his mouth moving over words I can't catch. I wonder why he's so far away before I note all the hands on him, too, pulling him backwards. Suddenly panicked, I peel the bodies apart and move towards him, my own expression mirroring his.

CHAPTER 33

THE END

*T*he bellowing crack of the gun has an instant effect. The crowd lowers and scatters amid screams and thundering footsteps.

My heart roars in my head and I lock on Archer's face. His gorgeous face is tipped back and coiled with agony, his hands twisted rough behind his back to immobilise him.

I remember how that feels.

A thick arm loops around his neck, the wicked black chamber of a gun pressing the skin on his temple. His eyes never drop from mine.

Archer! I mouth. Four more men close in on him.

Run, his lips command, and my feet obey. The delicate straps of my heels grip my feet and I cant kick them off, but I manage to clatter awkwardly towards the door at the foot of the stage. The heavy door slams open, the hallway behind filled with men. I can't hear them move across the floor over the loud rasping of my breaths, but they all wear the cold blank expressions of purpose. Desperately I seek Archer again.

In slow motion, every movement plays out with infinite detail. Archer manages to break away from the thugs. His eyes hold mine as I stand in the threshold, stricken fear and frantic ambition launching him towards me. Always my hero, saving the day.

Not today, though.

A deafening sound barks out through the din and my ears scream in protest. Archer's tenacious expression is interrupted by silent astonishment, his mouth seeming to pause on an unfinished train of thought. He blinks at me, seeking answers I can't give.

There's a black mark on the side of his head. So out of place, I focus on it. It looks more like a...

My heart lurches. It's a bullet hole. My scream strangles.

His lips lift in a faint crooked smile, all the love we cultivated over the years shimmering from him. The men no longer surround him. They've stepped away, but he just stands there, frozen and alone. His mouth opens, as if he's tasting my name, but it won't obey.

Archer!

He frowns in confusion, and I can only watch helplessly as he struggles to draw a breath. And fails. He tries again, his shoulders lifting with effort.

No no no no no! A noise is dragged raw from my deflated lungs. The sound of my heart shattering into a million pieces.

When confusion mutates into alarm, Archer tries to take a step, but his eyes lose focus and fall blank. His demeanour startles, then softens. Crimson swarms from the hole in his temple. Horror steals my breath and I crumple to the ground in sync with Archer. The tiles jar my arm as they break my fall, but the hard floor is unforgiving of Archer. Too far away for me to catch him, his head lands with a sickening crack, blood pooling beneath him, and his empty expression doesn't change.

"Archer?" My throat rips open with the force of my fear and my ears ring.

They killed Archer!

His dim and vacant eyes don't shut me out.

Like a flood, the mist crashes in, swallowing the scene, hiding Archer's lifeless body. It reaches out with wispy tendrils of numbness, sedating my tortured, bleeding heart. Erasing everything.

The world around me evaporates.

* * *

"How far away is he?" A rough voice interrupts the gloom in my head.

"Later this afternoon. He's wrapping up another job. He says to make sure she can't get away and not to tell Malcolm where we are. He doesn't want him stealing his glory."

I attempt to crack my eyes without drawing attention, but the effort splits my skull. They hear my groan.

"She's with us. Carl, tell the boys to keep alert."

"Shouldn't we, like, not use our names and wear masks or something?"

The light stabs angrily into my retinas and blurs the room. The taller blur's head shakes and his laugh barks. I blink to clear my vision.

"It won't matter, Carl. She won't be talking to anyone once Tony gets what he needs."

I'm not meant to leave this place. I try to bend over the cold twist in my guts, but find ropes biting into the flesh on my wrists that anchor me upright in a steel chair. My ribs strain against my pounding lungs as panic builds. Spots buzz around behind my eyes as the rope reminds me at every inhale that I can't escape. *This is it. The final chords of my song are the too-shallow breaths of my terror.* My song was meant to end with Archer, grandchildren at our feet.

Archer! My insides pull together. Frantically I reach out to the thread that binds me to Archer to reassure me he's okay. Something is wrong, and I need to know Archer's okay.

Where is he? He'll come for me. He always does.

"What's she doing?"

"I think she's freaking out."

My sight sharpens in time to see the baffled face of one man swipe a palm out. Pain crashes through me as he lands a stinging slap on my cheek, and I cry out in shock.

"What the fuck, Carl?" The tall man barks.

"I heard that a slap stops a chick going hysterical. And look, it works." Carl's smug tone lingers as I stab a glare at him. He's right. The heaviness that crushed my lungs broke off and interrupted the exploding rhythm of my pulse. I open and close my jaw through the throb to see if he broke it, because my neck burns with the strain of the impact. He squints into my face and breathes rancid decay on me.

"She's a pretty thing, ain't she? Do you think Tony will mind if we loosen her up a bit?"

My stomach seizes violently at the thought of his foul hands on me, and he leers down my cleavage with another decomposed breath in my face. I summon moisture into my dry mouth and spit at him, then cringe away as he raises a fist.

"Jesus, man. Just get away from her. I don't know what the boss man wants to do with her, but for Christ's sake don't beat the shit out of her before he gets what he needs."

I freeze when the sound of approaching footsteps reaches the door.

Flynn stumbles into the room, almost crashing into Carl and his sidekick.

"Flynn, are you okay?" I dart my concern over him, relieved there's no obvious injuries, my gratitude that he's unhurt crashing with the regret that he didn't escape. When I'm met with silence I find his eyes again, and my heart collapses.

Flynn doesn't wear the face of fear. He's not trembling in panic. He's not stiff with tension. His shoulders square and his head lifts. Flynn looks at me with cold blue eyes.

"Flynn?" My voice breaks over my plea, and his eyes narrow.

"Tony says you're to watch her. Billy and I have to pick him up but we're not gone long. He's counting on you."

Silent tears track down my cheeks, and I can't wipe them away. I watch with disbelief as my best friend nods briefly and leans back into the corner of the room as the door snaps closed, leaving us alone.

I break the silence.

"What have you done, Flynn?" I let him hear the pain of his betrayal.

He throws a glance over his shoulder, sidling up to the door with his ear pressed against it.

"I'm sorry." He huffs, pulling away from the door.

"Sorry for what?" I growl through clenched teeth.

He tries the handle, but it doesn't give. His knuckles whiten as he jams his grip down, but it's futile. He turns around, finally meeting my glare, fingers stabbed through blonde hair.

"My...my father wanted to meet you. I should have known something was off. He got in contact with me and asked me to bring you to meet him. I...I was so hopeful to reconnect I agreed without asking how he knew we were friends. I told him we'd come, but he was impatient and although I didn't tell him, he obviously found out where I was."

I crinkle my eyebrows.

"I'm not quite following, Flynn. What has your father got to do with anything?"

The colour drains from his face and his hands rest behind him on the wall for support.

"Tony is my father, and the guys that took you are his men. He's some crime boss or something, I think, at least, that's what it appears... I don't know what his interest in you is, though. I knew something was off so I made a call to Simone. She was on it, but... "

His face contorts with a conglomeration of guilt and anguish.

I close my eyes against the tsunami of certainties flooding

my mind. It all makes a sick kind of sense. The sly cruelty of Flynn's father. The spontaneous desire to reconnect with his son coinciding smoothly with the police interview and my assignment being handed in. And the nature of why Flynn's little sister had disappeared from his life without a trace. My stomach curdles. Flynn's father is involved in the same barbaric syndicate as Kurt. But there's more. There's something important in the mere layout of the room. The tables set up just so, the laptop at just the right angle on one of them. It's so terrifyingly familiar that it chills my bones.

I level my gaze on him, dreading the repercussions of what I'm about to tell him.

"Flynn, I need to explain something. You were right. Your father is an evil man if he's mixed up in this. This fog in my head I've been trying to shift is why I'm here. Tony is involved in a child trafficking ring that's remained all but undetected for years. The fog has been cloaking memories that can bust it wide open. Your father brought me here to find out what I remember."

Comprehension, like the fingers of shadows crawl into his expression.

"Do you remember enough to tell him?" His question jerks.

Hopeless tears tickle my lips, and my sigh wobbles. "It won't matter whether I can or can't, Flynn."

His head whips from side to side, his adam's apple bobbing.

"He wouldn't, Rain. He wouldn't do that, and you're wrong about the trafficking, too." His whisper is there to convince himself, and I let it sit between us for a few minutes. Then...

"Untie me, Flynn. Please?"

In the silence, Flynn works the ropes. Too tight, he only manages to loosen them a little, one ear angled at the door in case they return. My wrists throb as the blood flows again.

"They were supposed to leave the door unlocked so I could free you and I could get you out of here, but they locked us in..." The desperation in his tone bruises me.

"Flynn."

I lick my dry lips. "How old was your sister when she disappeared?"

The colour leaves his face translucent and I hear him choke.

"Flynn!" He's trapped in the hell playing out in his head. He holds his palms splayed in front of him and stares at them in frigid horror.

"Flynn? Help me?"

He stiffens like he's just noticed me and shifts an empty look on me.

"I'm frightened, Rain. I could never stand up to him. He'll hurt me. He'll hurt you."

His forehead collapses in agony. "He…the guys, Rain. They killed Archer."

CHAPTER 34

THE PROGRESS OF TERROR

I remember. How could I have forgotten?

My wail tears my decimated heart from my chest. I heard the shot break the night. I'd felt a little something inside of me creak, groan, and come apart. A something that existed inside of me that was fused with the man I love, now only the barest whisper of a distant memory.

"Archer!" I scream until my lungs collapse, believing that somehow as long as his name is on my tongue he's still alive somewhere, hoping that it could rip apart the fabric of time and anchor him to me. With a large gulp and tears streaming, I call out, over and over, for the man who loved me and never gave up.

Behind my eyes, Archer smiles. He leans his head on his bicep so he can watch me without the pillow obstructing his view. The olive chest begs to be touched, and I let my fingertips worship the valley between his pectorals. His skin is mine. I know it's satin texture, I know the scent of earth and spice that belongs to it. I know it better than I know my own. But my attention turns. I can't deny the allure of his eyes. Like a secret garden, those green gems sparkle with warm promises.

"I'll love you with my last breath. I am yours. You're my reason for being." The black velvet voice touches my heart like a sparkling memory.

Before it all turns sour.

Archer. The tears fall again at the thought. We never stood a chance. The secrets, the lies, all flavors of obstacles relentlessly working to keep us apart. In the end our fate was sealed, and there wasn't anything we could do to change it.

What were the last words he said to me? I search my memory, but grunt in despair from my raw throat. The fog rolls in like a silent assassin, stalking the image of Archer's face. It curls over his chest, sliding over his face until I can't see his beautiful mouth. The crippling agony dulls with the image.

Take away the hurt, I can't live with this pain. I don't want it.

His strong, straight nose evaporates into gray nothing, and the ebony mass of tousled hair is erased.

I lock on his eyes. The intensity of his feelings for me lingers in those magnetic orbs. They are Archer.

"*I love you, Rain. You are mine.*"

Then they, too, retreat into the haze.

No! I can't forget. I can't allow the anaesthesia to take him away. If I have to spend the rest of my life half alive, I will do it with Archer's beautiful eyes showing me he's mine. I give a mental shove, but the fog won't give.

I won't let you take him. I launch my rage, driving into the gray. I feel it give, like punching a wall of air, before it expands again. I try again, and again. And again.

The warm embrace of peace expands over me and I begin to wonder just what I was trying to do.

* * *

Everything is green. I'm aware it's an important colour but I don't understand why. It envelops me. I'll protect you. Its not even a voice. It's an emotion that assures and promises, and I sink into it. I'm so warm and safe and I feel the intrinsic urge to curl around, snuggle deep and cocoon myself in this feeling. I stare in awe at the darker centre, watching the emerald deepen into a mossy shade that heats my blood. I move towards it, needing to touch it, but it pulls away. I'm aware suddenly it's an eye, and it blinks languidly at me. There's so many emotions in it that it steals my breath. It's the most beautiful thing I've ever seen. My heart throbs like it's just held the secrets of the world, and I reach up, finally able to touch the eye.

The eye becomes one of two gems set in the face of a man. He smiles and I can feel all the things he's trying to say.

I need you, *I tell him. He smiles softly and I feel it in my veins. I move towards him, but he steps back at the same time. I'm confused. I try again, and again he retreats. My body fights and once more I reach out, and this time he stays put. His smile blows out and he lifts a palm to stop me.*

Yes, keep fighting. You're stronger than you think. *His voice echoes in my head while his beautiful lips remaining still.*

I feel the strength burn through me and my finger touches his face.

Lightning flashes in my skull.

The face freezes in shock, a scarlet stream cascading down the side of his face.

NO!

His eyes shudder and a light goes out in them, my chest ripping open as I watch. I follow the slow arc of his face with scorching helplessness, until it cracks against the floor, eyes glazed over, crimson pooling on the smooth floor.

Archer!

I jerk into awareness at my own strangled scream, consumed by an avalanche of grief and desolation. It doesn't cauterize the despair that blankets me.

Archer!

Then the blessed fog creeps in and plucks away the heartache.

And the memory.

The anaesthesia not only dulls the pain inside me, it also takes the edge off my fear.

Tony leans into my face. Flynn wears a mark of purple and

yellow on his eye for releasing me. It was a test, and Flynn had failed.

Tony could have been handsome if he wasn't so cruel. He looked like Flynn, only Tony's angles were harder, sharper and much more aggressive. His eyes, as if Hell itself turned blue and froze over. Even the air frosted around him as if whatever warmth should have been around him recoiled from his evil.

Unable to recall the details they need, I'm transferred to a small concrete room where time becomes fluid. It drains away, and I lose the ability to measure its passing as one day bleeds into the next. I have no idea how long I've been kept, but Carl and the other brute burst in with rough hands and rancid breath and secure me to the chair in what I refer to as 'the office'. I glance curiously around the room. It appears to have had a previous life as an outdoor laundry, with the uneven gray concrete floor with evidence of repair where the plumbing would have been. For a second the layout seems familiar. I'm placed to one side and an old wooden L-shaped desk off to the other. A high window thickened with years of cobwebs and scum sits on the wall opposite the desks, a chunk of clarity in the bottom corner where a missing square of glass allows wind to whistle through. I focus on that when Tony demands answers that continue to elude me, watching the emerald green leaves outside sway and bend. There's something so soothing about the color.

"What did you tell them?" He snarls in my face.

I scan the room for Flynn, my stomach twisting in fear when I notice his absence.

"Where's Flynn?"

Tony's malicious smirk widens.

"I thought we would…question him separately today."

Watching them beat Flynn rips my insides apart. He locked his focus on me in a silent reassurance as I watched every blow contort his defiant face. I watched the bruises pile up on his face, his flesh split beneath their knuckles and begin to knit again. If only I could remember, they'd lay off him. They'll kill me regardless, but Flynn might just have a chance if only this fog would clear. The parts of my past I've somehow exposed remain in my memory like mental bruises, but around them, the haze is more dense, a shroud of deep green that refuses to budge. If I could just clear it, Flynn might be safe.

But the pain will kill you.

I wish Archer would come and help me shift it. I wish I knew where he was. The fog shudders and I lose the fight to move it.

Who is Archer?

"I can't remember!" I cry in frustration.

Each time he interrogates me, Tony's hostility builds. His face purples and contorts as pain explodes on my cheek.

"What did you tell them?" Again.

"I don't know!"

Slap!

"What do you remember?"

"Nothing!"

SLAP!

"Tell me!"

SLAP, SLAP, SLAP.

I taste blood, the sharp copper flavour coating my tongue. Liquid fear chars a track over my raw cheek.

He looms so close I can see every separate hair in his eyebrows with crisp clarity.

"I have to ask you, Credence," he murmurs in my ear, his finger coated in oily evil running the length of my cheek.

I shudder violently, my skin retreating from his touch.

"Do you keep silent because you are enjoying this treatment? I'm right, aren't I? Kurt always had the knack of finding the pretty ones, the ones who were the picture of shattered innocence; they are always the most fun to break because they fought like cats. And you had to ruin it. Oh, the buyers wanted you, sweet

Credence. There were some pretty generous offers for you. But I knew where you would go. I had all four of you earmarked to go to Forbidden Fruits. You see, I have...a personal interest there and I can, and do, sample every girl we get, as often as I like. I was so pissed off that you managed to sabotage us."

The contents of my stomach roars to my throat and I swallow hard to keep it down. The thought of him touching any of us makes my blood curdle. Through the fear, my anger weaves upwards. This filthy man intended to do cruel and brutal things to my sisters and me. His eyes sparkle with cruel arousal as they travel down but when they reach my chest, they dull over, his lips twisting in distaste.

"But look at you now. A woman's body. Ugh! Nobody would pay good money for that. Is this why you're playing me? You regret your missed opportunity? Too bad."

He falls back in a squat, elbows on knees while he inspects me, a frozen sneer on his face.

"Do you know that your name, Credence, is also an alternative word for acceptance? What a bitter irony that is because you refused to accept your fate, and when you managed to thwart us, you refused to accept what happened. They should have named you Pernicious. A much better fit in my opinion."

My rage blooms under his arrogance. How this man can wear Flynn's face and be so evil? My aching body strains with fury.

"I messed up your sick, demented plans? Good! I wish I'd killed you instead of Kurt, because at least up until the end, he was good to us. You aren't capable of anything but depravity. You wanted me to simply accept the barbaric things you planned for us? Is that what Amelia did, Tony? Did you give her a kiss on the cheek and waved her off when you placed her into the hands of men you knew would hurt her?"

His eyebrows shoot upward and he stills. Good, I've hit a nerve. His eyes glaze over and a smile tugs the corner of his mouth.

His response is barely audible, but it chills me right down in the darkest parts of my soul.

"Oh, dear Credence…If only you knew…"

When his eyes refocus, they are so glacial the air fairly crackles with frost.

"Just tell me, Credence, what did you tell them?" Tony roars.

It's useless. After so much time, nothing comes. Bruises have flowered on my body in brilliant violet. I've watched them fade to a pretty plum, then a dirty yellowy brown as it fades. Then watch as others bloom in its place.

Every day buries me deeper under a blanket of despair. I listen to them talking. They don't need to keep their business dealings private because they make no secret that they intend to kill me. It's just a waiting game now, to see who will break first. Tony leaves the men in charge while he's off ensuring that his shady partners have a back up plan. The fact that their compounds haven't yet been invaded means I didn't tell the authorities everything, and they're highly invested in finding out just how much I've managed to reveal to Simone.

They have nothing but time.

I wonder how many weeks are hidden between the layers of beatings I've had.

The only times I see Flynn are when he stands restrained and beaten in the corner below the broken window while Tony attempts to force answers from me.

I jump when Tony slams his fist onto the desk. He jams his forehead against mine, and terror renews.

"I'm done with this bullshit, Credence. This has been…fun so far, but if you don't start talking soon, I'm going to have to insist you do."

His sour breath makes me gag, and I grunt in pain when I yank at the ropes that bite into the infected cuts on my wrists. My skin burning with fever is a new advancement, but the yellow discharge has been seeping and throbbing for what seems like years.

"You need to start talking, Credence. Now."

"I. Don't. Remember!" I gasp.

Tony pulls back his hand and I turn my face to offer the cheek that smarts the least.

Tony doesn't slap me.

His balled fist sinks into the soft skin below my ribs.

The pain travels the length of my body and back again. It empties my lungs, prevents me from drawing breath. My mouth chews at the air that eludes me, but nothing happens. I can't pull air. His cruel smirk is swallowed by darkness.

CHAPTER 35

THE LAST ASSIGNMENT

The cold bite of forged steel meets the bare skin between my shoulders, and the firing mechanism clicks.

"You're a dead man, Frostbite."

Axel flops his bulk down on the cot so hard the springs squeal.

Without turning, I coldly correct him. "I heard you coming, Axe."

"Did not." He snorts.

"That stupid belt buckle of yours clicked at the door, and you're as subtle as an elephant. You have exactly four dollars and twenty cents jangling about like a siren in your pocket, and I can tell you, you're not getting lucky with me, so the condom you're stashing in your back pocket won't do you any good."

I listen with satisfaction as he empties his pockets.

"Christ, man, you're friggin lethal!"

I shrug nonchalantly.

"Its what I'm trained to do." Flat fact.

I feel Axel's intentions as soon as he shifts. I dart a fist behind me and yank the pistol from his grasp. I take it apart, then reassemble it in a blur of fingers and the comforting crunching of metal as he moves in front of me.

"What's with the ink?" His question twists my guts as I snarl.

Axel shrinks back, uncertainty radiating off him. He would have lost whatever bet the boys had going, paying penance by attempting to win the story of my tattoo.

"It's nothing."

It's not nothing.

On the contrary its a masterpiece of bereavement, a testament to the cavern that exists where the brightest rainbow used to. It's a beautiful piece, my ink, beginning with a treble clef, the simple notes in the shape of raindrops sprawled across a rolling stave in the careful design of the notes that once convinced me 'You have already won this war.'

"What the fuck happened to you, bro?" *His tone of wonder jams my teeth together. But I won't tell him. I prefer to be alone, walk through the days without making conversation or seeking company.*

I freeze when the flashbacks fold in on me.

Her lashes lift to me, the love burning in her eyes enchants me. I run my palm over her flawless skin as she stretches like a cat. She is a vision of curves and beauty. I touch her because after all this time I still feel it's too perfect to be real. My angel, salvation for my soul.

"I love you, Archer." I can't respond because a mere mortal like me can't be this lucky. Then it reaches the next plane as she draws me closer, and I taste heaven on her lips and euphoria inside her body.

"Rainbow" my heart calls and she answers. Or maybe she IS my heart.

I read the reports. Except for that one listed death that haunts my every waking second. I searched the files to see if they'd listed her as Rain Harrison or Credence Bowman, only to find no name listed at all. Just 'civilian' like she wasn't my world. They tell me it's classified.

It took two days before they informed me of her death, and it took another four of constant supervision to make sure I wouldn't keep attempting to rip out the tubes and monitors that controlled the swelling in my brain.

Those bastards in the club chipped a chunk of my skull, leaving me instantly unconscious with a permanent soft spot and white stubble where the pigment never returned, but I spent the next two months hunting down anyone who was a threat to her. I uncovered the details of those responsible, and my team methodically and meticulously closed in on them all. When they'd been processed and prepared for incarceration, I returned under the cover of darkness and sent them to hell with retribution in my veins and destruction my only objective. I know what it feels like to feel air puff against my fist where a pierced a lung emptied around my knife hilt. I've seen the transformation between fear and deliverance in the twist of a neck. I've watched grown men beg for their lives with their children's names on their lips as I extinguish their light without regret.

With resentment in my soul and nothing left to lose, I've become the ultimate killing machine.

* * *

I pull my ankle over my thigh and boldly scrutinise the Director. He thrums his fingers on the expensive oak desk.

"What is the directive?" I demand. His fingers stop.

"Why do you think it's another assignment?" He asks. I roll my eyes, barely maintaining the farce of respect I'm supposed to portray.

"Don't insult my intelligence, Director. This last operation has wrapped up, the choppers have been working overtime transporting the superiors to secret meetings, and there's a sealed envelope containing the details in your jacket pocket you're wondering how to hand to me."

The man reclines in his leather seat at my arrogance, bringing his fingertips together.

"Archer Marraton, I can see why they say you're the best we have. Many reports have crossed my desk detailing your skill and fearlessness. You are very impressive."

"I'm not fearless." I correct him, and lean forward with a brutal

scowl. "I just don't give a shit."

He stares at me for a long while, and I watch as an odd contemplation registers on his wrinkled face before he erases it, fishing out the envelope. He slides it across the surface of the desk and gets to his feet, moving towards the door.

"You have two days to consider the proposal, Archer. As always, once accepted there is no revoking your decision. I will meet with you then for your answer and a debrief." He smirks from the doorway. "Don't leave the complex."

I narrow my eyes. The complex is a fortress; utterly impenetrable. He thinks he's funny. I think its a challenge.

Alone in the office, I peel open the envelope. Iran. For two years, working closely in the seedy underbelly of a corrupt country, liaising between their version of the Mafia and government officials.

My real job is done, though. I've poured everything left inside of me into inflicting cold justice on the criminals who stole Rain from me, and now I'm finished. This assignment may as well be a shiny, cocked gun with a bullet baring my name in its chamber.

My lungs expand with the same cruel despair that walks with me in the place Rain should be. It doesn't cease, this darkness that eats at me more with every second that passes. It will never heal, but it will end, in a strange country with a bullet in my head I'll never see coming. One I will receive with relief. If I can't spend my life in her arms, I will instead seek the cold arms of oblivion.

I sign my own death warrant with a scratchy black pen without hesitation. They won't accept it for another two days, so I post date it. There's no need to think about it. My final assignment. My life will snuff out at the hand of unscrupulous gangsters, my body dumped or discarded, my demise documented as a 'civilian loss' to hide their failure and another agent would be sent as my replacement to meet the same end.

I think of Heather with regret. I can't face her, knowing I was the one who couldn't save her foster daughter. It's the last twinge of life in my dead heart. Instead of facing my catastrophic failure, I bury myself away in this complex so I don't have to see Heather *break. Losing Rain drowned me in a darkness that won't stop bleeding, and right now I'll pay the ultimate price to put an end to this emptiness. I'm not the best because I'm fearless. I'm the best because I hope that behind every door I open will be the one that sends me into the merciful embrace of death, to sink into the arms of my girl one more time. But all I've managed was to cut down Rain's enemies instead.*

I never got a chance to say goodbye to Rain, and I can't face the judgement and disappointment of the woman I love like a mother, either.

I'm no longer a man.

I accompany my hollow footfalls to my dorm where I ignore the soldiers huddled near the door, stretching out on my bed to stare blankly at the ceiling. They speak in sharp, urgent whispers that I don't bother tuning into.

Until Axel looms above me with heavy concern chiselled into his eyes.

"Uh, Frostbite…uh, the boys were saying there was something between you and Credence, that true?"

A dagger buries itself deep in my chest and twists.

I silence him with my fingers biting into his neck.

"Fuck, man!" He croaks. "Just asking…"

I shove him away and roll from him, rubbing the mortal wound in the cavity beneath my ribs that keeps on stinging.

I listen as his footsteps retreat, muttering "Dunno why they'd want to keep it from you then."

My ears prick.

"Keep what from me?" My tone is a threat.

"They wouldn't say, just that Guy overheard the director on the blower this morning. Mentioned Credence and agreed that it was best to keep the information from you."

I sit, instantly tense and alert.

"What information? Did he specifically mention my name?"

Axle turns fluidly for someone of his bulk.

"Guy said he heard the Director say he needed to ensure Archer doesn't find out about Credence, and mentioned another assignment in the middle east. I don't know any more than that, though."

What does that mean? What is it that I shouldn't find out?

The ache inside anchors with a million tiny hooks, each sharpened by raw possibilities in my consciousness.

* * *

As soon as the men fall asleep, I move through the hallways silently, as if through a vacuum to the reinforced metal door that holds the answers I need. The moonless night barely hears the soft ping as the locking mechanism fractures. The door gives easily, swinging open like an invitation to hell.

A light shiver shakes me, causing me to freeze momentarily. Its the first time I've actually felt *something since I lost Rain.*

Hope.

I make the outline of a document spread open on the desk before I turn my attention lower. The steel cabinet crouches like a wolf beneath the desk and I drop to my knees to challenge it. It's one of those new issue systems with the high tensile mechanisms, theoretically theft proof, and I mentally reprimand myself for not paying closer attention to the new additions when the usual methods I try don't open it.

I work the lock relentlessly, determined to find out what it is they don't want me to know, and what part Rain plays in it. That's the concerning piece of this puzzle. Rain's death should have put an end to any secrecy, so the desire to hide information from me suggests something darker going on. Would it be the details of her death? The brutal final moments they refused to disclose to me, the lack of any concrete facts that sent me into a spiraling agony of my own blood thirsty theories?

I pause, swallowing the lump in my throat. Would it make my grief worse, knowing those details?

"Hey."

The faint whisper startles me and I spin with murder in my coiled brawn.

Silver eyes catch the barest light and I sense, rather than see, Axel's hands lift in surrender.

I've worked with this guy a thousand times before, and he's probably the only man in this pit of clowns I'd go close to trusting, so I know he's not here to rat me out. What he is doing here is a mystery, until I feel him shuffle beside me, his hand against my arm voicelessly requesting room. I hear the soft metal sounds as the internal gears resist and then give beneath Axel's efficient fingers.

The drawer rolls out and I snap on the tiny pencil light that spears the darkness with its sharp beam. Fingers gliding over the manilla tabs, I hover over the fresh, bold ink on a stiff new folder.

Credence Bowman.

CHAPTER 36

THE HONESTY OF INK

he notes are dated the same week that I was recovering in hospital.

Credence Bowman, location unknown. Identity of captors possibly Mikhail Gorvich or Tony Burgess. Strong links to trafficking rings across southeast Asia and Russia.

I forget being quiet. I slap the file open on the table and dig through the papers like a starving man.

Notes from a month and a half ago.

Notes from a week ago, all stating that Rain's location was unknown, not that she was deceased.

Axel's fingers grip sheets as he rifles through them, and when I hear his muffled gasp, I snatch the page from him.

My flashlight sears the words to memory.

Credence Bowman, location confirmed and reported at the abandoned butter factory in west Macclesvale, building C9. Confirmed captor Tony Burgess, instruction to capture and interrogate.

No evidence that memory has been restored in full or part.

The time stamp was yesterday morning, barely an hour before I met with the director.

She's still alive!

Interrogation witnessed and reported to be excessive,

confirmation that termination of captive is imminent.

They know she'll be killed and haven't sent in a team to get her out!

And they don't want me to know because I'm more useful to them when I have nothing to lose.

I choke on cold betrayal, and Axel's attention zeros in on invisible wound in my chest I rub, realisation slowly dawning on him.

"Oh, shit, man." His expression softens and settles on me.

They underestimate me. The complex holds me only because I allow it. I absorb my surroundings to form an escape plan. Behind me, Axel extracts a sheet of paper from a file, folding it carefully into his pocket. I don't bother cleaning up the documents spread over the desk. Let them see how pissed off I am.

Axel's bulk shadows me as I reach the window, and I fight the urge to refuse his company. He helped me, and the set of his shoulders warns me any argument I make will be futile, anyway. Wordlessly, he snaps out glass cutters and scratches a wide circle in the director's office window. Silently, we seek out the perimeter.

I'm a finely tuned machine of vengeance, and my smile doesn't reach my eyes as I drop down from the branch overhanging the razor wired cyclone fence into the undergrowth and smell the damp earth under my feet. Axel lands beside me with barely a sound.

We just busted out of their impenetrable fortress.

The undergrowth separates before us as if it detects the urgency in our haste. I slide my gaze over Axel in my periphery, unsure what drove him to accompany me here, and why he helped me break into the files in the first place. I maintain distance from all of my team because I know firsthand the vulnerability of friendship. With unwavering determination I can eradicate the foe without a thought for any other. But once you grow to care for another, the determination and focus divides and weakens until you are left sacrificing your heart to an enemy blade.

A rifle barrel breaks out from behind a thicket to our left, a soldier's face following it out.

"Dorian! Stand down!" Axel barks.

The soldier stands firm, shoulders and feet square and braced. His expression is unyielding.

"Not today, Axel. Sorry, we have our orders, and you're a traitor."

"No, Dorian, not a traitor. I wouldn't do that. I'm just a guy helping a mate. Come on, man. Just let it go. You saw nothing."

"The big guys are here, Axe. They're watching, and I need this. You know I do. And they know you broke into the files."

Dorian crunches off the safety, cold satisfaction stretching his smile. Axel and I step back.

"Listen man, I understand, and I'm sorry. I am. I thought we were brothers. But you need to understand I still live by the code, and I can't let you take us in. They deceived us, Dorian, and we are going to do what we should have done months ago. Take down the bad guys and save Credence."

With hands fanned above his shoulders, Axel steps closer to Dorian. The soldier huffs and glares, attempting to step around his bulk. And that's when he does it.

Axel's hands are a blur of choreographed purpose. The fluid enchantment of a body moving with flawlessness is a dance I'll never tire of.

Dorian crumples to the ground the moment Axel hits his pressure point. An easy manoeuvre, but Axel's chest heaves and breath hisses with unspoken history. Axel pulls the rifle one handed, aiming at the unconscious soldier, and I simply watch. When a brother has a score to settle, you don't interfere.

The echoing crack sends the birds into the sky. The unconscious soldier doesn't even tense with the impact. Crimson oozes from the tiny cave in Dorian's shoe.

We're coming, Rain.

"Why are you here?" I frown as we move through the forest.

"I owed you one." He shrugs those huge shoulders.

I let silence return as I remember. The scene was like every other one we'd stormed at first. My team had burst in and secured the enemy with an ease born of repetition. We'd become complacent, no longer securing wrists as we began leading them out. What we hadn't expected was the second wave of bodies streaming through every entrance we hadn't bothered protecting. We all wore some of our own blood, and some of my team were slaughtered. I'd disarmed my opponent, the knife still in my fist when I happened to glance at Axel. His bulk made him an obvious target, and while he was gaining the upper hand on his rival, another foe stood across the room, pistol cocked and trained between Axel's eyes. It was the only time I interfered. The knife left my hand with a low snarl, embedding in the enemy's temple, the gun clattering uselessly to the floor.

"And Dorian?"

Dorian was a good soldier, one dedicated to climbing the ranks, always seeking a leadership role. He was always passed over when promotions were handed out, but a shot to the foot like that would compromise his ability to move, and even a slight decline in his skill set has the potential to end his career.

Axel's frown hinted at deeper reasons.

"I owed him one, too."

* * *

The old blue Ford sedan growls to life with a twist of wires and Axel and I head for the old butter factory. Axel reads over the document he'd shoved in his pocket in the office, and I frown as I watch him carefully smooth it out on his thigh, refolding it before returning it to his pocket.

"You know after this, our career's pretty much over?" I ask.

Axel nods. Short. Sharp.

"What made you throw it all away? You know I don't give a shit if you settled our score or not."

His bulk fills half the car. If it weren't for my training, the sheer *size and muscle mass of this guy would terrify me. Except there's a softness in his eyes, like beyond his hard shell is a man who follows his heart.*

"I realised I was fighting for the wrong side."

And he says no more.

* * *

"I love you, Archer." *The heavenly apparition smiles her secret smile. The one she saves for me, because for some ungodly reason she's convinced I'm good enough for her.*

I'm so sorry, Rainbow. I miss you so fucking much, and I can't stop thinking about the time I wasted trying to stay away from you.

My throat burns.

Christ it hurts. It just aches and aches and never lets up. The only time it loosens it's hold is when I feel enemy flesh separate beneath my rage, when I sacrifice another life in her memory.

I can smell her.

I couldn't protect her. *The guilt eats at me like acid.* I can't let her down again.

We leave the car and slide against the concrete walls of the old butter factory. It looms like a place of dead things, where hopes and dreams struggle to survive in the cracks of the paths and within the thick concrete walls. I can't switch off. The frosty clarity I possessed in the complex has evaporated.

I again have something to lose. Rain. The realisation that nothing will ever be the same again, no matter the outcome, no matter what scene greets me weakens my knees. I see my fractured fear reflected in the pewter eyes of Axel and it occurs to me just how fragile and mortal we really are.

I frown, but can't manage to summon the glacial invincibility that for months perched on my shoulder. It's gone. Rain is my sole purpose, my only destination, but she's also my crippling weakness.

My throat scratches with doubt.

For the first time since I met her, I question my abilities.

What if I make a mistake? What if I hesitate, and that fraction of a delay causes the destruction of Rain? At my hand?

Shards of dread so loud they're deafening embed themselves in my stomach.

I'm wrenched from my angst by Axel's paw on my shoulder. He lifts his head at the building to the right.

Building C9.

She's here.

My heart in my throat, I nod.

* * *

The window is so dirty it may as well be a continuation of the wall, but there's a corner broken out. The bottom corner, where I can see inside if I reach up with my toes and steady myself with my fingers. My mouth is a desert.

She's there! *Face stained with tears, the fresh blood oozing from a gash on her neck where Tony presses his blade. The urge to burst through the window and annihilate the man almost sends me dizzy. But his expression...He's enjoying this darkness way too much, and he's not yet ready to end the game.*

I have time to think. Rain sits with the courage I know better than my own heartbeat. She hasn't given up, never will. The ache presses against my chest, and I rub where it hurts. My heavy swallow is so noisy Axel frowns, but he moves silently into position by the door.

Look at me, Baby.

As if she hears my thoughts, she looks toward the window.

I'm here, Rainbow, I've come for you. Like I always will. Like I promised.

CHAPTER 37

BEYOND THE FOG

*T*here is a briefcase sitting on the desk where the laptop should be.

Why should there have been a computer?

That's my briefcase!

The one that holds all my memories in the staves, my life between the treble clefs and codas. My emotions lyrics in HB grey lead.

Why would they want that?

I centre my attention on the light filtering in through the tiny hole broken out of the window as I twist and pull at my wrists and ankles. They burn and saw against my flesh but don't give.

They're tighter than before.

Before?

Before!

With a gasp that detects the wonder in my contemplation, I remember. I remember being in a sharper version of this room, and look beside me as if I expect to see Willow and Katherine on either side of me. Bound the same way. I keep working the rope and fire up my recall.

It's my birthday. My sisters wear expressions of helplessness and horror as my arms twist painfully behind me. The tattooed man taps at the keyboard and Kurt snaps impatiently at him over my head.

"It's not opening, Kurt. Did you change the combination on me?" He frowns.

"No I didn't you moron, and its a password, not a combination!" He blows out his irritation.

"I'm putting it in, but its not working."

"Christ Andy, we did a run-through yesterday. They're expecting us to have the cameras running by now! Just get it done already!' His anger makes me feel like my arm is ripping out of its socket.

I move my arms but my wrists are so tender I hiss.

"Flynn? Do you think we can go home, soon?" My mouth is parched and my throat burns.

His head whips around to mine, confusion painted thick on the canvas of his expression.

"Uh, what? Remember, Rain! Fight the fog!"

Beads of sweat pepper his face, his focus wild and defiant on the man in front of him. Waves of despair pound into me as he holds his chin up once more and clenches his jaw as another blow finds his stomach.

I listen to the footfalls with an absent interest, while Flynn lurches backwards to the door. The man who walks in is an older copy of Flynn. Tony. My stomach knots with sticky dread that I can't entirely understand.

His eyes are a predator's - glacial ocean blue - as they hover inches from mine.

"Well now, girlie, you've caused a bit of a problem for us, haven't you?" Tony's voice grates like broken glass.

"What do you want?" I wince as my words sting my windpipe.

Tony squints.

"You know what I want, Credence. I want to know what you know. I want to know *who* you've told, and *what* you've told them. If you're a good girl, I might even let you live."

I frown, bewildered. "How can I tell you what I know, if I don't know what it is I'm supposed to know?"

Tony hisses impatiently. I glance over at Flynn. He looks like he's going to be sick. He props himself against the wall, bent over with his arms wrapped around his stomach. So weak from the attack, the guards don't even bother holding him. They know after all this time he's incapable of anything but fighting for air. Six of them today, all leaning against walls and furniture with tedious expressions.

"She's a nut job, Tony. I think whatever is locked in her head even she can't access." Carl mutters. Tony spins away from me and prowls to Carl, thick fingers digging into his neck as he slams him into the wall.

"She's remembered enough to tell the cops, you idiot. She's given enough for them to stop the Five-Sevens, and it's a matter of time before the rest fall, too."

Five-Sevens. The faint flutter in the fog tells me I'm supposed to know what that means. My gaze swings to my briefcase, trying to find the connection I know exists. I'm so lost in my focus that I jump when Tony fills my vision. His face has purpled and his expression boils.

"Don't waste my time, Credence. What do you know? Did you tell them who came to the meetings at your house? Did you tell them about your boyfriend? Kurt?"

My heartbeat snags. I strain into my memories, but nothing comes.

"Leave her alone, Dad. She can't remember." A small, breathless sound blisters from Flynn's mouth.

Tony sends a contemptuous glare to his son.

"Jesus, kid. You're a goddamn embarrassment. I give you one job, bring the girl to me, and you couldn't even do that. Shut your whiny, sorry arse and stop distracting me!"

I watch Flynn recoil and break. The only time his father reaches out to him, and it's all for his own selfish purpose.

The snake snorts and rolls his eyes.

"For Christ's sake, look at you. It's fucking pitiful. You even screwed me over when you were born with a cock. Even those faggots didn't want to buy you in the end. Just a waste of air."

Tony stabs his attention back to me at the same time as a searing sting bites my neck. I drag air noisily, adrenaline hissing through my teeth. I hadn't seen him pull the blade. My pulse gallops.

I know this terror. The glacial certainty that nothing would ever be the same in another moment.

The chilling sensation of flesh parting beneath the knife, every nerve hyper aware of the steel invading my body. My eyes blow, focusing on the tiny chip missing from the corner of the widow. I need to see outside before I die.

Instead of a glimpse of foliage, the green in the window is solid. Iridescent. It's a hue that glows with familiarity. It flutters suddenly, sending awareness into my lungs.

Someone is watching, steady and committed. I lock on its comforting presence as I feel my brain begin to filter, and chronologically sort through fragments of broken thoughts. The familiar green that colors the fog collides with the green I'm absorbing from the window, and taste the tang as clarity begins to expand.

Tony's going to kill me.

Kurt is going to rape me.

He sold his daughter, and tried to sell his son.

He's filling an order for eleven year old girls.

He killed Archer.

Lightning explodes in my brain, Archer's green eyes suddenly crystal clear. The same shade as what filters in through the broken window. They stay with me, saturating me with the love that lives there. The love that cuts through and burns bright and doesn't relent.

I killed Kurt.

"What. Did. You. Tell. Them?" The promise of death hangs on his words.

"I…can't remember." I stutter, but even as the words leave my mouth, my thoughts begin to solidify. The blade heaves and my skin splits, and my hands still won't reach up. My cry gurgles.

The rope cuts into my ankles when Tony slams the blade into the chair between my thighs with an impatient snarl.

The eye in the window blinks. That's all it does, but there's an honest comfort in it.

Tony replaces his knife with a hand gun while my lungs heave in terror. He cocks the gun, tracing the outline of my body in the air.

"Rain!"

Even as I turn to the cry, Tony suddenly disappears behind a wall of Flynn. My head jerks to follow. Flynn's body jars with the force of his fists, the snarl of rage a wild sound rent from broken lips. Tony stumbles, but only partly in shock. All his son's pain, all the mental and soul deep scars his father branded him with is a weapon more powerful than his exhaustion. Hope bursts to life in my chest, because Flynn is winning. He's bent over Tony, split knuckles raised and ready, feral justice lighting his expression.

Crack. My ears ring as Flynn stiffens.

No, no no! This is NOT happening again!

But the fine spray of moisture that bursts in my face, and my friend's muted grunt, signifies otherwise. Boneless and spent, Flynn slumps to the floor.

"Flynn!" I scream and strain against the ties that bind me.

Flynn's eyes are squeezed shut, skin so pale I can see the layers of unborn bruises rising through his skin. He grunts softly, arms trembling around his stomach, as if it takes every last bit of strength to hold himself together.

"Don't leave me Flynn!" I sob, and my heart burns.

Flynn's guttural groans fill the room and Tony smudges blood from his bust lip with the back of his wrist. He dismisses the writhing body of his son, cold attention back on me.

"We'll play something different, if you enjoy games. I will ask a simple question, and if you don't answer, I get to make you scream." His sinister smirk sizzles.

"What's in this briefcase?"

He raped Sarah and Willow.

"My…my music."

"See, I think you're lying, and I'm rarely wrong. Let's have a look, shall we? I can do this one of two ways. You either tell me the password, or I shoot it open." And my blood freezes as he produces the wicked black sheen of a hand gun.

Wait, The password?

"It's not a combination, it's a password, you idiot." Kurt tells the man to try the password again. What is it? "It's the same as the run-through we did yesterday. It's eleven-eleven."

Eleven-eleven. Five-Sevens. Five girls at seven years of age to fill the order. Eleven-Eleven. *Eleven girls just turned eleven. Broken in on their birthdays for their buyers to view via the dark web.*

The eye in the window expands in my mind, the emerald orbs hover and hold, and I reach out to them with a mental pulse. The fog darkens and fizzes, tiny embers of vibrant green growing and building. And clearing.

Until it explodes into a million fragments, taking the haze with it.

"It's eleven-eleven." My voice is clear and strong as I look past Tony, and back through time. Then I lock a desperate stare on the blinking eye, conveying leaden meaning.

"The password is eleven-eleven."

The password has been at my fingertips this whole time. Every time I recorded my lyrics, my briefcase sprung open with the holy grail.

The shimmer of excited spittle gleams in the corner of his mouth until the case clicks open and it's contents are revealed. Tony growls as he snatches sheets of music from the pile, sending them see-sawing weightlessly to the floor.

When the case is empty his eyes burn with demented rage. I see my death in them, and calm acceptance settles over me. It's the oddest sensation, to feel tranquility while every reborn nightmare crashes and bucks to the surface. There's a reassurance in it, knowing that my pain belongs to me again, and I've already survived it. As Tony snarls and shows me the hollow finger of his gun, the irony isn't lost on me. The fog doesn't come.

CHAPTER 38

INTO THE FRAY

J've felt the cold blade of vengeance at my neck so many times I've lost count. Searing lead searching for vital organs, leaving puckered, angry scars on my flesh. I watched my reflection in the eyes of a thousand men with murder on their minds without remorse, or hesitation. It came so naturally to me that fear for my actions never entered my mind.

But it takes every coiled muscle to send a simple text with my quaking hands.

Axel lifts his eyes from my phone with a furrowed brow at me, and I nod, silently sucking in a breath. A man with trepidation in his heart is a soldier without weapons. I have to keep my head for Axel.

But she's here, and she's everything, and there is no way I can lose her again.

Time reaches for miles and I shoot agitated glances at my phone until I'm reassured the message went through to Simone.

Tony's concentration is interrupted by several soft pings and chirps around the room, and I'm aware of hiss thugs brandishing their phones. The oily weapon shifts as Tony reaches into his own pocket, lighting his face with the harsh glow of the screen.

"What the fuck?" Flynn's father stills as he scans the information. The gun lowers and Rain fights against her restraints to shift out of the firing line.

"Tony..." Carl's voice squeezes out.

"Boss?" The other goon makes a choking sound.

Flynn moans at Rain's feet. I glance at him, instantly overwhelmed by the stark difference between faceless casualties on a battlefield and a friend. I've shared meals with this man. I've heard the gentle intentions of his soul and know there is no malice in him. I've handed over trust to him to keep my reason for breathing safe. Yet here he lies, betrayed and damaged by his own father.

I will never be able to erase Flynn's pain from my mind. In the deep blue pools of his eyes, the faces of every life I've claimed stand in cold judgement. But Flynn's pure soul seems to mute them, jailing them behind his faith in me, and I finally understand. Flynn holds the cure to the moral disease of my past.

I need him.

"Keep it together, Frost!" Axel breathes.

I clench my jaw and nod, but my mouth is a desert and my humanity burns and labors.

"You fucking whore!" Tony curses, tearing my attention back inside.

His back faces me, his goons lining the walls offering an open combat zone. They are a carbon copy of the million other trained dogs I've seen before, low intelligence and even less alert, otherwise they'd catch on to Rain's glances constantly sweeping my way. Its a situation I've seen so many times I could finish them all in forty seconds with my eyes closed.

But not today, because Flynn is hurt, and Rain could get hurt, too.

Axel knocks his knuckles hard against my shoulder, gesturing urgently.

Puzzled, I slide my eyes back to Tony. Skin purple and swollen with unleashed fury, he stabs the gun at Rain's defiant, courageous glare and curls a thick finger around the trigger.

Axel yanks me to my feet and shoulders through the door before I can blink. Seven heads swivel towards us, Mouths agape and eyes bulging, and I should have taken Tony out that first second, but I freeze in place. The room reeks of fear. Rain and Flynn's fear, and I feel the guilt of not protecting them in my bowels. It stiffens my bones. It strips me of every skill I acquired. With the grace of a trained killer that suddenly eludes me, Axel doesn't hesitate. He knocks the weapon from Tony's claw and begins to pick off the henchmen.

Adrenaline punches through me and I feel the training consume me. So easy now, I swipe at Tony's neck, but he ducks aside. I snag his arm, snarling with the force of snapping his bones. He drops with a blood curdling scream and twists so the kick I aim at his throat shatters his jaw instead.

Stars explode in my vision and I spin to find a thug behind me, an iron bar raised above his head ready for another blow. I kick his legs from beneath him, catching him before he hits the ground, listening for that familiar wet crunch of his neck breaking. He slumps to the floor, but I'm already sinking an elbow into the gut of another man. The blast of pain clears my head, and I shake off my fear.

Once more I'm a honed machine, processing criminals the way I'm programmed. My knuckle strikes the vulnerable pit of a temple, and another foe meets his maker.

I check on Axel as I smear the trickle of blood from my eye. He's got three on him, but his stance is primed. He's under control.

Then it all turns sour with one word.

"Archer?"

The word reaches into my chest, winds around my lungs and grips my heart. Everything but her empties, and I scramble over, landing on my knees before her.

Her gasp rattles with raw incredulous hope.

She blurs as my hand finds the soft flesh of her cheek, smearing blood like war paint in its path. My throat aches with the sheer relief of touching her again.

"Rain!" My voice shatters at her feet, and I can do nothing but take my fill of her. My heart.

"Archer, look out!" She sobs, but I can't break my thrall. She's mine.

But the next breath I take fails, and so does the next one. I watch my hand leave the warmth of her face as it jumps to my throat.

My nails dig at where the rope bites into my neck, skin bulging around it. My mouth hangs wide, uselessly snapping for air. The heat from my enemy scorches my back when I lever against him and find my feet.

My lungs burn with the force of trying to pull oxygen. My fingers frantically reach behind me. Rope, twisted and locked tight with a fist of stone. I can't budge either of them.

There is no sound I can make. It's an end that finds me waiting in silence, the thug letting my life ebb without a single word of victory. Just like me, he waits.

When my vision begins to float away, the blood slamming against my skull like its about to burst right through, Tony's face leers at me.

"So this is the famous Archer? You're the name that struck terror in the hearts of my men around the world?"

He laughs, and it's so very far away, even as he's close enough that I can feel his breath.

I watch Axle's blur in my periphery, and he's struggling, too, but no matter where I move my eyes, I can't see Rain.

And I can't have that.

With the last of my strength, I heave backward, against the blinding agony of the rope, and hear the satisfying crack of my head connecting with Tony's. I snap back again and I'm rewarded by the crunching resistance of his nose breaking.

The constriction weakens and I grab behind me. The barest hope flickers when I explore the knot. The fist is gone. On the edge of consciousness, my vision darkens as I snatch at the rope fibres. I yank weakly, but its just enough. A thin string of oxygen trickles into my lungs.

Oh, the agony of scrambling for more. I suck it down with dragging gasps, the awful sounds like a miracle to my ears as my *sight slowly returns.*

Axel's punches have lost their power, but he's holding his own. Just.

I'm horrified at how badly I shake. The thought of having my life stolen from me when I haven't grown old in Rain's arms fills me with a fear before unknown to me. I blink away the last of the darkness and snarl. The air shifts around me, every layer of armor I've built to enable me to disassociate with the enemy falls useless at my feet. The soldier in me lays down his weapons and turns away with the knowledge I'm no longer the cold assassin I have been. From the moment I made the promise to Rain to protect her, I've stepped into a role that was never supposed to be mine. I manipulated Simone into sharing Rain's secrets, I bullied the elite forces until they agreed to arm me with the skills I needed to achieve my directive. I sent my team into dangerous battlefields just so I could bathe in revenge I felt entitled to.

Now, Rain is here. No more secrets. No more vengeance. I've done my bit, and now that the password is exposed, so has Rain. The ghosts in her eyes are as much my fault as the lesions that colour her skin, and the thought catches in my throat. This is the last battlefield I'll step foot on. Its time for us now, she and I, nothing coming between us ever again.

Tony, face bloodied and arm shattered, has managed to retrieve his gun, but he's not after revenge for the injuries I inflicted. He lifts a shaky arm towards Rain. Her eyes light on me, the face I know better than my own twists in a beautiful agony that shreds every one of my nerve endings.

My feet move with instinctive clarity. Every step bringing me closer to my girl, my destination, my final objective.

My snarl is deafening as I reach for Tony, silently beg Flynn for forgiveness, as one last time I give myself over to my training.

One last time I feel flesh give beneath unforgiving hands.

One last time the crunch of broken bones grinds in my ears.

One last time I know the slump as a body slackens and drops to the ground.

I close my eyes on Tony's still expression, taking my final breath as a killer. Its a bittersweet moment, the growl of my brother in arms as he, too, finds victory behind me. In the silence that follows, I bring my eyes to her and I'm ensnared by the deliverance in Rain's expression.

I throw back my head and roar, a sound that grips my soul and gives voice to both the darkest agonies and the triumphant wings of a destiny of our own design.

It's the last battle cry that will ever leave my lips.

My war has ended.

CHAPTER 39

AFTERMATH

*T*wo months pass in the blink of an eye. In the wake of any massive upheaval comes the inevitable aftermath we are left to sift through. Bitter sweet ballads and the dark notes of endings.

For thousands of girls, the future waits to be re-written. Simone is able to infiltrate the previously impenetrable computer program with the password, exposing thousands of illegal trafficking rings across the globe with the strike of a key.

Around the world, girls are led out of their prisons and out into the sunlight for the first time in years. The people Archer and his men had found are a mere drop in a poisoned ocean. The bulk of the compounds are infiltrated easily, but the last half dozen are located locally. Simone will oversee those ones. Within those last few is the paperwork evidence needed to ensure every person who had a hand in the ring are held accountable.

Flynn carries ghosts, the kind that linger in the shadows of human cruelty, and change a person. The bullet wound reminds him like my tattoo that the betrayal of blood leaves the deepest scars. The same blood that ran through the veins of the man who sold his sister pulses through his own, and he's struggling to find peace with it as he seeks out his sister. With a drive that borders on obsession, Flynn begins to wade through the dead ends and false documents with Simone to find Amelia. Archer's initial distrust of Flynn is long gone, replaced by a strange need to protect him. Somewhere in that room with his father's body and his pooling blood, Flynn has become important to Archer.

Axel and Archer began as brothers in arms but evolved organically into family. Axel saved Archer all over again the day the soldiers came to drag Archer back into service to honour the assignment he accepted before he knew I lived. On the precipice of disaster, Axel produced the only thing that would free him. Archer's signature. He had the foresight to take the signed contract when they were searching for the files that inevitably led them to me. Heather was so taken by him that he's moved into my old room for the time being.

It's taken longer than I thought to shrug off the chains of our journeys, but the comfort Archer and I find in each others arms is a salve that knits us back together every time we verge on breaking beneath the weight of our pasts.

Archer's deep green orbs find mine and smile. That green, the only antidote to the haze that imprisoned me, and the only shade I need. The fog receding made for some painful nights, but in Archer's arms, heartbeat grounding me, I'm making it through. The worst is behind us and we're collecting notes for our next song. We are finally free to breathe.

My life will never be ordinary. I crave the cascade of mismatched notes that will always be the song of Archer and me. Those imperfections are what I thirst for. Our song begins all over again, every sharp and sour note blending just as perfectly, only this time at a slower tempo. The pitch of Archer's flaws fuel me. Excite me. With an understanding that needs no voice, I know he, too, needs my broken tones to follow the sound of the wind. He is mine and I am his.

Movement near the door catches my attention, and I gasp. A tall, slender woman with familiar auburn hair pulled back in a sensible pony tail stands uncertainly by the door. Her eyes rimmed red, shadows under her eyes dark.

Simone, the woman who betrayed me. Betrayed me so she could protect hundreds of children around the world. And her crime? Withholding information I was already in possession of. It's all so trivial, and holding tightly to trivial things causes the most damage. I let it damage Archer and me. I won't make the same mistake a second time.

I launch into Simone's arms and hold her so tightly my wrists burn. Her breath whooshes out her relief and her tears soak my shoulder.

"I'm so sorry." I lament, and she strokes by back.

"I am, too, Rain. The last thing I wanted to do was hurt you, but they gave me no choice."

"I know." And I do, because in this messed up existence, it's the truths with the greatest pain that make the most sense.

* * *

In the last two months we have discovered our own version of normal. We found a beautiful home down the street from Heather and purchased it with the savings Archer had accrued, and the generous payout Aaron insisted upon after he broke my contract and closed the club permanently. Each of the four rooms had its own ensuite added. There was enough left over to purchase The Broken Keg.

We take over the pub from Zack when he retires in a couple of months.

Axel has become an essential part of our lives. He's moved into one of our spare rooms, deciding to stay after Simone offered him the position within the police force Archer refused.

And now a new song begins. We needed waitressing staff for the pub, and our family wasn't quite complete. After some detective work by Simone and a few phone calls, its finally happening.

Stones crunch under the tires of Simone's sedan. Archer squeezes my hand and I glance at him gratefully when he shoots me a reassuring smile.

Old sneakers lower to the gravel warily, followed by the loose fabric of grey tracksuit pants. Floppy shirt buttoned right up to the collar, and the orange hue of cheap bleached hair covers the face I've pictured countless times.

I leave Archer's side and lean in before she's fully unfolded from the car, throwing my arms around the slender body beneath.

"I've missed you so much. Welcome home!"

Searching the familiar face, I take stock of the newer demons that lurk there, and my heart breaks. Her beautiful eyes, haunted but holding on, meet mine.

And Willow smiles.

EXCERPT from PRUDENCE

Chapter 1: Willow

T have a bed. So sinister yet so alluring, I'm hesitant to crease it with more than a careful caress. I draw my knees to my chest and take in the queen bed with its crisp white sheets and royal blue cover. I feel like I've walked onto a set for a photo shoot. It's magazine immaculate.

I wish I could fall into it feeling as safe and serene as the models in those magazines.

But I know it's a vicious trap with razor teeth.

A beautiful lie.

I leave it skulking in my space like a hungry wolf, resisting the urge to strip it down and dismantle it on the spot. I'm not ready for the questions that would come from that. It stands taunting me as I pile my old bedding in the far corner of the room.

The sigh squeezes from my chest as I drag my blanket over my shoulders and I find some kind of comfort on the thick carpet.

I blink into the dusk. I have two weeks before I start work. Fourteen days before I can break out of this invisible cell I've existed in for so long. Fourteen days until I can be done with toxic homes for good. My nerves jerk excitedly. I can't recall the last time I was enthusiastic about something that I didn't have to compromise to get.

So far.

It's not that I doubt Rain's intentions, it's that she still appears naive enough to believe that good things just happen. But I know better; everything has a price, and the costs always bite deeper than she could ever understand.

But a job? This could change everything. If I am just able to hide the broken pieces of me, I'll appear normal, like everybody else. Just a normal seventeen-and-a-half-year-old girl with a job and a permanent address.

I feel a smile threaten. In every home since I was twelve, its been my job to cook and clean, so waiting tables is one thing that I'm certain I can do. I can take orders with perfect recall and deliver an armful to set the different dishes before the patrons who ordered them.

My smile blows out and sits on my cheeks.

A shriveled seed of hope inside me sends up a tentative shoot.

* * *

I hear the deep growl of the motorbike roll in and the hulking footsteps cover the distance to the house with the sharp crunching of stone. Climbing quietly from my nest I creep to the window. The curtain slides aside and makes room for my curiosity. The forest giants surrounding Rain's home break up the moonlight, so I catch only fleeting glimpses as the man moves in languid, arrogant strides towards the house. He shifts his bulk as if it's liquid, graceful and purposeful like a smooth dance.

Holy hell he's a big man.

I hear my own swallow and my mouth slackens. The leather on his jacket creaks as if it's failing to constrain all the muscles fighting against it. He's so tall and broad that my heart races.

He could protect me.

He could kill me.

His steps break and for a second he's as still as stone, head to the ground, and my gaze is glued to him as he turns his face slowly towards my bedroom window.

My stomach smashes against my ribcage and I jail my breaths.

Hidden behind the curtains he can't see me, but he knows I'm here.

Also by Rowena Spark

STAND ALONE ROMANCE

HER WHOLE HEART

STEALING BRYNN

SCARS OF CREDENCE SERIES

PRUDENCE (BOOK 2)

RETICENCE (BOOK 3 - COMING SOON)

www.ingramcontent.com/pod-product-compliance
Lightning Source LLC
Chambersburg PA
CBHW030615120726
47904CB00006B/1903